GW00482056

This book wouldn't have come into being without the help of my Editor, Margaret Jarvis, my self-publishing guru Alba Lewis and the support of my wonderful husband and family. Thank you all, you've made dreams a reality.

The Return of the Queen

Chapter 1

Darkness had fallen, deep and putrefying, reaching out its hand and ravaging everything it touched. Food turned to ash in people's mouths, wine to acid, crops withered and the flesh crumbled from the bones of the livestock. The land was filled with wailing and screaming, despair for everyone, young and old, who were giving their lives to stop the wave of evil that stalked the land. But the Rebel King advanced, relentlessly slaughtering all those who opposed him, with his armies of the night, men and women with hearts of darkness and souls full of hatred. They burnt homes and farms until there was nothing but devastation, the Rebel King's lust for power and belly full of hate driving him onwards to the heart of the Kingdom, in his futile search for the only one with the power to end his avenging campaign, and it consumed him to the point of madness.

In the midst of all this bleakness, there was a grand courtyard, proud and square with stone walls as high as the clouds and iron gates that swung over the stone floor when opened. In the very centre stood a great willow tree, its roots spreading far across the land and deep into the earth like the circulatory system of the world. Its silvery branches, adorned like tides of glistening water pouring silently out of a vast urn, brushed the stone floor and created another world beneath its foliage, quiet and still. The wise King Lucius visited the tree daily, offering up his very heart and soul to the mighty being. He would run his old hands across the pitted bark, smiling gently as he remembered days past when he was in his youth, full of zest for life, his love and his kingdom. By now his smile had vanished – all he could think about was his kingdom as it was now, the endless warring that had savaged the land for the last three years, the child that had been taken from him, the friends he had lost, the pain his people had endured, all over the power buried deep in the roots of this very tree. He wondered if the tree knew how much blood had been spilt to protect it, to keep its sanctuary safe. The King gazed up through the branches, the soft light casting a mottled shadow on his face. It had finally come to this; he had no more to give, there were no more men for the fighting, no more banners to raise. The Rebel King had reached the inner sanctum, he had reached King Lucius' door, the mighty willow tree itself.

"Sorry, old friend," his voice little more than a whisper.

He closed his eyes, feeling the gentle breeze that filtered through the leaves, he smelt the sulphurous air, once so sweet, and readied himself. The mighty axe he had was no match for the grand tree before him, but with all his strength he slowly carved a groove in the wizened trunk. Though it was a cold day beads of sweat formed on his back and brow, and he let them roll down his face like the tears he longed to shed. For hours he slugged away at the old tree; with each cut he felt its pain course through his aging body, before finally it let out its last death cry and slowly toppled to the ground. The King fell to his knees, dizzy with the exertion and emotion, as the gate to the courtyard slowly ground open and a greying man entered. The man stopped for a moment, struck by the scene that confronted him, before dashing to the King's side.

"My Lord, what have you done?" he asked, helping the King to his feet.

"What had to be done, Hart. Forgive me, I beg you."

"But what will become of us, without the tree? The crops will wither, the animals will perish, and your people will die. Your Majesty, I can forgive you, but what about your kingdom?"

"We will have to work once more, like our forefathers and theirs before them. I couldn't let the tree fall into my enemy's hands; he would have obliterated our entire world. I have given us a chance to survive," replied the King, his face growing hard.

"People will die," repeated Hart.

"But how many more would die if all this power is consumed by the Rebel King?" The King's reply was cold, he knew he had made the right choice, the sacrifice was worth it. He himself had made a sacrifice so great that his faith had wavered, if only for a moment.

"Bring fire, we must burn it," instructed the King,

"But my Lord..." began Hart.

"Just do it."

Hart bowed deeply, obedient as ever, then turned and left. King Lucius gazed at his fallen comrade, his eyes quickly searching across the broken boughs. When Hart returned, with several other men in tow, he found the King cradling something small in his hands. He came closer but the King shied away like a small child hiding something precious. He whispered gently into his hands then lifted them to the sky as if setting a bird free.

"Your Majesty?" murmured Hart.

"Burn it," he said and wrapping his cloak around himself he swept past Hart.

Hart turned to follow, passing his torch to the man next to him who nodded in acknowledgement. The tree took a few moments before it was ablaze, smoke billowing from its sappy wood. As ordered, the men watched until they were sure that all of the mighty giant had caught fire, then they closed the heavy iron gates, never to enter again.

Outside the courtyard the last of the King's Guard had gathered and were milling about in the darkened hallway. They shifted about uneasily, all dressed in the same royal green, weapons at their sides and grim expressions on their faces. Hart was surprised there were so many of the King's Guard left, they were losing the battle and they knew it. Hemmed in on all sides by an encroaching evil, he would have not have blamed them if they had fled long ago, but they were truly loyal men, steadfast and faithful until the bitter end. As the King approached they dropped to their knees, heads bowed in respect. The Monarch made his way to the middle of the group of men and commanded them to rise; he wanted to look into the eyes of the men who had dedicated their life and soul to him and his family. He wanted to honour them by talking to them on the same level, not as ruler and subject but as one man to another. Gazing around at the war-weary faces, he spoke to them as he would a dear friend, as he would speak to Hart, and they listened respectfully, awaiting orders. As the directions were administered men disappeared left and right into the heavy shadows that now filled the once sunlit castle.

Finally the King stopped in front of a young man dressed in black, a hood pulled down over his face. The man instantly dropped to his knees, bowing so low he could feel the chill coming off the cold stone floor. Hart drew his breath in sharply through his teeth and stepped forwards, a fierce look in his eyes.

"Son," he murmured angrily under his breath. But the King held out his hand to stop Hart.

"Get up, boy," he said quietly, "It takes a lot of courage to come before me at a time like this; you have deeply grieved your father and he is my dearest friend.

What grieves him also grieves me. You must have something important to say?"

The man stood, removing his hood. Two penetrating dark eyes blazed passionately from the cold, hard face of Sir Hart's only son.

"My Lord, let me be her protector," he asked, his voice strong and determined.

Hart made to speak, but again the King silenced him. Hart glared at his son and clenched his hands so tightly into fists that his knuckles turned white. The King paced the now empty hallway, the sound of his boots reverberating off the harsh stone walls, while the young man waited silently.

"What are you willing to sacrifice to protect her? Why are you better than the man I have already chosen to keep her hidden, after so much thought and deliberation?" challenged the King.

Hart saw his son shift on the spot a little, before replying, "I will give you everything I have, my life if so be it."

The King came to a stand-still in front the young man, "To protect her, you will have to give her up. If you can do that then I believe you will have truly given everything."

Hart watched as his son swallowed hard and looked the King directly in the eye. He half expected his son to back down, overcome by his own selfishness and arrogance.

"Very well, my Lord, for her I will I do as you ask. Her life is worth more than any feelings I may have," he replied.

Hart bit his lip as he watched a new expression come over his son's face. It was barren and emotionless, as if he had buried his emotions along with his desires. It seemed as if a little bit of his soul had been taken away along with his freedom to be with the woman he loved. The task of a King's Guardsman was purely to protect the King and his family at all costs, including one's own life. There was no time for family, or life outside of the Guard. Your fellow Guardsmen became your only friends and there was very little time for anything other than training in the art of war, sustaining peak physical condition and protecting the King. It bred a type of person that was cold, hard and emotionless. A warrior.

King Lucius took a small knife from his pocket and reached out his hand towards Hart's son, who without hesitation placed his hand in that of the King. He did not look as the King sliced into the soft flesh on his palm, instead he fixed his eyes on his father. The King then did the same to his own palm, clasping their hands together so that their blood mingled and his loyalty was sealed. Hart's son gazed blankly at the King's face and pictured her face one last time as he locked his love for her away forever.

"Now we must go," said the King releasing the man from his grip, "Hart, take your son to her. I don't expect to see you again unless the worst has happened. Goodbye, dear friend, you have been my truest ally and strongest comrade."

King Lucius reached out and clapped his old friend on the shoulder before pulling him into his chest.

"Here, take this. It's from the willow, keep it safe. Just in case she doesn't survive," he whispered pushing a small pouch into Hart's hand.

Hart nodded, tucking it into his cloak, then he and his son bowed deeply before the King, before turning on their heels and leaving the King's presence. Hart barely managed to hold his tongue until they had emerged from the castle walls and out into a deserted market place. He sat down heavily on a wooden bench and clasped his head in his hands. His son watched him, unwilling to be the first to speak.

"What were you thinking?" Hart growled, his words echoing off the stone walls.

"I love her," he replied.

"And you think that's enough? Do you really understand what you are giving up, boy? Being part of the King's Guard is dangerous enough, but this too! You are putting yourself right in the line of fire, right in front of the Rebel King's face. You are still so young."

"Father, I am a man now," he glared down at the old man before him, "You just don't want to see that."

"Son."

"If that is where she is, in the middle of all this darkness, then that is the only place I need to be. I need to protect her."

Hart's son turned away and headed towards the castle stables; there was a long journey ahead and there was no point lingering in this abandoned shell.

"This is not the life I wanted for you, my son," murmured Hart before following him.

Back in the hallway a man with a scarred face and crimson eyes slipped unseen from between the courtyard doors wrapped in a leather cloak to protect himself from the flames. He paused and looked down at the small bag in his hand; he marvelled at how something so small could hold so much power. Feeling its satisfying weight in his hand he hid it in his cloak and disappeared into the darkness.

The King watched as Hart and his son rode away from the castle; he stood leaning on the window sill, his eyes fixed on the two figures as they gradually got smaller and smaller. He continued to gaze out the window even after they had disappeared into the bleakness of the kingdom beyond. A gentle voice pulled him out of the depths of his thoughts.

"My King."

He turned to see his wife, the Queen, standing in the doorway. Isabella was more beautiful now than she had ever been, time had been on her side. He loved the way she still took time to have her maid braid her hair every morning and to apply her makeup, to make sure she looked every part the Queen she was. But now she looked pale, as if the last of her fight had gone. With a quickening pace she crossed the room to her King and embraced him; the castle was desolate except for the two of them. He drew her into his arms and placed a kiss on top of her auburn hair. Being this close to her he noticed her fiery hair was now streaked with silver. He wondered when that had happened. His thoughts were interrupted by a deep roaring sound as if the very earth was being torn apart; the very foundations of the castle shook and mortar cascaded down from the walls.

King Lucius embraced his wife tightly, covering as much of her tiny body with his own as he could, as the very fabric of the castle started to come apart, great chunks of stone shaken off the walls and smashing on the ground all around them. The king looked down at his Queen - she was trembling and her eyes were wild with fright, he could feel her heart pounding in her chest.

"My Lord," she murmured,

"It is done," he said.

On the cold harsh road to the Grey Man, the oldest mountain on the border between St. Dores and the Greylands, Hart and his son felt the earth tremble. They struggled to calm the horses, fear in the animals' eyes as they pounded the ground, joining the melee of tremors underfoot. Lord Hart looked back in the direction that they had come, a deep sorrow in his dark eyes. His heart pounded hard and slow in his chest and he breathed in the bitter air, the sight of the crumbling castle choked him. He couldn't speak, nor could he look away, as much as he wanted to. The castle had been his home for many years and it had stood for hundreds of years before he had come to live there. His son had been born there one warm summer's morning, his wife had died in his arms shortly after. So many memories, heart-wrenching and comforting at the same time.

"It is done," murmured his son, watching his father gazing homewards longingly. He turned back toward their destination - that was where his longing lay, his heart's desire that could never be fulfilled. He felt an emptiness at the pit of his stomach, a churning unrest that he knew would never settle. Lord Hart turned to his son and rested a large, weathered hand on his shoulder.

"Come, my son, let's go to her, we must keep her hidden and safe until it is time is right. She is our one hope for the future."

Hart's son spurred his horse on and his father fell into stride next to him. They rode in silence for a while before the son turned to his father.

"I don't understand why we couldn't have sealed the Rebel King into the other realm," he asked quietly. Hart reined his horse in sharply.

"How could you say such a thing? How could we inflict the Rebel King on a realm that doesn't even know of our existence?"

"I just thought..."

"You didn't think my son, just like you didn't think when you mixed your blood with the King's. You are his for the remainder of your life, however long that may be. We don't know when she will be ready to return, this is only the beginning."

Hart saw his son groan inwardly and he turned his horse away, kicking it to a gallop. He shook his head before following him, leaving the King and the life they had known behind them

From the shadowy branches of a large tree, the man with crimson eyes watched them ride away, a wicked grin on his face.

Meanwhile, deep in the heart of the Grey Man on the border of St. Dores a young woman, no more than sixteen years old, shivered as she undressed and climbed the hard, stone steps into a large stone container filled with a thick, clear liquid. She felt the eyes of her guardian on her, but she felt no shame at her nakedness. As royalty she was used to being dressed and undressed, and now her body was no longer her own it was the property of King Lucius; it belonged to the people of her kingdom and she had a duty to them, a purpose. As she dipped her toe into the liquid she was pleasantly surprised to find it was neither cold nor warm; it felt as if she was floating on air as she slowly lowered herself into the liquid. The sounds of her guardian's voice singing a gentle wordless melody drifted in and out of her consciousness as she closed her eyes and lay herself down until the liquid covered her completely. As she felt the liquid flood her mouth and nose, she opened her eyes wide, fighting to take a breath. The silhouette of a man loomed over her and she tried to sit up, thrashing her arms and legs, but they felt leaden, and strong hands were pinning her to the bottom of the casket. Panic surged through her body and with all her strength she fought against the hands that held her, until finally she succumbed to the lack of oxygen, her consciousness faded and she was left with nothing but dark oblivion.

A moment later her eyes wrenched open, a dazzling white light surrounding her, voices bombarded her and she felt sick. Aware of a low but constant humming, she tried to sit up but her body felt heavy and weak. She shook her head, trying to focus her bleary eyes on something, anything, trying to suppress the overwhelming urge to vomit. Eventually the room and the people came into focus, the stone walls of her hideout in the mountain fading away, as her consciousness crossed over into this world. It had worked. She opened and closed her hands, wriggling her fingers, as if to test them out, and to her surprise she was holding something. Before anyone could take it away she tucked it into the pocket of her clothes. Now all she had to do was wait to be called home.

Chapter 2

Emma Dores had come to admire the empty side of her bed, the crisp ironed white bedsheets, the perfectly plumped pillow, the unrumpled duvet. In fact, she would go as far as to say she respected the vacant left-hand side of the bed; it signified dignity and self-worth, an absence of one-night stands, drunken accidents and embarrassing mornings. Emma did not acknowledge the crisp lines as a sign of her lack of a meaningful relationship, her loneliness and how sometimes the total silence of her flat when she returned home from work made her cry.

The left-hand side had remained empty for several years now, and when Emma stirred in the middle of the night she would often sleepily reach across and push her hand between the cold, refreshing sheets. A small pleasure in her small life. Tonight was like any other, and rousing momentarily from her sleep she reached across, smiling to herself at the coolness that enveloped her fingers, before turning onto her back. Suddenly her eyes wrenched open and a scream escaped her lungs. She dived across to the empty side of the bed in terror, pulling the duvet over her head like a small child. She could have sworn there had been a man's face just inches from her own, but when she gingerly emerged from the blanket and rubbed the sleep from her eyes she found herself staring into the same darkness that accompanied her every night.

"Fool," she muttered, trying to reassure herself, running her hands through her hair. She didn't move from the empty side of the bed, instead she settled down onto the unused pillow and tried to focus on the faintly glowing hands of her watch. 4.15 am, too early to get up but now the good night's sleep she had anticipated would be ruined by a couple of hours of light, erratic sleep in which she would be keeping one ear open for her 6.30 alarm. Emma sighed and pulled the duvet up around her chin. She felt cold and restless but eventually she must have drifted off into an uneasy sleep, the empty side of her bed dishevelled and occupied for the first time in years.

After the night's events Emma overslept. The snooze button on her phone evaded her fumbling fingers and she switched it off accidently. Instead of lying there with her eyes screwed shut, pretending she was still asleep, waiting for the trill of the alarm, Emma drifted back to sleep. Thirty minutes later the 7.00 am train shook the single-glazed windows of her flat, rattling her awake. Cursing, she threw the covers back and dashed across the room to the ensuite. A decision lay before her, breakfast or a shower? Although her body would not appreciate being deprived of the most important meal of the day, she felt her customers wouldn't appreciate the smell of her unwashed body. Plus a few less calories in the day certainly wouldn't have a detrimental effect on her figure.

The shower was hot and brief. Emma washed her hair, relishing in the guilty pleasure of overpriced shampoo and conditioner; she didn't care what anyone

15

said, it made her feel special. Out of the shower and wrapped in a towel she ran an anti-frizz serum through her hair and debated whether to battle with it today. She knew if she scraped it back into a tight bun, by the end of the day her unruly curls would have escaped from the clutches of the hairband and crowned her head in auburn fuzz. Au natural today she decided and began applying a little makeup. She was peering into the mirror and carefully sweeping the mascara brush over her pale eyelashes when she thought she saw something dash past the slightly open door. She placed the mascara brush on the edge of the sink and crept towards the door. Taking a deep breath, she flung the door open only to find her bedroom empty, exactly how she had left it fifteen minutes ago.

Shaking her head and rolling her eyes at her own ridiculousness she returned to her makeup. By 7.30 she had made it out of the apartment and downstairs to her car. Fortunately it was under cover and the previous night's frost hadn't quite reached it. She opened the boot and flung her bag into it, before clambering into the driver's seat. The cold engine took a moment to start before rumbling into life and Emma pulled away. Luckily the book shop she owned with an old friend was only a short drive away on the high street.

Emma had known the co-owner, Nicholas, since they were children. Their families had been friends ever since she could remember, although Emma's memories didn't stretch back as far as most people's. At the age of sixteen Emma and her parents had been involved in a car accident, and her parents had died. She had walked away from the twisted wreckage physically unscathed, although mentally she shut down. Her brain decided that the best way to cope with the loss of both parents in one catastrophic event was to just forget; to forget everything prior to the crash, to forget her friends and family, her home town, her name and even the faces of her parents. It was as if she had suddenly come into being as a sixteen-year-old girl, alone and confused, with nothing but the clothes on her back and a cutting from a willow tree which she had refused to relinquish to anyone. All she remembered was Nicholas; though she didn't recall his name at first, there was something about his caring face which settled her soul.

His family agreed to take her in and become her legal guardians. At first she refused to be separated from Nicholas, finding her way to his bed every night where he would sleepily roll over to make space for her, one arm around her and her head on his chest. Although the odd sexual thought crossed his mind in the depths of the night, he never acted on his impulses; she made him feel sad and all he wanted to do was ease her sadness and his along with it. Slowly she let herself be separated from him, fitting into his family's everyday life, remembering her mother and father purely through photographs, being told the things she liked and didn't like, until she turned twenty-one and inherited the money her parents had in savings and from the sale of their house and possessions. At first Emma had tried to convince Nicholas' parents to take a large portion of the money as a way of compensation for the second teenager they had never expected to have, but they had point blank refused.

'Why would we want payment for looking after our own daughter?' they told her, for they too had lost someone, a daughter who died just before her first birthday from a rare childhood illness. Emma did not remember her, but she was told that she used to play with the baby and bring her little presents. So instead Emma and Nicholas had decided to invest the money into their joint dream, a London bookshop, named 'Dores and Penn'. Now at the age of 26, Emma had been running the book shop together with Nicholas for 5 successful years. She enjoyed its quaintness and the mile-high stacks of books crammed into every nook and cranny, though she often wondered if one of the stacks fell on her whether she would ever be found again.

She pulled into the side street behind the shop, parked, opened the car door and shuffled out between the bins, trying not to touch them too much, or brush against the mildewed wall. She swung her heavy bag out of the boot and rested it on her hip as she reached up and brought the boot lid down with a slam. She had been doing some accounting at home to pass the long wintery nights; numbers had never been Nicholas' strong point - he liked literature, books and women. Emma however enjoyed the satisfaction of straight columns filled with neat numbers that all balanced at the end of the page. She was happy to take on the responsibility. She locked the car and trudged over to the back door, fumbling in the cold for her keys. She made a mental note that the back door needed oiling as it creaked open and she stepped over the threshold, taking a deep breath. The smell of books, old and new, mixed with yesterday's freshly ground coffee was so intoxicating, so wonderful it made her smile inside and out. The small storage room at the back of the shop was home to a sink, a couple of kitchen units, a coffee machine, table and chairs and a small fridge that hummed noisily, but it was all they needed. It was the fridge that she made a beeline for, dumping her stuff on the floor and rubbing her hands together.

"First things first," she said to herself, bending down to look for the ground coffee.

She then reached for the cupboard and pulled out a rather coffee-stained green mug. Nicholas had given it to her when they had opened the shop five years ago and she refused to part with it even though the handle had fallen off several times. It reminded her of him when he was away; it felt like a part of him was still there. She unscrewed the coffee jar, spoon in hand, only to discover it was empty. She tutted, remembering that she was supposed to have taken a little detour to the coffee house on the way to work this morning. She looked down at her watch, 8.00 am. She still had half an hour spare before she really had to be setting up the shop ready to open at 9.00 am. There was an express supermarket maybe a 5-minute walk away so Emma decided instant coffee would have to do for now, and grabbing her keys off the kitchen counter she checked her pockets for small change. Finding some in the depths of her coat pockets she headed out of the back door and into the cold.

The ground was icier underfoot than she had realised, and as Emma rounded the corner of the shop onto the side street she felt her feet slide from under her. As she fell she tried to grab onto something to stop her fall, but the wall was devoid of hand holds, not even a water pipe graced its face and Emma almost instantly felt the frozen ground rushing up to meet the back of her head. Pain splintered through her skull sending a cloud of stars in front of her eyes before the world closed in and she blacked out.

In the darkness Emma could hear voices, quiet at first but gradually getting louder and louder as she lay paralysed in the darkness.

"How long will it take?" A man's voice, cold and cynical.

"A day or so. She's been out for a very long time, it takes time to bring her back properly." This time it was a soft, female voice; it sounded familiar but Emma could not place it.

"We don't have that kind of time," said the man, sounding agitated.

Emma tried to open her eyes but she found them inexplicably firmly shut, as if she had no control over her own body. Suddenly she felt rough hands on her shoulders, shaking her. She tried to cry out, but her voice stuck in her throat. As quickly as the blackness had engulfed her, it began to evaporate and she could see the sunlight through her closed eyes. The shaking continued until she opened her eyes, half expecting to see a man and a woman, but instead a young woman was leaning over her, gently clutching her shoulders and calling to her, a concerned look on her face.

"Are you ok?" she asked, as Emma started to come to and realised she was still lying on the frozen ground in the side street.

Emma stared at the woman for a moment before remembering her manners, "Yes sorry, thank you."

"That's ok, I saw you fall as I passed by, looked like you hit your head pretty hard. Are you sure you're ok? Can I call anyone?" the woman asked with genuine concern.

Emma felt the back of her head, it was tender but there was no blood. She showed the woman her fingers.

"No blood, I'm fine, honestly," smiled Emma.

"If you're sure, maybe I should stay with you for a while?" said the woman, more to herself than to Emma.

"Honestly its ok, I have a friend I can call if I feel woozy, but thank you for your help."

The woman nodded and helped Emma to her feet, then saying goodbye she disappeared around the corner. Emma called out her thanks and decided to give up on the coffee for now and maybe try again later. She returned to the quiet shop and found an icepack at the back of the fridge. She placed it gently on the back on her head and sat down at the little table. Her head was incredibly sore. She knew if Nicholas had been there he would have made her go to A&E and sat with her until she was seen, despite her telling him he needed to be at the shop. But he wasn't here; he was thousands of miles away in the States with his current girlfriend, current being the optimum word. Nicholas was sweet, caring and funny, not to mention handsome. His soft blonde hair and deep brown eyes had won many hearts, but he couldn't settle on just one girl.

"There is too much variety in life, too many beautiful women to love," he would say laughing, "I need to sample it all!"

He and Emma had locked lips once, after one too many celebratory drinks in the dusty shell of their shop, keys pressed tightly into their hands. They both had instantly vowed never to do it again. She and Nicholas loved each other like brother and sister. He was her constant and unchanging Nicholas and his fleeting heart was all part of who he was, yet she knew his feelings for her would never change. One day she hoped he would find the girl he couldn't let go of, the one who would capture his heart like a butterfly.

After a few moments Emma got to her feet and once more began rifling through the cupboards. She was sure she had seen some painkillers in there somewhere. Eventually her fingers closed around a small cupboard box from which she extracted the last couple of pills and swallowed them with a glass of water.

The day passed slowly and uneventfully; Emma made a good number of sales and accepted an order of books she was expecting, but she was distracted. The throbbing in the back of her head, though somewhat dulled by the painkillers, bothered her and she couldn't get her head around the voices she had heard. Where had they come from? Her own self-conscious maybe? The man in her bedroom and then the movement in the mirror kept playing on her mind. She felt foolish even considering the idea that she had actually seen someone, but she couldn't shake the odd feeling that had overcome her whole body. It was like a chill had totally consumed her, making her hair stand on end, and it was unpleasant, it made her feel uneasy. Maybe it was because of the bang to her head, perhaps she was a bit concussed, needless to say she wasn't looking forward to going back to her apartment alone.

At 6.00 pm she flipped the closed sign, locked the front door and had a quick tidy before making her way out to the car. The evening had grown bitter and she shivered as she locked the back door and shuffled over to the car, pulling her coat tightly round her. She opened the car, threw her bag onto the passenger seat and slid into the driver's seat. The car took a few attempts to start but when it finally choked into life she glanced in the rear-view mirror out of habit then did a double take, spinning round. But there was nothing there, just the vacant back seat.

"This is getting silly, maybe A&E wouldn't be a bad idea," she muttered to herself. Slowly she pulled away, the car already losing traction on the icy ground. She headed for her local supermarket, not wanting to go straight home to her silent apartment, choosing the bright lights of the food aisle instead. She spent half an hour or so looking for something that would take her fancy for dinner, before settling on chicken and new potatoes. Healthy, lean and bland. As she passed the turning for the hospital she almost slowed down, but dismissing the idea as quickly as it had popped into her head she continued her journey home.

Emma parked the car and made her way up the narrow stairwell to her flat. It was only on the second floor but she liked to think that by taking the stairs she was counteracting the effect of the cakes and chocolates that regularly found their way into her cupboards. She hesitated at the door, keys hovering by the lock. She took a deep breath - surely there was no one in her flat and it would be exactly how she had left it that morning. She felt her body tense, despite her rational thinking, as she plunged the key into the lock. The door swung open to reveal exactly what she had expected, nothing. The life of a singleton sat before her in the gloom. Emma flicked the lights on and walked into the flat, shutting the door behind her and dumping her stuff on the sofa. Heating on and then into the kitchen to prepare dinner.

Before long Emma had dimmed the living-room lights and was washing up in the bright lights of the kitchen. She poured herself another large glass of wine and washed down a couple more painkillers before picking up a tea towel and beginning the drying up. The theme tune to her favourite programme began playing in the living room and she turned, plate in hand to watch it from the kitchen.

The sound of breaking china echoed through the flat, bits of broken plate scattered across the kitchen floor leaving Emma standing still, clutching the tea towel. Sitting at her dining table was the same man she had seen in her bed that morning. Her chest tightened with fear, her heart beating hard against her ribs. He hadn't looked up when Emma had dropped the plate; instead he continued to stare avidly down at something on the table, although Emma could see nothing there. Although she couldn't see much of his face, she was sure it was the same man. A chill ran down her spine as she tried to make her body obey her but it refused. He moved his hands over the table as if he was studying something, his dark hair falling around his face and obscuring her view of him. Finally her body seemed to remember it could move, and as she forced herself to step into the room towards the phone he looked up. His deep, dark eyes burned into hers for a second and he was gone.

Chapter 3

Panic swept through Emma's body, and she was shaking almost uncontrollably as she reached for the phone. As she dialled she was unable to take her eyes off the spot where the man had been sitting just moments before. She listened to the familiar trill of the phone at the other end, then there was a click as the phone connected and a man answered.

"Emma?" said a sleepy voice at the other end of the phone, sounding distant and far away.

"Nicholas," said Emma trying to speak calmly.

"Are you ok, my girl?" He asked, a worried tone entering his voice, "it's unlike you to call me, not at this hour, you normally text."

"Sorry, I forgot about the time difference."

"Emma, what's wrong?"

"I'm fine, I mean I'm not. I just..." her voice trailed off.

"Emma?"

"It's just I thought I saw someone in my flat."

"When?"

"Just now, he was here and then he was gone."

"A man, did you call the police? Is he still there? Do you need me to come home?" Nicholas sounded frantic as he bombarded her with questions.

"Well, no."

"No to what?"

"All three," murmured Emma, realising how ridiculous she sounded.

"So, let me get this straight, there was someone, a man, in your flat but now he's gone and you didn't call the police. Emma are you feeling ok?" Nicholas' voice returned to its normal pitch and tempo.

"I fell in the alley behind the shop, banged my head. Maybe that's all it is," Emma sighed, feeling silly.

"Go get yourself checked out," said Nicholas, "call mum if you're worried about being alone tonight. Don't you call her on a Monday anyway? I'm sure she would come over."

"Yeah, you're right, as always Nick, sorry to bother you."

"Anything for my girl."

"You shouldn't talk about me like that, what's her name? Jenny will get jealous."

"Penny and nah she won't, don't think it's going to work out anyway. I'll be back in 10 days, maybe sooner if you need me?"

"Don't rush back, but make sure you come over when you're back, ok?"

"You'll be my first stop. Penny is staying here for Christmas, so we'll do Chinese and movies, ok?"

"Sounds good, see you soon, and be nice to that poor girl, don't break her heart. Love always," said Emma smiling to herself.

"Would I ever do such a thing?! Take care, my girl, see you soon," replied Nicholas, hanging up the phone.

Emma felt more relaxed after speaking with Nicholas, her hands had stopped shaking and her voice was steady. She picked up the phone and dialled her adoptive parents. As she waited for them to answer she decided not to tell them about her fall or about the man in her flat; instead she had her usual 20-minute catch up that always made her feel happy and safe.

Putting down the phone Emma returned to the broken plate, grabbed the dustpan and brush and started clearing up. She couldn't help glancing over her shoulder at the dining room table every now and then. When she was finished she settled down in front of the TV with the rest of the wine and a blanket, only to wake up at midnight, the TV still chatting away to its unconscious audience. Sleepily she switched off the TV and headed for the bathroom, taking off her makeup and brushing her teeth before climbing, exhausted, into bed. The sheets were freezing and it took several minutes of shivering before Emma warmed up enough to drift off to sleep.

Emma sat up in bed, threw back the covers and groaned. She swung her legs out of bed and grabbed her phone off the bedside table. 5.42 am. Great. She had hardly slept at all, tossing and turning, waking up what felt like every 5 minutes. Rubbing her eyes, she made her way to the bathroom, and seeing that she was up so early she decided to have a bath instead of her usual in and out shower. She sat on the edge of the bath watching the steam rise from the hot water, before reaching for the bath soak and glugging a large amount under the tap. She watched it foam and fill the small bathroom with the gentle fragrance of coconut milk and honey. She smiled - after the terrible night she had had she deserved a little indulgence, a little relaxation. Checking the temperature with her hand, she swirled the water around until she was satisfied that it was ready, then began to get undressed.

The hot water was almost scalding and she could feel beads of sweat starting to form on her forehead, but that was how she liked it. It felt as if it was washing away all the events of yesterday and last night, making her new again. She shuffled down, submerging herself to wash her hair, lingering under the water for a moment or so, eyes screwed shut against the water and soap. As she started to sit up she suddenly felt something heavy on her shoulders. Two large hands were gripping her tight, pushing her down, stopping her from reaching the surface. Emma wrenched her eyes open, trying to get a glimpse of her attacker through the soapy water; she could just about make out the dark outline of someone leaning over her. She struggled and thrashed, desperate to break free, the surface tantalisingly close, the precious oxygen she needed only centimetres away. As she felt the last of her breath escape her lungs, rushing away from her in a smattering of small bubbles, the hands released her and she pushed herself up as quickly as she could.

Emma emerged coughing and spluttering, her breath hoarse and shallow. Gasping for air she looked around the room for her attacker; she could feel tears burning in the back of her eyes, a mixture of fear and relief. She slowly climbed out of the bath and wrapped herself in a large towel. Looking around the room for a weapon, she spotted the nail scissors and after deciding they were a better option than a toilet brush she crept towards the door brandishing the scissors.

Emma pushed the door open a fraction, revealing a thin slice of her bedroom, but from her limited view the coast seemed clear. She opened the door fully to an empty room. With her heart pounding in her chest, she quickly opened the door to the living room, thrusting the nail scissors in front of her. All was quiet and dark. In a few strides she had made it across the living room and to the front door where she flicked the lights on. Nothing. Her empty wine glass was still on the side table, her blanket draped over the armchair where she had dozed last night. Still unable to shake the unnerving feeling that she was not alone Emma walked over to the glass and picked it up. The last room to check was the kitchen and she decided she might as well put the wine glass in the sink. She strode over to the kitchen door, glancing at the dining table. Something caught her eye and she did a double take, she was sure she had seen those eyes again, smouldering and dark. The next step sent a searing pain through her foot and she trod on a missed piece of broken plate, then she felt her feet go from under her as the floor rushed up to meet her.

"I'm not dressed," was her last thought as she fell, her head hitting the floor hard as she blacked out for the second time in less than 24 hours.

Chapter 4

Emma caught glimpses of faces in the darkness - they would rush at her with a burst of white light and then disappear again, obscured as if seen through frosted glass. Yet she could hear their voices clearly, slicing through the oppressive blackness, quiet at first but getting louder with each flash of light.

"It's happening too quickly," said a woman anxiously.

"She's strong, she'll be ok," replied a man, his voice deep and quiet.

"It's been 10 years," Emma heard panic beginning to creep into the woman's voice.

"Exactly, we are running out of time, it has to be now. It's been too long," murmured the man.

There was silence, resounding and deep. It was unnatural, pressing down on her ear drums and stretching out in front of her in a vast expanse of nothingness. Suddenly a blinding light filled Emma's vision and she struggled to open her eyes. Slowly the light began to fade and she managed to bring her hand to her eyes to shield them as she cautiously opened them. She pulled herself to her feet and found herself standing in a dried-up riverbed, the white light bleaching everything around to sepia. She turned on the spot but as far as the eye could see there was nothing but blue sky and white-washed earth. Panic set in as she took in her surroundings, was this Heaven? Was she dead? She could feel her heart pounding and her breath came in short sharp bursts, so maybe she wasn't dead. But then what was going on?

"Where am I?" she murmured under her breath.

She buried her head in her hands, in the hope that when she took them away she would be in her living room, sore, cold but home.

"Emma," her thoughts were interrupted by a voice behind her. Slowly she withdrew her hands and turned around to see an old man, dressed in a long white robe.

"I'm dead," she said, squinting at him as he approached. There was something familiar about the gentle smile on his aged face and as he got closer her reached out a hand to her, his skin mottled like crepe paper winding its way round his bony fingers in tattered sheets.

"Emma," he said again, his hand still outstretched.

Emma backed off a little, a worried look on her face.

"Oh, my child," he whispered to her, stepping forward and taking her hand with a strength she didn't expect. His touch was soft yet firm, she found it surprisingly reassuring.

"What is going on?" she asked.

"Slowly, slowly," he murmured, "let's walk."

Without letting go of her hand he began walking, leading her somewhere yet nowhere. She looked down at herself for the first time and realised that she, too, was wearing a white robe. She brushed it down as she walked, feeling the fabric between her fingers. She was about to ask the old man about it, when he spoke.

"Don't worry about the clothes, it's not important," he smiled, "think of something else if you'd prefer?"

Emma's mind instantly went to a hideous dress that Nicholas had brought back with him from the States last year. It was an awful emerald green and covered with tiny gold stars, far shorter than anything she would have picked out. She had worn it for an evening so as not to hurt his feelings. As she thought of it, it appeared on her body in all its hideousness.

The old man laughed, "Well that's different, I think I preferred the robe."

Emma smiled gingerly and the white robe appeared again.

"Here will do," said the man coming to an abrupt stop. Emma looked around, this spot was exactly the same as the one they had left, in fact it looked identical. Dry earth surrounded them, stretching out to a cloudless sky.

"Now I have some explaining to do, so have a seat if you will," the man gestured to a bench in front of them which had definitely not been there a moment ago. It was a crude bench, covered in graffiti and carvings, just like the one at the local park that she and Nicholas used to play in.

"So what shall I answer first?" he asked her once she was seated.

"Where am I?" asked Emma.

"On the plains of your mind."

Emma looked at him in disbelief, "Ok, and who are you?"

"Part of your mind, your subconscious if you will," replied the man calmly, not at all phased by Emma's disbelief.

"So, I'm in my own mind talking to myself. I must have hit my head harder than I realised. If I close my eyes I'm sure I will wake up back on my dining room floor," Emma laughed, trying to convince herself. She closed her eyes the way they did in the movies, counted slowly to 10 and then cautiously opened them again.

The old man was still sitting patiently in front of her, a serious look on his face. Emma tried opening and closing her eyes a few more times for good measure, but every time she opened them, much to her disappointment, nothing had changed.

"Ok," she said finally, "I'll play along. So if you're my subconscious why are you, you?"

"I don't have to be," smiled the man, "I can be anyone you want me to be."

Before Emma's eyes the man became Nicholas, then her adoptive mother, her adoptive father, her next-door neighbour, her friends from college. Hundreds of different people appeared and disappeared in front of her, some she recognised, others she didn't.

"I can even be you," said a tall woman standing before her.

Emma gazed up at her from her seat. There certainly was a strong resemblance but this woman was tall and slender, like a bowing willow tree, with long wavy auburn hair and bright green eyes. Freckles were scattered across her small nose and there was a knowing smile on her thin lips. She was striking, handsome even, unlike the models plastered across the magazines she read, yet there was something very alluring about her. She held herself with confidence and boldness, as if she could hold her own.

"That's not me," Emma laughed. Where was the little round tummy and the cloud of fuzzy hair?

Without thinking she ran her hands down her body, feeling it beneath the robe. Startled, she had to look down, running her hands again and again over her body. She couldn't believe what she was seeing and feeling. Her stomach was flatter, her bust smaller, her face longer.

"I...a mirror," she managed to say.

"But I am your mirror," replied the other Emma.

"But I... how can this be?" asked Emma, faltering as she struggled to speak. Her mind raced, she was so confused already and she still half expected to wake up at any moment. The woman sat next to her and placed a hand on her shoulder.

"Shall I explain?"

Emma could do nothing but nod.

"Close your eyes."

Emma obeyed. Images began flashing in front her of eyes, faces and places, quickly rushing past in her mind's eye.

"Forget all you once knew. The world you once knew, the home you once lived in, the people you knew, they have all been your hiding place for the last 10 years of your life. There has been such turmoil in the world you were hidden from, so much fighting, so much death and darkness. Your father and mother had to hide you before it was too late, before the man that savages our land found you and destroyed you too, just like your brother. Your brother was murdered when he was only a young man, then the Rebel King killed your mother and your father, but not before your father cut down the Great Willow Tree, the source of all power in St. Dores and across our world. He sent with you a cutting from that great tree."

Emma saw the image of an ancient willow tree and pictured the little tree she had cultivated from the cutting she had refused to give up after her accident, in her adoptive parent's garden.

"Do you remember?"

Emma opened her eyes, shaking her head.

"Close your eyes again," said the other Emma softly, "your father sent protectors to watch over you while your body was in a deep sleep in our world and while your conscious took form safely in another. But now the time has come for you to return, to restore the willow tree, give us our hope and peace back, to take your rightful place as Queen."

"Queen...?" stammered Emma, her eyes flicking open, "I think you've got it wrong. This is clearly a dream, or my body's way of dealing with a head trauma; I'm probably in a coma somewhere."

"You had to believe the other reality completely, that is what kept you safe. You have been hidden for 10 years, that's a long time, but you will remember your life here soon enough."

"But how? My body, my life. I had a bookshop, friends, what about my brother?" Emma felt herself choke a little as she thought about him.

"It's all real in a way. They are real, it was you that wasn't. Did you ever wonder why you couldn't remember your parents? Why it seemed that you just came into existence at the age of 16 with no previous memories?"

Something struck a chord with Emma and she looked up at her double, a serious expression on her face. In an odd way things seemed to be starting to make sense. She had never felt like she fitted in, even as an adult. She had never found love, never had close friends, she lived alone. But what was most significant was her distinct lack of childhood memories. She had a vague recollection of being loved, wanted, but by whom she wasn't sure. The doctors had told her it was due to her accident. The accident?

"Wait, the accident? Did it ever really happen?" she asked.

The woman shook her head, "Not to you as such."

"So what happens now?"

"Well, you will start to remember, slowly at first, but it will come and you will forget the other life you had and the people you left there will forget you, it will be as if you had never existed. But now we need to wake you up; I think they are ready for you now."

"Wait, I still have so much to ask you. I don't understand. This can't be happening. It's too ridiculous," stammered Emma, standing up and pacing a little, "who is waiting for me?"

"Your protectors, your people and your guardian. She's been with you these 10 years, keeping your body safe."

Emma gave her other self a look of disbelief, and pushing her hands into her hair she sat down again.

"So, if I am really to believe this make-believe, how do I get to them?" she asked. Emma hated to admit it but she was actually a little curious despite her disbelief.

"Drink this," the other Emma replied, holding out what looked like a glass of water that had appeared from nowhere.

"What is it?"

"I have no idea, we're in your mind," laughed the woman.

Emma took the glass and smelt it. It had no noticeable smell and she was about to drink it when her other self stopped her.

"One last thing," the woman said, placing her hand on Emma's free hand, "your real name is Emelda, Princess Emelda. Get used to it quickly. Now drink."

The other Emma pushed the glass towards Emma's lips and she automatically drank deeply. The liquid had no taste and she didn't feel any sensation of drinking. For a moment she wondered if she had actually drunk anything. Then she felt an almighty fire raging down her throat and into her stomach; her throat seemed to close and she couldn't breathe. She heard the glass smash as she dropped it; clutching at her throat she was swallowed by darkness. Her body twitched and convulsed in the blackness and a feeling of nausea overwhelmed her. Images flashed through her mind once more, constantly changing, never stopping for long enough for her to get a good look. Faster and faster they came, the same few people and places, over and over again. Her memories, her family, her home all came rushing back so fast she couldn't configure them, yet with each fleeting image she felt like she was waking up, like she was coming alive again. Her body was still convulsing and she felt vomit rising in her throat. Then one image fixed in her mind: a boy of 16 or 17 laughing a deep cruel laugh, and blood everywhere. Someone somewhere was screaming; it was blood-curdling, making her skin crawl.

 Emma opened her eyes, sitting bolt upright, the terrifying scream resounding from her own mouth. She could feel her chest aching with the intensity of her cry. Yet in her distress she could feel gentle hands on hers, quietly calming her, until the noise faded and Emma took a deep breath. It was then she really looked at the woman before her, a very old woman, older than anyone she had ever seen. Her long wispy hair hung down her back like a silver waterfall and her face was lined like an old map but her eyes were gentle and comforting. She spoke softly to Emma.

 "Your Majesty," she said gently, caressing Emma's hands as a mother would a child, "breathe deeply, take your time."

 She turned and called to someone who waited behind a screen that separated Emelda from the rest of the room, "Indira, bring me that towel, would you?"

 There was a shuffling behind her and Emma looked over the woman's shoulder to see a younger woman, with skin like the night and hair of gold, rushing to find a suitable towel from a shelf carved into the actual walls. Emma's eyes went from the woman to the room she was in. It was gloomy, lit only by an array of candles that cast shadows over the stone walls. They were all nestled into the face of the wall and little hollows had been carved for each one of them. She felt as if she were in deep in the bowels of the earth, hidden away from everything. As she looked around she saw a small bed in the corner of the room, as well as a little table and two chairs, a few of the things needed for a basic level of living.

"Your Majesty," said the old woman once again, startling Emma, "can you hear me?"

Emma nodded slowly, focusing her eyes on the old lady. It seemed to take ages for her body to respond to the instructions she was giving it and she wasn't sure if she could even speak. She moved her hands a little at her sides but found them tied fast; she peered down and saw that they were wrapped in many thin branches; in fact, her whole body from the waist down was intertwined with the woody tendrils of a tree. She felt panic rising as she struggled to break free but the tree would not let her go.

"Emelda please, be still, my child. They will only hold you tighter, we just have to wait, they are adjusting to your change in state of consciousness, just as you are," explained the old woman, "watch and see."

Emma glanced down, her heart still pounding, resisting the urge to struggle. Before her eyes the branches started to withdraw, creeping down her arms and legs, setting her free once more, until finally they became nothing more than a small cutting which glowed faintly, a little bud clinging to the side of it. It looked familiar and Emma frowned at it.

"I know it," she managed to say, her voice little more than a whisper that stuck in her throat.

The old woman brought her mouth close to Emma's ear so that only she could hear, "That is all that is left of the Great Willow, it has sustained you here for the last 10 years. It is the source of all power and life, it belongs to you."

As Emma stared at the little bud, the same great sadness she had felt when she had seen the image of the Great Willow overwhelmed her and she felt tears burning at the back of her eyes. She tried not to cry, but it was no good, the tears flowed silently down her face.

"Come now, not all is lost, you are our hope and the time has come for you to come back to us," smiled the old woman.

She held her hands out to Emma, who gingerly took them and stood up in the stone vault she was in. Her legs felt like jelly and she fell down again, almost smashing her head on the back of the container, but the old woman was nimble and strong, she caught Emma's head and eased her back up to sitting.

"Slowly, slowly," she murmured.

Emma tried again and this time her legs held her weight, she stood for a moment clutching the woman's hands before finally stepping over the edge of the container and down a small flight of stone steps. She collapsed into the warm towel and the woman's outstretched arms at the bottom of the steps and was ushered over to the bed. She was overcome with uncontrollable shivering that made her teeth chatter in her skull so loudly she was sure she was going to deafen herself.

"It's ok, it's all normal. Your body is just getting used to sustaining itself again. It will be over soon, there's no rush," the woman reassured her.

"You are my guardian?" Emma managed to stutter.

"Yes, your Majesty."

"Please call me Emma."

"Emelda."

"Yes, Emelda."

38

The name sounded funny coming from her own mouth. She repeated it under her breath over and over until it finally sounded like her own.

"What's your name? I'm so sorry I can't remember," asked Emelda.

"Sophia," she replied, "and this is Indira, she is one of your protectors, she is part of the King's Guard."

Indira stepped forward out of the shadows and knelt before Emelda, who shifted nervously, unsure of what to do.

"Please," she said, "don't kneel for me."

"But you are Princess Emelda, our last hope, I am honoured to serve you," replied Indira.

Emelda smiled politely back, "Thank you."

"Come eat and drink a little, my girl. It will help no end," said Sophia gesturing towards a plate of bread and cheese, a tall glass of water next to it.

With trembling hands Emelda brought the glass to her lips and took a sip. It was cold, refreshing, bringing her parched throat back to life.

After a moment Sophia took her hand in her own, "Are you ready to bathe?"

Emelda nodded and Indira disappeared for a moment before returning with a small metal bathtub. She placed it before Emelda and then disappeared again only to return just as quickly carrying two buckets of steaming water. She emptied them and then went to fetch more until the bath was filled.

"Come now, your Majesty, before it gets cold," said Indira holding out her hand to assist her into the bath. Emma climbed cautiously into the scalding water, gasping as it took her breath away.

"Is it too hot?" Asked Sophia, concerned.

"No, it's wonderful," replied Emelda, sliding deep into the water so she was submerged up to her neck. She felt down her chest and stomach and all the way down her legs before pulling up, horrified. Ten years of hair growth was bristling up and down her legs, and probably under her armpits too. The thought appalled her.

"Do you have a razor?" she asked Sophia quietly.

Sophia looked puzzled. Then she broke out into a laugh.

"Men use a razor blade, but women use this, should they desire to be hair-free like a baby," she grinned, beckoning to Indira who brought over a basket of pots and bottles. She rummaged around and pulled out a pot of a sticky amber liquid.

"Wax," laughed Emelda.

"Would you like me to do it for you?"

"Please."

As Emelda bathed, Sophia busied herself with strips of soft cotton and warmed the wax in the hot bathwater. The soothing aroma of warm beeswax soon drifted through the air as Sophia worked quickly and efficiently, removing all the unwanted hair until Emelda saw her body shine like silk. As the water began to cool Sophia produced more soaps and perfumes and washed her from head to toe. Emelda felt like a child again but it wasn't an unpleasant experience and as the water soothed her body and soul and Sophia scrubbed she felt strength returning to her limbs. She felt a keenness returning to her mind, a sense of purpose and determination. Emelda felt as if she was returning to herself; Emma was fading away and Emelda was emerging once again. The future Queen was being reborn.

Sophia laid out her clothes on the bed then produced another thick towel and Emelda climbed gracefully out of the bath, her feet no longer stumbling over each other, her legs strong and in control of her movements. She felt a difference in the way she moved and walked that didn't feel out of place.

Emelda stood, letting the towel fall to the ground. This woman had seen her naked for the last 10 years, what did it matter now? She climbed into her undergarments and shirt, surprising not only herself but Sophia too. Her fingers remembered how to fasten the delicate buttons and tighten the black leather bodice. Sophia held up a pair of slim looking trousers, a quizzical look on her face.

"The King's Guard had these made for you; they said they would be better for travelling in. Not very ladylike if you ask me," said Sophia.

"It's ok," replied Emelda, "I'm used to wearing things like that."

"Very well, your Majesty," said Sophia helping Emelda into them.

She smiled as she thought how funny Nicholas would have thought she looked, dressed in such dated clothes. Thinking about Nicholas, the smile faded from her face. He would be forgetting her already. She felt tears building up once more, but with all her might she choked them back. Sophia fastened the trousers neatly around Emelda's waist and stepped back, a satisfied look on her face. Just then she remembered something and scuttled off, returning with a pair of slim leather boots and socks.

"They are beautiful," said Emelda, instantly reaching down for the boots. They were soft and supple, with a gentle heel for walking.

"Please, let me, your Majesty," said Indira stepping forward and taking the boots from her hand. Carefully she slipped the socks over Emelda's small feet, followed by the boots. They felt like a second skin, she had never worn anything so fine and beautiful. She looked up at Indira, smiling with glee.

"Boots fit for a Queen," murmured Indira.

Sophia then brushed and plaited Emelda's hair, pinning it off her face.

"Your Majesty, there are two more of the King's Guard waiting outside. They will join me in

41

accompanying you to the encampment," blurted Indira, as if she could not wait any longer.

"An encampment?" asked Emelda,

"Where those loyal to your father, the King, have gathered to relinquish the land from the Rebel King's grip once and for all. They are growing vast in number but they still need a leader, a figurehead if you will, someone to fight for, someone to bring back the Great Willow and restore this land to its former glory," said Indira.

Emelda was a little put out to be called a figurehead, as if she was of little use other than to sit on a gold cushion and be paraded around for the soldiers to see. She felt it a slight amongst all the compliments. Indira turned and left the room once more and Emelda took a moment to gather herself and straighten out her clothes. It seemed to her that this world was real enough and the idea of waking up on her living room floor was becoming more and more of a distant thought. She closed her eyes and took a deep breath as there was a knock at the door. She stood anxiously, her pulse racing, unsure of who was about to enter the room.

"I know its's a lot to cope with, but I know you'll take it all in your stride, Princess. Now call them in if you will," encouraged Sophia.

"Come," Emelda called out in her steadiest voice.

Indira entered first followed by two men cloaked in black; they all bowed deeply, before one of the men dropped his hood to reveal his face.

"Allow me to introduce myself," said the unhooded man; with white blonde hair and startling blue eyes, he had a gentle, smiling face, "I am Christian."

He stepped forward taking Emelda's hand in his own and boldly pressed it to his lips.

"Your Majesty, I will protect you with my life, it was what I was born to do," he said, a grin spreading across his sweet face.

"Thank you," said Emelda, relinquishing her hand from his grip, a little taken aback by his forwardness. Indira rolled her eyes at him and shook her head as Christian stepped back.

"Please excuse him, your Majesty, he is a representative from the Greylands. They clearly don't know how to show their superiors the correct level of respect. There must be no end of immortality in their armies if they are all like him; he thinks he is all things to all women," remarked Indira.

Christian made to complain at the insults he had just received, but he was silenced by the third member of her Guard. He dropped his hood and took a single step forward. Their eyes met.

"You," murmured Emelda, fear gripping her chest.

She started to back away, shaking her head, her hand clasped to her breast. The man made no attempt to approach her or reassure her, instead he watched her, his narrowed, black eyes unfaltering. Emelda shook her head again in disbelief. It was him, the man who had been in her flat. She hadn't seen much of his face, but those eyes. Never had she seen eyes like his, so hard and cold, emotionless. Just the way that night she had felt them burning into her, and as much as she had wanted to look away she couldn't.

"No," she whispered, "no."

A sudden realisation came over her and her head spun. She reached out to the little table to steady herself.

"You tried to drown me!" she cried.

The others looked at him, horrified looks on their faces.

"What is she talking about?" asked Indira.

"I have no idea," replied the third Guard coldly, "we have never met before."

Sophia approached Emelda and took her hand, but she refused to take her eyes off the man in front of her.

"Things get mixed up in the transition - in the blur between the two realities things are bound to get confused. There is no way that he would have tried to drown you, I have never left your side so I would have known," Sophia's voice was quiet and calm and it reassured Emelda.

"Maybe," she said, not letting go of Sophia's hand.

"Your Majesty, Kasper," said the dark-eyed man, before stepping back.

Emelda remained where she was, watching him. His face was definitely familiar, despite his denying they had ever met before. He was striking with dark hair that fell around his face and brushed the nape of his neck, where the top of a deep red tattoo could be glimpsed from beneath his clothes. A large scar ran across the left side of his face, silvery against his pale skin. He reminded Emelda of a character from one of the Japanese magazines that Nicholas had liked in his youth. He had pored over them for hours, absorbed in the adventures of warlords and samurai, but secretly she knew he just liked the hourglass shaped women with overly large breasts and skin-tight outfits.

"Forgive me, Sir, it has been a confusing experience and I am still not quite sure of myself yet," she said, scrutinising his face, "are you sure we haven't met before?"

"Yes, Princess."

"Don't worry about him," smiled Christian, "he's always grumpy. Are you ready, Princess?"

"I think so, but please just explain to me one last time, just where we are going and what I have to do?" smiled Emelda, trying not to let her worry show.

Kasper turned to Sophia and pulled her to one side by the arm, "I thought she would remember everything, I thought she would be ready."

Sophia shook herself free and straightened her clothes out, "Brute, you pushed for her to come back so quickly a few things must have gotten lost along the way. You didn't give her enough time!"

"We don't have enough time," although his voice was calm, Emelda could hear a hint of anger creeping in. His voice was definitely familiar - she was sure she had heard it before but in a totally different context, and those haunting eyes stirred something in her that she couldn't put her finger on. There was no doubt in her mind that he was not a stranger to her.

"Will she remember?" he asked,

"Yes, but..." began Sophia.

"Then she will have to remember on the way, we don't have time to sit around and play house while she fills in the blanks."

He turned to Emelda, ignoring Sophia's protests, "For your transition back to our world you need to regain all of your memories and forget all of those you made in the other world. Otherwise you are of no use to us, half in one world and half in another. If someone finds the body that you spent the last 10 years hiding in, they could tear you away from here again, take your consciousness back to that other world. We have to move fast, I wouldn't know how to bring you back again."

"How much do you remember, Your Majesty?" asked Indira.

"A lot of things," she replied.

"Any hazy bits?"

"Some, but there is one memory that worries me. A boy," replied Emelda.

"Your brother?" suggested Indira.

"Maybe, I remember that he was killed as a young man, I remember the blood. But there is something else, it makes me feel cold." Emelda shuddered unconsciously.

"We need to go to the encampment," said Kasper, interrupting her, "let's pray that seeing your kingdom will help you remember."

Chapter 5

Sophia provided Emelda with a thick fur cloak, wrapping it around her shoulders and giving her a gentle squeeze. She also gave her a bag containing food and a small hunting knife. Emelda thanked her deeply, kissing her small aged hands. Sophia had given up 10 years of her life to watch over Emelda's static body. She had seen her grow from a teenager to a woman before her very eyes. She was like a second mother, her secret mother. Although she remembered very little about Sophia, Emelda knew her heart would always hold a great warmth for her and it made her sad to think she might not see her again. They clasped hands for a moment longer. Sophia gently pressed a glass vial on a necklace into her hands and Emelda glanced down at the precious object. It was the little glowing twig and bud from the chamber her body had been kept in. Sophia smiled as Emelda nodded to her and tucked it quickly out of view.

As they left the small chamber where she had spent the last 10 years of her life, Emelda sighed. Although she remembered almost everything about her past, she still felt as if they were someone else's memories, she had no attachment to them. Her memories were of London, the bustling streets and bright lights, her bookshop and her adoptive family. However even now as she thought of them she struggled to picture their faces, all except for Nicholas'. As they began to wind their way out of the centre of the mountain through damp and dimly lit tunnels she vowed to hold on to Nicholas' memory as long as she possibly could.

Emelda followed as close to Kasper as she dared to get, still unable to shake the unnerving feeling she got from him. She could feel Indira and Christian following close behind her, not more than an arm's length away and it made her feel a little claustrophobic. She longed for fresh air and sunlight, even the wind and rain on her sheltered skin. They walked in a silence that was broken only by the sound of their feet on the tunnel floor. Emelda was sure that the others could hear her heart drumming as loudly as she could.

Eventually Indira broke the heavy silence, "Your Majesty, things have changed a little since you've been asleep, the world won't be as you remember it."

"That's ok, I'm not sure what I remember anyway," replied Emelda. She wasn't really listening, instead she was running her hand along the wall of the tunnel. The stone was damp, cold and refreshing. She hadn't felt anything in a long, long time and she wanted to feel everything again.

"We have formed a stronger alliance with the Greylands, which will be unified by your marriage to Prince Eric Grey," remarked Indira carelessly.

Emelda stopped and whirled around; she could barely see Indira's expression in the gloomy but she was sure it was one of cruel pleasure.

"What?"

"Speak to Christian, he is, after all, Prince Eric's representative," replied Indira. Emelda heard Kasper scoff up ahead.

Christian came to her side and fell in step with her. He began to explain her fate to her, in his gentle, boyish voice.

"Our two lands along with a few other minor ones have decided to strengthen our alliance, to avoid another decade of war and darkness. We don't want any more men thinking they can overthrow the monarchy and take power anytime soon, and a wedding is always the best way to bring nations together. We have watched each other fighting against evil from behind our own borders for too long, Princess; unification is the way forward. A sharing of ideas and theologies as well as crops and materials - we need to build a better world, a safer world," explained Christian.

"I understand," murmured Emelda, not meeting Christian's eye.

"I know for a fact that Prince Eric is handsome, with skin like an angel and hair like silver, and he has soft blue-grey eyes that melt women's hearts," Christian laughed.

"Do you know him well?" asked Emelda.

"He's my younger brother. I'm the bastard child of my father and one of the handmaids, so no chance of a royal marriage for me. But if you need any practice before you meet my brother I'd be happy to help out. I'm much better!"

He grinned, clasping her hand once more and pushing it to his lips. Emelda barely felt the soft skin of his lips before her hand was ripped from hers and he was flung out of the way. There was a thud as Christian hit the wall hard.

"That is enough, Christian. Prince or not, you should have more respect for your future Queen,"

Kasper's face was so close to Christian's you could see his hair move as Kasper spoke.

Christian held his hands up in defence, "Woah, relax, I was just trying to make the Princess feel more at ease. Think what she has been through and what is ahead of her."

"Come now," said Indira, placing a hand on Kasper's shoulder. He looked over his shoulder at her and their eyes met. Kasper relinquished his grip on Christian and glared at him. As he turned his back Christian rolled his eyes at Emelda and she couldn't help but smile. That had been all Christian wanted, to see a smile on the Princess's sad face, such beauty marred by such confusion and loss. He would not have wanted to be her for anything in the world.

They followed a path through tunnels that led out of the mountain that seemed to go on forever. The tension was thick and no one spoke again. Emelda tried not to breathe too loudly, worried that she would incite Kasper's temper again. She felt she would have withered under his looks of contempt. As she walked behind him she wondered why he had been chosen for this mission, considering that he seemed to feel so little towards her - maybe he was a good fighter? The strongest or the bravest? The quickest maybe? Whatever it was he certainly didn't seem the kindest. She guessed it was a good thing, no emotions meant no weakness.

After Christian's revelations about her future, Emelda's ideas of being a Queen in her own right slipped away. She had thought that maybe she would be more than just a figurehead, a producer of heirs, a contract payment. However her job was to unite the Greylands and St. Dores so that Prince Eric could take control of her kingdom. Though she found it hard to remember her kingdom, she had an overwhelming sense that it was hers and that it was being taken away from her before she had a chance to even set foot in it. She was to be an accessory to someone else's future, a possession to be couriered and delivered. She was sure that was how Kasper saw her anyway, nothing but a package. Her heart sank and she hung her head.

It wasn't long before Emelda felt a cold breeze tugging around her ankles and blowing the stray bits of hair across her face. She pulled her cloak tighter around herself, regretting her desire for wind and rain.

"Here we go," said Christian, as they came to a halt at the end of the tunnel and were faced with a wall of rock. He gently moved past her, letting his hand brush hers.

Kasper looked over at Christian as he took his place next to him and together they placed their hands on the stone wall and pushed. Slowly it began to grind backwards, before there was a loud clunk and a whirr of cogs. The door began to slide to the right out of the way, seemingly on its own. Emelda watched in awe, wondering how something so heavy was moving on its own.

"It has a mechanism that means it can only be opened from the inside; it was put in place once you were safely sealed inside," explained Indira.

A flurry of wind and rain greeted them as the door fully opened. Emelda squinted against the harsh rain and pulled her hood up to cover her face as much as she could.

"It's not far to the nearest village, but if we wait much longer the night will be upon us and we will have no hope of making it down the mountain," called Indira over the battering rain.

Kasper and Christian nodded and they emerged from the tunnel out into the elements. Outside was deserted, a barren shelf on the side of a vast mountain. Emelda had expected to see guards and outposts set up to protect her. Instead she had been left with Sophia as her guardian and she wondered how valuable she really was to them. As she dashed out Christian spent a moment closing the door behind them before quickly returning to the group.

"This way," shouted Indira, "Princess, the path down the mountain is steep, be careful. I will walk behind you - Kasper and Christian will lead the way."

Carefully they began their descent down the water-logged mountain, the wind constantly pulling at them, trying to wrench them from the mountain-side. Emelda tried to focus on the dim lights of the small village they were headed for but her feet kept slipping on the soft ground and wet rock and she ended up staring at her own feet, not watching where she was going. Every time she looked up to make sure she was still following the others, her hood dropped down over her eyes and she had to keep pushing it up out of the way. Her legs felt heavy and she wanted to cry at her own ineptitude. Stumbling along at barely a crawl she made it half way down before her foot hit a rock. Somewhere between shifting her damn hood and trying to keep an eye on the men in front of her she lost her footing. She cried out in pain and sat down hard on the soggy ground, feeling her own hot tears mixing with the cold rain on her face as she threw her hood back over her face in shame. What kind of Princess was she that she couldn't even make it down a mountain path?

Frustrated, she rubbed her foot and looked for a handhold to pull herself up with, but before she could even move, there was someone in front of her and then a large hand clasped her own, gently pulling her to her feet. Emelda tried to look up at her rescuer, but she could see very little through the driving rain, the pressing night and her ridiculous hood, and he already had his back to her, his dark cloak and hood concealing his identity. Emelda went to release his hand but instead the grip tightened and he began to lead her down the mountain, slowly and carefully. Emelda was sure it had to be Christian; she doubted Kasper would have stopped to help her, especially with such gentleness. There was no doubt in her mind that the lone figure up ahead was Kasper. She squeezed Christian's hand a little to say thank you, her thumb carelessly rubbing across his fingers that were rough yet warm; after a moment he returned the gentle caress. She stumbled once more, gripping onto his forearm; he made to turn but she called out to him to carry on, she was ok, and so he continued on.

Emelda was wet and shivering by the time they reached the base of the mountain, despite the cloak she was wearing. She breathed a sigh of relief as her feet found flat ground again, and stood a little taller against the rain, enjoying the stinging cold now that she wasn't concentrating on not falling. As they walked she felt Christian's hand slip away, a ring on his little finger cold as it brushed along the edge of her hand and then he was gone. The two men continued in front and Indira came alongside the Princess, her hand in the small of her back guiding her forward, but to Emelda it felt more like a push than a hand of guidance. She tried to quicken her pace so that Indira no longer touched her, but she seemed unable to get away from her. It was dark and it was hard to make out much more than the shapes of buildings, most of them dark and quiet. A few had hearths and lamps that shone brightly in the darkness, creating long shadows. The sound of music and voices carried on the wind as they made their way deeper into the village, where more and more houses had lamps lit.

They turned a corner and were confronted with the heart of the village. A large inn shone like a beacon in the night, lamps in all the windows, music and voices pouring out. It brought a smile to Emelda's face, the thought of warmth, dry clothes and something to eat and drink; she felt herself pick up the pace. She reached the door just behind Kasper, who turned and barely looked at her from under his hood, before he placed one hand on the door and pushed it open. She was about to enter when he blocked her way with his free arm and beckoned the others forward.

Christian entered first, followed by Indira but Kasper didn't remove his arm; instead they stood barely touching in the pouring rain until Indira reappeared and nodded at Kasper. He pulled her cloak down so she could barely see and made sure it was buttoned up to her chin before gesturing for her to enter. With a sigh of relief Emelda dashed into the inn; the smell of stew and ale hit her along with a wave of warmth. Her stomach rumbled noisily. She had barely eaten anything since she had woken up. Her stomach had been churning too much with anxiety, and until now she hadn't thought about food.

No one seemed to notice them enter the inn and Indira quickly led them over to a table in the corner, far away from the music and the people dancing. After checking that no one was paying them any attention, Kasper allowed Emelda to take off her cloak. It felt wonderful to be warm and dry again, and she couldn't help but smile.

"Can we eat, please?" asked Emelda as her stomach called to her again.

"Of course," said Christian giving her a knowing grin. He turned in his seat and looked around the bar, before he caught the barmaid's eye and beckoned her over. She sauntered quickly over, a suggestive smile on her face.

"Stew and ale all round, miss," ordered Christian, his eyes wandering up and down the girl's body as she walked away. Kasper banged his fist down hard on the table, making Emelda jump. Christian spun round, a look of innocence on his face.

"What?" exclaimed Christian,

"Remember who you are for five minutes, please," growled Kasper.

Christian shrugged. Emelda looked down at the table, not wanting to meet Kasper's eye. Instead she focused on Kasper's hands, still clenched on the table. As the barmaid appeared carrying the food, she noticed he was wearing a small silver ring on his little finger. Had it been him guiding her down the mountain? Her anxiety about him told her otherwise. She was still unable to shake the feeling that they weren't strangers, that he had been the one drowning her in her own bath tub. He was not to be trusted, not yet, he made her nervous.

The food had barely touched the table before Emelda pounced on it like an animal. She couldn't hold herself back, it smelt so wonderful and her stomach was gnawing at itself.

"How ladylike, Your Majesty," sneered Kasper.

A wave of embarrassment overcame her instantly and she stared down at her food. She began carefully picking out bitesize pieces of meat and vegetables from the stew with her fork and eating them slowly. She had to be mistaken - this couldn't be the same man that had carefully and considerately led her down the mountain less than an hour earlier, the touch of his hand still lingering in her mind. After a moment she looked up from her plate.

"It's been ten years since I ate anything, please forgive me, Sir," Emelda said quietly.

Kasper looked at her and nodded but said nothing, turning back to his food instead.

"Don't worry, Your Majesty, I like a woman with a good appetite," said Christian reaching across the table and touching Emelda's hand. It was Indira's turn to scold Christian as she jabbed him hard in the ribs.

"Men," she muttered rolling her eyes.

As Emelda sat nursing her ale, she thought about the journey that lay ahead of her and wondered what Eric Grey was like; if he was anything like Christian then she could see herself being ok. It wasn't the future she would have chosen for herself, that was for sure. As an independent woman in the other world, she was used to having the freedom to make her own choices. Her thoughts drifted back to her real parents, the King and Queen, their faces as she had said goodbye so many years ago, knowing that this might be the last time that she would see them. She remembered saying goodbye to someone else as well, a goodbye that was just as heart-wrenching, yet somehow different, but she could not remember their face or even their name. Yet she remembered crying the whole way to the Grey Man, her head in Sophia's lap, the old woman gently stroking her hair and letting her tears soak into her skirts.

"Your Majesty?" asked Christian, interrupting her thoughts. He held out his hand to her. Emelda smiled up at him and placed her hand in his. She glanced down at Kasper as she got up and he met her glance for a split second with a flicker of his black eyes before turning back to Indira, who in turn got up and covered Emelda's head with a fine scarf. She adjusted it a little, making sure that she was unrecognisable as the Princess and released her. Christian led her gently by the hand to a space at the back of the hall, closer to the music but still out of the way. Emelda glanced around at the couples and small groups who all seemed to be doing some kind of traditional dance.

"Just follow me," he said, taking her by the hands and parading her around and around their little corner of the room. Emelda tried to copy his steps and eventually her feet began to fall into time with his and she began to relax, letting out a little laugh. It was a like a release of tension, dancing and laughing as she bounded around the room. A couple of times she stole a look at Kasper but every time he was in deep conversation with Indira, their body language relaxed and intimate. For some reason, she felt a slight pang in her chest, which she quickly shook off, turning her attention back to Christian's gentle face.

Kasper glanced sideways at Christian and Emelda, his eyes drifting over the curves of her body. Laughing at himself, he returned to his conversation with Indira.

Puffing and panting, grinning from cheek to cheek, Emelda finally raised her hands in defeat and they returned laughing to the table. She watched as Kasper and Indira quickly broke apart as they approached, putting a more acceptable distance between them. There was a scuffle as hands retracted across the table and Kasper coughed loudly and for a moment the Princess thought he looked guilty. Indira's eyes darted between Christian and Emelda, then she stood up abruptly. There was no guilt on her face, instead a look of satisfaction and knowing.

"I'll sort the rooms."

The others nodded and she left. Emelda took a long, slow drink from her glass, the mild ale warming her stomach and quenching her thirst. She watched the people dancing, joy on their faces, and felt uplifted. It had been a long time since she had had so much fun, since she had been carefree like this. The other world was different, she had always been on the edge, never quite fitting in and now she knew why. She didn't let her mind dwell on the severity of the situation she was in in this world. Tonight she would be enjoying herself for maybe the last time in the foreseeable future.

It wasn't long before Indira returned.

"I have procured two rooms; it would seem they are busy, people have heard rumours that the Princess is coming and that the Rebel King's reign will end soon. People are celebrating," she told them.

"Getting a little ahead of themselves, aren't they," muttered Kasper, his eyes meeting Emelda's for a moment.

Emelda swallowed hard, "I will be Queen."

Kasper looked away, "We have been too careless tonight. The fun is over, Your Majesty, from now on we must be more cautious. I have arranged for horses to carry us for most of the journey. I'm assuming you can ride?" He did not wait for an answer, carrying on giving out orders, "There are two rooms - Indira you will share with the Princess."

Christian looked mildly disappointed but didn't say anything. Emelda climbed the staircase behind Indira, her long, golden hair swinging in its long braid, which was made up of hundreds of tiny braids that covered her head like golden rope. It was breath-taking, but not subtle. Emelda wondered how she managed to be covert with such a striking feature. She was not sure how she felt about sharing a room with Indira, there was something about her haughty attitude that put Emelda on edge.

They parted ways with the men at the top of the stairs and once inside the room awkward tension filled the air as Indira insisted that Emelda take the large double bed to herself. As one of the King's Guard she claimed she could sleep on top of nails if she needed to so the floor was no hardship. Emelda tried to persuade her that there was plenty of room and that she was more than happy to share. But Indira insisted that it wasn't proper for her to share a bed with royalty, plus she had no need for comfort. After that remark Emelda gave up; she was too tired to argue and Indira was clearly too stubborn to accept her offer, so she quickly stripped down to her undergarments and shirt and climbed between the cold sheets. As an afterthought, she rummaged around in her bag and placed her small knife under her pillow. She heard Indira scoff quietly but she ignored her, turning toward the fire that burned in the small hearth, enjoying the warmth on her face. Indira removed her bow and quiver of arrows, before bundling her cloak into a pillow and lying down on the floor between the bed and the door.

Emelda tossed and turned for a bit despite being exhausted. The light of the fire made long finger-like shadows on the walls.

"Want me to put the fire out, Princess?" asked Indira, sounding annoyed.

"No, I like the light," replied Emelda.

"Very well." Short and curt.

There was a moment's silence, before Emelda spoke again, "Indira?"

"Yes, your Majesty," came the reply.

"Are there many women in the King's Guard?"

"Not really, go to sleep now, Princess." Indira spoke to her like a naughty child that was refusing to go to sleep.

Emelda lay in the flickering darkness, the light of the fire slowly ebbing away, giving way to a deep blackness she had never experienced before when living in a city in the other world. Her mind raced with the memories that had come back to her; she felt as if she would never sleep, but before she knew it she had drifted off into sweet oblivion.

Even in her sleep she wasn't given any rest from the countless memories that bombarded her mind, but most vivid of all was the memory of a young boy, who she assumed was her brother, yet she couldn't see his face. They played together, running through long grass behind her castle, chasing each other with childish innocence. She could feel the grass between her fingers, smell the sweet flowers and freshly cut hay. She smiled and laughed as he caught up to her, and wrapping his arms around her middle pulled her to the floor. Together they lay hidden, breathless, watching the clouds form horses and swirling waves. As the sun beat down on her face, she was happy, pure and fulfilled. She felt his fingers brush against hers, her heart skipped a beat, and though they had held hands many times this was different. She was now older, wiser, womanly. She turned to face him and screamed. Blood poured from his eyes, his nose, his mouth. Then she was inside the castle, the floor was awash with blood, her brother was gone and she was screaming.

She awoke with a start, cold with sweat and trembling. She pushed back the sheets and made to get up when a hand reached up and grabbed her wrist from the floor next to the bed.

"I need to use the bathroom," said Emelda, and the hand released her from its grip.

"I will come and find you if you do not return in 5 minutes," said Indira sleepily, and rolled over again. Emelda doubted she would still be awake in 5 minutes, her breathing already deep and steady.

She slid out of the bed, reaching for her cloak that hung beside the smouldering fire and fumbling in the pockets for the willow before making her way to the door. Though it made her shiver, the fresh, cold air felt good against her clammy skin, and taking a deep breath, she crept out of the door. Outside the room all was quiet and dark, a couple of dim lamps were all that lit the long landing. Silently she padded towards the bathroom and opened the door. Above the basin was a small mirror with an ornate frame and she caught a glimpse of herself in it. The face that looked back at her took her by surprise - for a moment she thought there was someone else in the room. Expecting to see a bush of dishevelled auburn hair crowning a slightly round face, she was taken aback by the handsome woman that stared back at her. She had forgotten how different she looked here. It was as if her skin had been stretched over a better, more proportioned model, instead of being squashed into the frame she was used to. She had never thought of herself as ugly before, but average and maybe a little overweight. She could still see the face she knew well, but it fitted better in this mould. Satisfied, she ran some water and dabbed it over her neck and chest, washing away the nightmare, before drying herself with a towel that smelt like lavender. She inhaled the scent of the towel, fresh and clean; it jogged her memory but she couldn't pinpoint how. Taking one last look in the mirror she fastened the willow in its little vial around her neck and tucked it out of sight. She realised she had probably been longer than the allotted 5 minutes and opened the door to leave. She jumped as a figure in the darkness stood waiting for her.

"Kasper!" She gasped.

He looked momentarily surprised, his expression quickly returning to its usual coldness. He didn't say anything, just looked her up and down. She felt exposed, hurriedly pulling her shirt down as far as she could.

"I needed the bathroom, I was just..." she began to explain, but he interrupted her.

"You'll catch a cold wandering around dressed like that," he said, "I suggest you get back to your room, Princess, it's also not very dignified for someone in your position."

With that he turned and left. Acutely aware of her half-dressed state Emelda hurried back to her room, opening the door as quietly as she could, and climbed into bed. She pulled the covers up as far as she could, muffling her gentle sobs. She fell asleep as the tears dried on her face, the dim light of the dawn starting to sneak through the curtains and tiptoe across the room.

Chapter 6

Emelda awoke to an empty room, the sound of her companions' muffled voices barely audible through the wall. She crept out of bed, grabbing her cloak and pressing her ear to the adjoining wall, straining to hear what they were saying.

"What were you doing, letting her wander around in the middle of the night, half naked?" said Kasper angrily.

"She needed the bathroom, what did you want me to do?" There was a tone of disbelief in Indira's voice.

"Half naked, you say?" murmured Christian sleepily.

"Shut up!" growled Kasper.

Emelda pictured him reclining on the bed, still half dressed.

"I'm not her babysitter," retorted Indira, "if you're so concerned you sleep in her room next time."

"I know you're not her babysitter, but that girl is important to the Kingdom - think what she signifies. She will bring unity and peace, and then we can all go back to our lives." Kasper's voice had softened a little, but

Emelda could still hear him straining to control his anger.

The sound of movement in the room signalled the end of the conversation and she dashed back over to the bed and pulled the sheets up to her chest. 'That girl', his words echoed in her mind, reiterating the fact that she was nothing but a commodity. The bedroom door creaked open and Indira peered round it, she looked the Princess up and down.

"You're awake, Your Majesty, my apologies for not being here when you woke. Do you need any help dressing?"

"No thank you, Indira, you can wait outside," replied Emelda surprising herself with her curt tone, "I don't need a babysitter."

Indira nodded briefly before backing out of the door. Emelda climbed out of bed for the second time and slowly got dressed. Indira and the others could wait for her - it was her prerogative after all as future Queen to have people waiting on her. She plaited her hair loosely and gathered up her belongings before heading for the door; she opened it and found Indira waiting patiently for her.

"I'm going to have breakfast; I imagine you will be joining me, I couldn't possibly manage on my own," Emelda's voice was sharp, and uncharacteristic of her.

As she turned away Indira grabbed her wrist and pulled her back a little roughly, "Your Majesty, forgive me but it is my job to protect you. Whether we see eye to eye is inconsequential; either way I will be at your side until we deliver you safely to Prince Eric."

"And where exactly is it you are taking me?" asked Emelda, trying to shake her wrist free, but Indira's grip was strong.

"I...," she faltered a little, "the exact location has only been divulged to a select few."

"So how will my people know where to find me?"

"Everyone knows that people are gathering at the Southern Woods, but it is vast, no one knows where exactly," explained Indira, "Let's go eat. The men will be waiting."

Emelda nodded but said nothing, turning and heading downstairs ahead of Indira. Kasper and Christian were already at the table when they arrived in the quiet bar, but had waited for them before ordering any food. Christian smiled at her as she sat down and Kasper glanced up at her briefly before signalling for the waitress. He ordered porridge and honey for them all and it came moments later steaming in heavy wooden bowls. Emelda dipped her spoon in and raised it hungrily to her lips, she blew on it gently before savouring the hot, sweet taste.

"This wonderful," she murmured between mouthfuls.

"Have you never had porridge?" asked Christian, bemused.

"Of course I have, but I've never tasted honey like this, it's beautiful," replied Emelda.

After breakfast, they settled their bill and left the inn, Emelda donning her hood and face covering. Following Kasper, they made their way through the village towards the place where he had arranged to collect the horses. It was the first time Emelda had seen her surroundings in the daylight, and she was horrified. The whole town was grey, most buildings were still standing but many were abandoned and dilapidated. The people, mainly women and children, scurried between the buildings like timid mice.

"Where are all the men?" Emelda asked.

They all looked at each other; there was a sadness in their eyes.

"Dead, or gone to war," replied Kasper, his voice quiet.

Emelda didn't say anything; there was a stark contrast between the joy she had witnessed in the faces of the people last night and the reality that she had woken up to. Her heart broke for her Kingdom, though she could only just remember it. The place she had in her memories was so green, so free, so different, that she couldn't believe she was in the same land. She gazed around at the down-trodden faces of those around her, surviving in the shells of their former homes, scared of their own shadows.

"That's why you are here, Princess, to make a difference," said Christian gently.

Emelda nodded, looking into his eyes, seeing for a moment what the people saw in her.

"Here we are," interrupted Kasper, stopping outside a large stable a little way out of the village. The man who waited for them told them he had prepared his fastest horses along with some supplies they would need for the next leg of their journey. He brought out a stunning white horse and presented it to Emelda, who reached her hand out to it instantly. The horse looked at her for a moment before nuzzling her hand and whinnying happily. Emelda was happy to finally have something she knew she could do with confidence. As a teenager she had learned to ride on the recommendation of her adoptive mother, who had ridden as a girl and enjoyed the escape. She had spent many, many hours down at the stable and out riding. It was a freedom like no other. She murmured reassuringly to the horse and stoked its nose gently.

"You have a way with horses, Miss," remarked the groom.

Emelda nodded, not daring to make eye contact or speak; instead she focused on the horse. They walked the horses away from the stable and out of the village until the small desolate farmhouses gave way to open fields, crops lying rotten in the stony soil.

"I take it you can remember how to ride, Princess?" said Kasper.

"Yes," she replied.

"Well, that's something," he turned and mounted his own horse with graceful agility, leaving her a little in awe. Indira did the same, making ready to leave.

Christian, however, approached her, "May I assist you, Your Majesty?"

He offered his clasped hands for her to stand on.

"No, please, I couldn't," Emelda muttered, a little embarrassed.

"I insist, you must be tired still and it is quite an effort. Don't be embarrassed, you are our Princess after all."

Unexpectedly Emelda felt strong hands around her waist and she was practically thrown onto her horse. She watched as Christian's confused face disappeared below her and she thought she heard Indira laughing quietly. She steadied herself in the saddle before looking over to see Kasper returning to his own horse.

"We don't have time for pleasantries or ladylike decorum," he scowled, turning his horse and giving it a kick.

'That's not what you said last night,' thought Emelda angrily, her face glowing with embarrassment. Kasper's disrespectful attitude towards her and his double standards made her cross. He was so unreasonable, unkind and utterly indifferent towards her, but when Christian made a cheeky yet harmless remark about her it resulted in his being rebuked furiously. She watched him as he pushed his horse into a gentle trot and reluctantly followed him, the idea of a Prince with skin like an angel and soft eyes that melted women's heart sounding more and more appealing.

Emelda watched the country they were passing through, desolate and void of life, with a heavy heart. How could anyone cause so much damage? There weren't even birds in the trees or the rustle of creatures in the shrubby undergrowth; it was so quiet and still, so unnatural. They rode until she felt as if she would fall asleep in the saddle, the steady sway of the animal beneath her lulling her gently towards sleep and the failing light helping her on her way. She could feel her head dropping as she fought against sleep. In a moment of clarity she threaded the reins through her belt and wrapped them around her wrists in case she fell.

As darkness began to fall softly like a gentle blanket, Emelda felt her vision blur and her body begin to slide from the horse's back. She had been desperate not to give the King's Guard, especially Kasper, another reason to consider her an inadequate Queen and a burden. But her pride was her undoing as she felt the reins tighten painfully around her wrists as she fell. She heard the horse whinny before her head hit something hard, pain radiating through her skull. Without the strength to move blackness enveloped her. The sound of someone calling her name drifted with her into her unconsciousness.

As Emelda lay unconscious she dreamt the same dream as before, the sweet smell of grass, the soft hand of the boy and then the blood and screaming. When she finally opened her eyes, her throat felt dry and tight. She choked back the tears that had begun to build in the corners of her eyes. Her head pounded and she reached up to feel it. As she did this, pain coursed through her wrist and she cried out.

"Princess! You're awake," said Kasper, appearing at her side, a look of relief on his face.

"Yes," she murmured, pushing herself to a sitting position with her good hand and looking around. Everything swam for a moment and she almost fell back down again, but after a moment the horizon became level again and she realised she was sitting next to a small camp fire. On the opposite side the other two seemed to be sleeping; just Kasper and she were awake.

"How are you feeling?" he asked with concern, raising his hand to her face. She flinched a little and he looked taken aback.

"I just want to check your wound," he said, the usual coldness returning to his voice.

Looking into his eyes, Emelda nodded and let his fingers brush her hair away from her face. His tenderness surprised her and she felt herself tense a little under his touch. He moved a little closer to get a better look in the flickering firelight. She could feel the hotness of his breath on her cheek and she felt her heart skip a beat, her skin tingled. She felt utterly foolish, but as much as her head told her not to be ridiculous and that this man thought nothing of her, and she was just another thing to be delivered, a job to do, her body sang out a different song.

"It doesn't look serious, I think your reins slowed you down," he spoke softly, so close to her face she could feel each word.

Their eyes met, yet neither moved away, nor did he take his hand from her hair, instead it drifted down to her chin where he lifted her face up towards his. His dark eyes danced over her face in the fire light, landing on her lips. There was movement from the other side of the fire and Kasper let go of her suddenly as if she were something abhorrent.

"Princess, how are you feeling?" called Indira sleepily, clambering up to come and see her. Kasper pulled as far away from Emelda as possible as Indira approached, but Emelda saw Indira's eyes flicking back and forth between her and Kasper. She opened her mouth to answer, but Kasper cut across her.

"The Princess is fine," his voice emotionless and hard, all concern gone from his face.

Indira smiled, "I am pleased to hear it, would you like me to sit with the Princess while you get some rest?"

She placed her hand on his shoulder and looked down at him. Kasper stood up, ignoring her hand and turned to leave.

"Yes," he said and walked away.

Emelda watched as he lay down in the spot that Indira had just vacated and quickly went to sleep without even a glance in her direction. Indira knelt down next to her and reached for her wrist.

Emelda hesitated a little, but Indira leaned in and pulled it towards her. Emelda winced in pain.

"Forgive me, Princess," Indira said, and began moving her wrist, feeling the joints and bones.

"Nothing broken, just jarred from the fall. You are lucky it didn't break. I will bind it for you and give you something for the pain," she said, getting up and retrieving her bag.

She produced a bundle of tightly wrapped bandages and with quick, deft hands bound Emelda's wrist, then she handed her a small pot of what looked like crushed leaves and bark. Emelda looked down at it then up at Indira.

"It's a natural remedy for pain relief; it's all we've got until the tree is restored," said Indira reassuringly.

Emelda took a small pinch and popped it in her mouth; it was bitter and hard to swallow. Indira watched her struggle for a moment before pouring some water into a cup and handing it to her. She took a big mouthful, then another to wash the taste away. After a few moments she did indeed feel a lightness in her wrist and the pain seemed to ebb away a little. She thanked Indira, then wrapping herself in her cloak she lay down next to the fire and waited for sleep to take her. It didn't take long.

Chapter 7

Emelda was woken by Indira shaking her roughly by the shoulders.

"Get up quickly," she hissed at her, pulling her to her feet, "get to your horse fast!"

Emelda stood frozen, a scene of terror spread out before her. They were surrounded on every side by huge wolves, teeth bared, drool dripping from their mouths. She could hear them snarling and the horses braying and pulling against their tethers. She glanced desperately around for the men, her heart racing. She spotted them on the other side of the fire, swords drawn, staring down at their own set of encircling wolves. Emelda opened her mouth to call out to them but Indira pulled her by the arm and pushed her towards the horses.

"Quick, while their attention is on the men, get to your horse and get out of here," she insisted.

A hard shove in her back sent her flying towards the horses; she was only just able to stay on her feet, but she managed to get her body to obey her and she ran towards the horses. As quickly as she could she climbed into the saddle and looked back at Indira who had gathered up her bow as the wolves began closing in. There was a calmness about her as she stood, bow in one hand and an arrow in the other, waiting for the creatures to get closer. Emelda watched in disbelief as one wolf got within arm's reach, Indira's gold eyes trained on the animal, then they flicked towards her and the wolves turned, their eyes focused on Emelda.

Horrified at what she had just seen Emelda kicked her horse hard, the wolves closing the distance between her and them very quickly. Almost instantly she heard the twang of Indira's bow and arrows as she pushed the horse as fast as she could. The wolves growled and snapped at her heels, getting closer and closer. Her horse breathed heavily, snorting in the cold night air, as she urged it on faster and faster. She rode hard, her head close to the horse's neck, her hair loose and flowing. The cold night air on her face was refreshing and exhilarating and despite the terrifying situation she grinned to herself. She glanced over her shoulder - the wolves were still chasing hard behind her, but she could see her three protectors battling yet more of them in the hazy morning light.

There was a loud growl, very close to her heels and her horse reared up. Emelda held on for dear life and the horse came crashing down, trampling the wolf beneath its hooves. She cried out, kicking another wolf in the face with the heel of her boot and it whined, slumping to the ground, stunned. As fast as she could get rid of one another took its place, until she was surrounded. That was when she felt a sharp tug on her ankle and she was yanked from her saddle, landing heavily on the ground amongst the wolves. She felt teeth sink into her soft boots and tender flesh. Letting out a yelp of pain she kicked as hard as she could with her other foot, sending the wolf flying. It took several others with it, giving Emelda time to scramble to her feet, her hands searching for her weapon. Her eyes darted over the ground until she spotted her knife a little distance from where she stood; adrenaline and fear coursed through her body, turning her blood to ice. Taking a deep breath, she dived for the blade, narrowly avoiding an attacking wolf, and grabbed it before turning to face another attack. This time she plunged the knife deep into the wolf's neck - it let out a howl of pain and slumped to the ground. As she pulled the knife out she sensed movement on her right, but her body seemed to move on its own, remembering fighting skills from deep within her memory.

She had barely enough time to turn her blade towards her attacker before it was upon her, its jaws snapping at her face; she could smell its sour breath and feel its hot drool on her cheek. She twisted the blade deeper into the creature's belly, crying out, but it would not die. Finally she saw the light die in its eyes and it stopped snapping at her, dropping heavily on top of her. With the last of her strength she pushed the creature off and pushed herself to sitting, retrieved the blade from the animal's belly and wiped it on the grass. She had only a moment to catch her breath before more wolves took the place of those she had killed, closing in on her slowly. They smelt the blood, sensed her fear. Emelda pushed herself to her feet and readied herself one last time, her heart pounding in her ears, fast and deafening. She was not going to die, she had only just begun. She was beginning to remember who she was, who she was supposed to be, all she could aspire to be. Her ankle throbbed and her wrist hurt but she took up a defensive stance. The wolves snarled, hungry for her flesh.

With a fierce battle cry that sounded alien to her, she held her knife high, plunging it into the oncoming wolf. Creature after creature came at her, but soon they were too many, coming too fast. Just as she was being overwhelmed, she heard the twang of a bow and whistle of arrows heading in her direction, and the wolves started dropping around her. She could hear the roar of the men and the pounding of their feet on the ground as they charged at the remaining wolves; some scattered, others fell to their swords, but soon they were all dead or gone.

Emelda's heart pounded, adrenaline coursing through her veins and making her feel sick. She dropped to her knees, breathing a deep sigh of relief and tears welled up; she tried to hold them back but some escaped, etching lines down her cheeks through the blood and dirt. Staring at the ground she tried to control herself before any of the others saw her.

"Princess," came a voice from in front of her.

She couldn't bring herself to look up, not yet, she wasn't ready. She needed time to breathe, to get herself under control. She felt hands on her chin and she looked up to see Christian gazing down at her.

Kasper stood to one side, breathing hard, words stuck in his throat. He prayed that they weren't too late, that she was just in shock, that she hadn't bled out. He imagined her cold, dead eyes looking up at him staring into nothingness. Her body torn and bleeding.

"No," he murmured under his breath, he still had so much to say to her, so much to ask her.

Christian dropped to his knees at her side and brushed the hair and dirt from her face as if she were a child. His touch was soft and caring.

"You are still beautiful, even covered in dirt and wolf blood, Your Majesty," he smiled.

Emelda felt a smile form in the corners of her mouth and she wiped the rest of the tears away with the back of her hand.

"You know how to make a woman smile," she laughed gently.

Christian reached out his hand and helped her to her feet; she winced a little as she put weight on her ankle.

Now the adrenaline had subsided the pain was taking hold and the bite to her ankle stung. She clung onto Christian, reaching down to feel her ankle and her fingers came back bloody. In one quick movement, he gathered her up into his arms and began walking back to the campsite, despite Emelda's protests.

"I can walk Christian, honestly," she argued.

"No, Princess, let me carry you. We let you get hurt and we were supposed to protect you, carrying you is the least I can do. Just relax," he reassured her.

Despite feeling a little awkward she let herself be carried. She placed her arms around his neck, the gentle warmth of his body was comforting and she listened as his breathing slowed and his heart rate calmed. Once they reached the campsite, Christian placed her gently on the ground next to the remains of the fire.

"Thank you all, you saved me," she said.

"It is our duty to protect you, Your Majesty," replied Christian, but Kasper remained silent, watching her.

Christian went to get his bag and Kasper muttered angrily under his breath as he passed by, "That was too close, how did she get so far away from us?"

Christian shook his head and carried on while Kasper silently approached Emelda and bent down. He removed her boot and examined the puncture wounds on her ankle. She gazed around at the campsite, there was utter devastation. The ground was covered with the countless corpses of wolves, some hacked to bits, others littered with arrows. She looked over the grisly scene, her mouth slightly open in horror. Her eyes met Indira's briefly and she turned away quickly, there was nothing but anger there.

"So much blood," she whispered.

She realised that Kasper's hand was pushing her trousers up her leg so he could see more of her ankle, but as quick as a flash she batted him away.

"How dare you?" She reprimanded him, "I can do that myself, there is no need for you to touch me anymore that you have to. You have already overstepped the mark; remember I am a Princess and soon to be your Queen."

Kasper looked surprised for a moment, but the harshness quickly returned to his face. He rolled his eyes at her and got up.

"Very well, your Majesty, dress your own wound. I shall be very careful not to touch you in any way inappropriate to the mission," he said, grabbing the medical bag from Christian's hands and throwing it down at her feet, "here."

He turned and began gathering his belongings together; Indira followed suit while Christian offered his help. However, after the fuss she had made Emelda didn't feel she could accept help from anyone now. Christian smiled at her and began helping the others. Emelda washed the wound and bound it quickly, then sat watching the others. Her mind wandered to the look in Indira's eyes as the wolves had come after her; could she have been sending them to attack her? She had heard Indira's bow taking down the wolves as soon as her back was turned, so maybe she had just imagined it? She couldn't shake the uncomfortable feeling that Indira held more than just dislike for her.

She watched as they gathered the horses - only two had survived, however, hers and Kasper's - and loaded them up ready to go. Christian cleaned his blade before sheathing it and coming over to check on her. He smiled as he approached, his usual kind look in his eyes.

"Are you ready to go, Princess?" he asked.

"Yes," she replied, and gathered the medical gear into her bag along with her knife, before changing her mind and fastening it in its little sheath to her belt.

Christian helped her to her feet and she walked slowly over to the others. Emelda glanced at the one horse piled high with their food, water and blankets, whereas the other one stood wearing only a saddle. She was about to ask when Kasper spoke.

"You will ride, Princess," he told her.

"I can walk," she protested.

"You will be slow and we don't have time for your pride. Now get on the horse, Princess," he said forcefully.

Emelda's face twisted with anger and she opened her mouth to speak, then shut it again deciding it was not worth the argument. Christian carefully helped her onto her horse, where she tried to sit as proudly as she could, not daring to look down at the others. She knew she was weak compared to them. The time she had spent unconscious had weakened her body and though she could feel its strength coming back to her slowly, she knew she could not compare herself to the others. She knew, however, just from fighting the wolves, that she had once been strong, a competent fighter, bold and courageous. She just had to find that side of herself again.

Christian took her horse's reins while Kasper took hold of the other and led the way into the morning, Indira at his side. They walked for some time, Christian babbling away in his usual jolly tone, yet Emelda wasn't really listening. Instead she was watching Kasper and Indira up ahead talking animatedly, and although she couldn't hear them, she could tell by their body language that it was a familiar conversation; one between friends, maybe even lovers. She felt sad and lonely as she watched them, a little tightening in her chest made her sigh. Christian looked up at her, some bread and dried meat in his outstretched hand, and coughed to get her attention.

"Everything all right, Your Majesty?" he asked as she took the food from him.

"Thank you, I am fine, a little uncomfortable maybe," she said, not taking her eyes off Kasper and Indira.

She ate a little bread before speaking again.

"Do they have some special affinity?" she ventured in a small voice.

"I like that word 'affinity'," he laughed, "when you join the King's Guard you're not supposed to be involved with anyone. You are supposed to forsake all the privileges of normal life and dedicate yourself to the King and his family."

"Sounds lonely," she mused.

"I guess, but you are dedicating yourself to something, it's not like you are just living a life of abstinence for no reason."

"You seem to know a lot, doesn't sound like your cup of tea, though," she joked,

"I'm more of an honorary member of the King's Guard if you like. I joined shortly after Kasper, when the fighting started to threaten the Greylands' borders. And I wanted to see this Princess that all the fuss was about," he smiled, "when my father heard you were to return, and that enough people had gathered in your name to stand against the Rebel King, it was decided to unite the two Kingdoms. I have been sent here to protect you and the Greylands' interests. The rules don't really apply to me," he smiled.

"Just protecting your assets, then?" she asked curtly.

"I want peace as much as the next man for my country, for your country, and I will do anything to protect it. Princess, you are peace, a new start, the end of a decade of despair. Why wouldn't I want to look after you? You are so valuable in so many ways."

Emelda contemplated his words.

"Plus," he continued, "women like the idea of a night of passion with a man who will be gone in the morning to fight for his King and their freedom."

She had no doubt his boyish good looks and charms had got him passage into many women's beds but it sounded lonely. She smiled, thinking of how much he reminded her of Nicholas. That cheeky grin especially, it warmed her heart and she relaxed a little.

"You remind me of someone," she told him with a smile, then gesturing towards the two up ahead, "and you never answered my question."

"Someone you were close with?" he grinned at her mischievously.

"Not like that, my brother, in that life," she paused, "do you think he's forgotten me already?"

"I don't know, your Majesty, I think it takes time, like a dream you can't quite remember and then it's gone. How are your memories, if you don't mind me asking?" he said gently.

"Getting there, most things have returned, but I still feel like I am only just getting to know who I am again."

"Don't worry, Princess, it will come," he encouraged her.

Indira laughed and Emelda looked up to see her putting her hand on Kasper's arm, but this time he didn't shrug it off as he had before.

"And don't worry about them. It's nothing. Kasper's not that kind of man, he's true Guard through and through, and even if he was like that he wouldn't let it interfere with the mission."

Emelda nodded but his words didn't comfort her, "You've know him a long time?"

"One long decade."

"Oh," she was quiet for a moment, "how far to the encampment?"

"On horseback four days, but on foot, maybe a week or more," he said with a sigh.

"I see," replied Emelda, and they fell back into silence.

After half a day's travel, they stopped to rest and eat. Christian helped Emelda from her horse and walked her over to a clear patch of ground to sit. Kasper watched as Christian placed his hand round the Princess's waist and guided her; he felt a little riled watching them. The Princess's injury would slow them down further, and even though the wolf attack had not been her fault he found himself blaming her. As much as he told himself that that was the reason for his foul temper he couldn't bring himself to believe it. Christian said something to Emelda and she smiled, a gentle laugh escaping her lips. She nodded and he sat next to her, their shoulders almost touching; he removed her boot and waited for her to pull up her trousers before examining her ankle. Gently he redressed it, chatting meaninglessly as he always did, and then helped her with her boot.

Christian sat next to Emelda and pointed at the snow-capped mountain range in the distance. He explained that they were trying to reach it by nightfall so that they could camp in the caves at the base; they would make the ascent in the morning.

"Over the mountain?" she asked.

"No, no, through the mountain, you'll see. It would be preferable to get a decent rest in the caves at the base. It's a hard climb to the passage through the mountains and an even tougher descent once we get through. Don't worry though, here, let me get you a drink."

With that he got up and walked over to Kasper and Indira who were preparing some food. They looked up at him expectantly as he approached.

"The wound is starting to heal. There may be a little infection as it is a little warm to the touch but it's nothing that won't wait until we get into the mountain - the Brothers will sort it out," he informed them.

They nodded and Indira fished in her bag, "Here give her this. Double this time."

She handed him the pot of herbs again.

"What is it?" He asked dubiously.

"Pain relief and it should help with the infection, at least until we get there. I gave her some after she hurt her wrist," replied Indira.

Christian looked at Kasper, who nodded, "I actually prepared it. Eat quickly, we need to get moving again and reach a safe campsite, maybe start up the mountain if possible."

Kasper's word on the medicine was enough for Christian. He trusted his judgement and if he said it was safe then it was safe. He thought about protesting that Emelda needed a little longer to rest, but once Kasper had made up his mind on something there wasn't anything anyone could do about it. He was as stubborn as an ox and arrogant with it, but irritatingly he was usually right. Gathering some food for himself and the Princess he returned to her side; they ate quickly and when he offered Emelda the medicine she took some happily.

They were soon back on the road, Emelda in the saddle and the others walking. She was sure she could have walked, but her ankle was throbbing and the medicine was making her feel a little woozy, so maybe it was best she rode. Then again, she was finding the riding hard on her body; though her strength and stamina was returning to her, it was taking time. She was not the instant Queen that everyone seemed to expect. She had to keep reminding herself of who she was and that it was the Kings Guards' job to protect her and give her safe passage to her fiancé. However, she wanted to make it some of the way on her own two feet, as a Princess and future Queen, not carried on the backs of others as a weak and needy girl, not when she was starting to remember who she had been before. She reached up and loosened her cloak a little, an unfamiliar warmth rising in her body.

By the time they reached the base of the mountain, she felt as if she was glowing. Nausea swept over her in waves and she couldn't see straight. She clung onto the horse as tightly as she could, desperate not to fall again. As the light was beginning to fade Indira insisted that they made camp in one of the caves at the base of the mountain, though Kasper was keen to make their way to the safety of the mountain. He grabbed Indira by the arm and pulled her out of earshot of Christian and Emelda. After a few moments, Kasper returned alone.

"We will camp here," he said bluntly.

"Where's Indira?" asked Christian. Emelda dared not speak; there was anger smouldering in Kasper's dark eyes.

"Gathering wood for the fire and dinner. Let's set up."

No one else spoke, instead Emelda sat on the cold ground trying to keep her focus on the two men who busied themselves with starting a fire and laying blankets on the ground. Soon Indira returned with several rabbits and a large bundle of firewood. By this time Emelda's head was aching and she could barely keep her eyes open. She put her hand to her head, it was burning and damp. Muttering her apologies, she slowly got to her feet and almost fell down again. Indira was quickly at her side.

"Are you ok, Your Majesty?" She asked.

Emelda tried to look at her and reply, but Indira's face seemed to be swimming around in her vision, and a strange darkness kept coming over her. She mumbled something and with Indira's help she staggered over to a blanket where she lay down and closed her eyes. She just wanted to sleep, to drift away into nothingness. She could feel the sweat on her back, yet she felt cold, and pulled her cloak tighter around herself; eyes shut she tried desperately not to be sick. Drifting between feverish sleep and semi-consciousness, she dreamt the same dream she always did except this time she couldn't get away from the blood, she seemed to be drowning in it. Desperately gasping for air, she thrashed around, trying to get her head above the surface of the blood; she could feel her heart drumming against her ribs and her chest as if it was being constricted. She tried to cry out but when she opened her mouth more blood filled her lungs, metallic and thick. Somewhere she heard someone calling her. She turned around, desperate to see where the voice was coming from but all she saw was red.

"Princess! Princess!" came the voice again, quiet but urgent.

The blood began to fade into darkness, the voice getting louder and more fraught. She wanted to open her eyes and answer but her body wouldn't respond. She felt like she was burning, being consumed by flames. Her body hurt all over and she couldn't move.

"Princess!"

She tried to respond but all she could muster was a pitiful groan. She heard footsteps leaving her and return quickly with a second set. She felt hands pulling at her face, her skin and hair and in her mind, she saw demons cawing like ravens and clawing at her body, their sharp little nails piercing her skin, their filthy mouths sucking at her blood. She tried to shake herself free, fear suffocating her, then her whole body began to shake with the fever, yet in her delirium she heard Kasper's voice, serious and worried.

"This isn't good, we need to get up the mountain now."

Then Indira's voice rang out, "Ambush!"

Emelda felt strong hands lifting her up and she no longer felt scared. Instead of demons attacking her she was being held by an angel with fire in his eyes. She tried to open her eyes to see her saviour, but she couldn't, all she could do was rest her head on his chest and listen to the reassuring beat of his heart. She felt the thud of his feet on the ground as he began to run, the distant twang of Indira's bow and the clash of metal on metal. Desperately she tried to cling onto her rescuer but she couldn't make her limbs do as she wanted. Her head lolled back for a moment and her rescuer shifted her around so that he could hold her even closer. The rush of cold night air on Emelda's face revived her a little as she continued to slip in and out of consciousness.

She had no idea for how long she was carried but the sensation of floating and then the cold ground beneath her seemed to bring her into a more comprehensive state of consciousness. She felt a hand cradle her head and another brushing her sweat-soaked hair from her face, then gently her head was rested on the ground and he was gone. She lay there, breathing, eyes still closed, waiting for her head to stop swimming. Moments later there was a blood-curdling cry of a dying man and Emelda forced her eyes open, the star-spattered sky spun for a moment before she could focus on it. She tried to lift her head but she was so weak she could barely manage it. Instead she turned her head and tried to look around. In the darkness, she could scarcely make anything out, but she could hear the sounds of fighting and death, smell the metallic scent of blood in the air. Eventually she gained her night vision and she could see that she was hidden amongst an outcrop of rocks and shrubs, not far from the solitary figure of a man who was being attacked on all sides. The lone figure moved with a deadly grace, his twin blades catching the moonlight as they sliced through the attackers' bodies like butter. Emelda could hear the sounds of other fighting somewhere in the distance and assumed the others were still fighting too; she could smell the blood on the air and it made her think of her dream.

Emelda managed to drag herself into a seated position against a rock, not taking her eyes off her protector. She watched, her eyes heavy, as the last man dropped at her protector's feet with a groan and he stood for a moment listening, ready for another attack. Satisfied that no more were coming he sheathed his swords across his back and turned towards her. Noticing that she was trying to sit he broke into a run; dropping to his knees at her side, he placed his arm around her and helped her sit more comfortably. She collapsed into his arms, her eyes fixed on his face, and her vision started to blur once more, the fever returning with a vengeance.

"Kasper," she breathed.

"Princess," he whispered and once more gathered her up into his arms and began to walk.

Emelda rested her head on his chest and tried to hold onto him, but she felt her strength slipping away again and her breathing getting shallow, the crushing feeling returning. Pressed up against him she could feel his steady rhythmic breathing, he was calm and in control. She tried to slow her own breathing down, inhaling his smell of delicate lavender, but it was no good, she couldn't slow the rapid rise and fall of her own chest.

'This is it,' she thought, 'I'm going to die.'

She felt the ground beneath them start to rise up and she wondered how Kasper was going to carry her up the mountain; surely he wouldn't manage it. She ought to be walking - she tried to speak but Kasper ignored her, holding her tighter still and carrying on steadily forward. She closed her eyes, unsure if she would ever open them again, and drifted out of consciousness.

Kasper's body screamed with pain but he carried on up the mountain He could not stop nor look back, his eyes focused on a point up ahead. He cried out as his foot caught a rock and he almost dropped Emelda, but he clung onto her, steadying himself with one hand. After many aching steps, he reached the wide mouth of a cave and placed the Princess gently on the ground. He paused for a moment at her side and shook her shoulders gently, but she didn't respond, her body floppy and her breathing shallow. He wiped the sweat from his forehead and pushed himself to his feet.

"Brother Icka!" He called desperately, "Brother Icka!"

Kasper's voice was thin and weak, he was barely able to catch his own breath, but he carried on calling. His voice echoed through the cave but remained unanswered. Taking a deep breath, he reached underneath the Princess and hauled her up; he could barely feel her breath on his cheek now. A burning pain ripped through his arms and he cried out with the exertion. He stumbled further into the cave and took a deep breath, and with all his might he bellowed into the darkness, "Icka!"

"Please," he murmured, the words barely escaping his lips.

With the last of his energy gone Kasper dropped onto his knees and cradled the Princess's head in his arms. Her breathing was intermittent and her pulse was faint; he knew she was dying and there was nothing he could do. Then out of the darkness came the faintest of lights, growing larger and stronger as it came closer, followed by the sound of hurried footsteps on the cold stone floor. One light was soon joined by another and another until there was a sea of light bringing with it the reassurance of help. Kasper breathed a sigh of relief as the familiar face of Brother Icka appeared in the pale light of his lantern, whilst the other Brothers prised the Princess from his tired arms and carried her away. Kasper watched as her limp body disappeared into the darkness of the cave. He watched until he could no longer see the Brothers' lights bouncing as they ran. He slammed his fist hard against the cave floor before sinking to the ground, his head in his hands. He stayed that way for some time, waiting for his body to recover, waiting for his breathing to return to normal and his heart to calm down, yet he couldn't breathe away his fear. He felt a hand on his back and he looked up; Brother Icka was standing over him, waiting for him, a gentle yet concerned look in his eyes.

"Lord Kasper...," he began, stepping back as Kasper pushed himself to standing.

Kasper interrupted, "Please, just Kasper, Brother."

Brother Icka nodded, "Very well, but it's not good to keep secrets, they eat away at you from the inside, you know."

Kasper didn't speak, instead he gazed into the darkness after the Princess.

"She's alright now, she's stronger than you know," Icka reassured him, "shall we?"

"The others," said Kasper shrugging Icka's hand off, "we were ambushed."

"I have already sent some of the monks out to find them. Come now, you need to rest or you will be no good to anyone," Icka told him in a firm tone and placing a hand on his back he led him into the cave.

"And the willow?" asked Kasper.

"I will make sure it is safe, come now," Brother Icka told him. Kasper let himself be led away, glancing briefly over his shoulder and praying that Christian and Indira would make it unscathed.

Chapter 8

Christian breathed heavily, sword drawn, ready for another attack. The last few men had almost overpowered him; he was injured and exhausted, he had no idea where Indira was. He kept glancing up the mountain in the hope that Kasper had made it safely up to the cave. Christian hadn't been sure the Princess would last until morning. He had been surprised at her sudden decline; she had been fine only hours earlier, her ankle a little red but nothing to worry about. Christian looked around at the bodies that scattered the ground, organs sprawling out on to the earth and the stench of blood filling the air. There was a deep wound across his chest that was oozing more blood than he was happy about; luckily the adrenaline was still numbing the pain, but he wasn't looking forward to it wearing off. His eyes searched the darkness - at some point he and Indira had become separated and with her special skills, she wasn't easy to spot. He remembered the first time he had watched in awe as she had closed her eyes and taken three deep breaths before she let out a groan, her eyes opening wide and turning from gold to black. Her hair had turned black as well, and she had melted away into obscurity. It was terrifying, the ultimate killer's weapon, being invisible in the shadows.

The air had become still and there hadn't been an attack for some time. Christian began to relax, letting his heavy sword rest at his side. He looked around at the carnage. The men who had attacked them had been poorly equipped and disorganised. They hadn't worn the insignia of the Rebel King's Men, in fact he could have sent three skilled men to do the same job with a better chance of success. It hadn't taken long for Indira and himself to dispatch the first wave, while Kasper carried the Princess off to safety. Then Indira had disappeared too and he had been on his own. As he wondered if Kasper and the Princess had made it to the cave, he sheathed his sword and started to make his own way up, deciding to have a look for Indira on the way. He gazed at the faces of the men he had killed. He thought about having to carry the Princess all the way up the mountain; Kasper was strong but it was a long way for even him.

His thoughts were interrupted by the sound of an arrow being loosed. With a lightening reaction he turned just in time to feel an arrow whizz past his face, leaving a thin cut along his cheek. Pulling his sword from its sheath he faced his attacker, ready to fight, yet to his surprise he saw nothing but darkness in front of him. Trying not to breathe he listened hard. There in the inky blackness barely audible to the untrained ear was the faint sound of breathing, of a taut bow string and of a barely trembling arrow.

"Indira?" Christian called out to her, putting his sword away, "it's me!"

But she did not reply, nor did she put down her weapon, instead she appeared from the darkness like a spirit, adjusted her aim and stared hard at him.

"Indira?" He called again, confused.

She pulled the bow back a little further and was about to fire when the sound of singing filled their ears, strange and out of place on the mountainside. Then several men dressed in long brown robes appeared, negotiating the mountain path with ease. Indira looked at the men, then at Christian; she turned her bow on the men, before dropping it and removing the arrow. She turned to greet the monks, masking a look of annoyance. Christian watched as she shuddered and her hair and eyes returned to brilliant gold once more. Unsure of what had just happened he cautiously made his way over to the monks. Indira turned to face him, gave him a smile and beckoned him over.

"Come with me," said one of the monks, "the others will deal with this."

His voice was low and soft and as he spoke the other monks began to make their way further down the mountain and began quickly piling up the bodies, singing as they worked.

"Follow me. The Princess and Kasper are waiting for you," he said turning away from them and beginning to trek back the way they had come.

"Do you have any idea who attacked you?" asked the monk, "We don't get many people around here."

"Bandits," said Indira quickly, before Christian had a chance to speak.

"Hmmm...not unheard of I guess, these are desperate times," he replied, sounding unconvinced.

They continued to walk in silence, Christian hanging back a little, trying to make sense of exactly what had happened back there. Eventually he matched Indira's pace and grabbed hold of her arm. She tried to shake herself free but he tightened his grip.

"What was that back there?" he asked in a low voice, so only she could hear.

"What was what?" she replied bluntly, barely looking at him.

"You tried to kill me."

"I thought I saw someone behind you."

Christian let go of her arm and stopped for a moment, unconvinced, then he caught up with her again but said nothing, fixing his eyes on the entrance to the cave some way above them.

Emelda woke to the sound of voices nearby; one was Kasper's and the other she didn't recognise. Slowly she opened her eyes, wondering if she was dead; she had felt on the edge of another world not so long ago. She was sure she had been in a place between life and death; for a moment, she had sworn that she had seen the ceiling of her apartment before it had vanished again and she had felt what she thought was water washing over her body, cool and refreshing. Looking around she saw that she was in fact lying on a bed in a small room, with a little window. As she tried to move, her body responded, and carefully she propped herself up against the soft pillow at her back. With renewed strength, she looked around - the room was relatively bare and she was alone. The small window was shuttered yet the sunlight had managed to sneak its way into the room and a cool breeze filtered in with it. Emelda felt the urge to throw it open and breathe the fresh air in, to bathe her face in the bright sunlight.

Cautiously she swung her legs over the side of the bed and placed her feet on the stone floor; she drew her breath in sharply at its coldness. It was only then that she noticed her clothes had been changed and her ankle redressed. Her ankle still ached a little, but the pain was barely noticeable; her fever was gone and she could think with clarity again. She ran one hand through her hair - that too had been washed and brushed. She attempted to stand up, one hand on the edge of the bed, and slipped, a little cry escaping her lips as she steadied herself. The voices outside stopped and Kasper entered the room, looking concerned.

"Princess, you're awake," he sounded surprised, yet his voice was gentle, she had not heard it like that before.

He came straight to her side and placed his hand on her forehead, then gently swung her legs back onto the bed. His hand went back to her head again and it lingered there a little longer than necessary, before he realised what he was doing and quickly removed it. He turned to the man behind him and beckoned him into the room.

"Her temperature is normal, thank you, Brother Icka," he said with relief.

Emelda sat herself up once again and smiled at Brother Icka.

"Your Majesty, please allow me to introduce myself, as Kasper's manners appear to have failed him in his time of worry. My name is Brother Icka, one of the monks of the Royal Order. I run the monastery here; I doubt you have heard of us, but I knew your Father well," explained Brother Icka.

Emelda looked up at the man who had entered the room behind Kasper. He was on the short side but had a kindly face. His hair and beard were brilliant white and his skin lined with age, but his eyes still burned with life. He smiled at her as a father would a child.

"We are one of the lines of defence put in place by your father. Although we were here thousands of years before you were even dreamt of, King Lucius chose to hide you in plain sight of our monastery so that we, too, could keep an eye on one so precious," explained Icka.

"But you are just monks," replied Emelda, confused.

Brother Icka laughed gently, "Monks, warriors, healers. We are trained to protect and to defend, as well as being healers, but at the heart of it all will always be the Great Tree. Our job is to keep the water source, the living water, which feeds it, safe and untainted until such a time as when the Great Tree can be replanted and the land restored again."

"Yes, the willow tree, I remember," murmured Emelda, her hand went to her neck. She felt panic rising in her stomach as her fingers felt nothing but skin. She opened her mouth to speak but Brother Icka continued and she swallowed her words.

"It was a mighty tree and a conduit for the living water, absorbing it through its roots and spreading it across the land, making the earth fruitful and quenching our souls. Without it the earth is dry and our hearts are heavy," his words were poetic and heart-felt.

"Can't you make some sort of irrigation system or aqueduct?" Emelda asked.

"Then he would know where we are. If the Rebel King found us he would use the power hidden here to decimate this world. Think of how many people would die."

"But wouldn't he be destroying himself too?"

"Yes, but he is so blinded by power that he believes destroying your Kingdom, oppressing the people and ruling over the ruins will bring him satisfaction, that it will quench his blood lust. So far, he has succeeded; the only thing standing in his way, Princess, is you. "

Emelda shook her head, Nicholas' face coming to mind. She couldn't remember anyone else but he was still clear to her. There was so much at stake, so much resting on her shoulders, the alliance, the willow tree and now this apocalyptic prediction.

"Then I need to get better very quickly, Brother, thank you for your care so far," she replied, feeling determined. The fate that Brother Icka portrayed would never come to pass, not while she was still alive.

"Where is the willow? When I awoke it was gone," she asked trying not to let her concern show in her voice.

"Don't worry Princess, it is safe, I will return it to you once you are feeling ready," Icka told her kindly and Emelda felt herself relax again.

"Thank you."

"It is my duty and honour to serve you, your Majesty," said Icka bowing deeply, "can I recommend a visit to the Spring before you go, it is sure to restore you, Princess."

"The Spring?"

"The life-giving water that flows to the tree - you should bathe in it. I will leave you with Kasper."

Emelda thanked the monk again as he left, bowing and gently pulling the door closed behind him. This left an awkward silence in the room. Emelda had so much to say but she could barely look at Kasper. She couldn't find the words to even begin, so instead she breathed softly, hoping the words would find their own way out, but the silence held. She wanted to take his hands in hers and thank him for saving her life, for carrying her up the mountain with no consideration for himself. She wanted to thank him for protecting her, for even killing for her. But the words would not come, she felt tears welling up in her eyes and she forced them back. Kasper coughed a little and shifted on the spot.

"I should let you rest," he said quietly and started towards the door.

"No!" Emelda cried out with more emotion than she had intended, "I mean please don't go just yet."

Kasper stood by the door, his eyes fixed on her, waiting to hear what she had to say. Automatically she looked away, her eyes focusing on anything but him.

"Thank you," she murmured.

It was an inadequate thank you and she knew it; it sounded paltry the moment it left her lips. How did you truly thank someone for saving your life? She had never been in such a life or death situation before, never had to be grateful that she was still breathing. Emelda looked around the room - she could feel his dark eyes upon her, boring into her but she could not meet his gaze. She was still a little fearful of him and his changing temperament, despite all that had happened.

Finally, unable to put it off any longer, she let her eyes venture up towards his face. There was a strange look in his eyes, a mixture of relief and disappointment. Emelda thought about crossing the room to take his hand, but refrained, unsure what kind of reaction it would provoke.

Instead she spoke formally as a Queen would to a good and faithful servant, "You saved my life and I am indebted to you."

Kasper sighed as if he was expecting more from her, "It was my duty, Princess."

He looked as if he had more to say but instead he abruptly turned to leave the room; his hand was on the door handle before Emelda called out to him again.

"Thank you, Kasper."

Kasper did not look around; a moment of hope dwindled in his soul like a dying fire and he did not want her to see, nor could he bear to look upon her face when she still looked at him with uncertainty and fear.

"Get some rest," he muttered in response and left quickly, leaving Emelda alone in the small room.

He walked briskly along the carved stone corridor, fists clenched, his footsteps echoing on the hard floor. He had let himself hope and that was a fatal error; he had forgotten his promise to the King all those years ago, the promise sealed in blood that bound him eternally to the King's Guard and the royal family. Yet as he had carried her close to his chest in the moonlight, he had been unable to steel himself against the emotions he had put to rest a decade ago. He had wondered if she had remembered anything, but after their conversation it was clear she had not. Yet in him it stirred memories and desires; the soft touch of her hands around his neck, her face buried in his broad chest, warm and close. But she still looked at him like a stranger, someone to be wary of, there was not even a flicker of recognition. Kasper could taste the bitterness of his disappointment as he pushed open a small wooden door and emerged into the blazing sun.

He found himself facing the centre of the monastery, a large courtyard hewn out of the mountain itself and open to the sky. The rocky mountain face was made up of brilliant white rock that almost hurt his eyes to look at in the bright midday sun, but the effect was spectacular. A beautifully constructed monastery hidden in the mountains safe from all eyes but those of the birds. Kasper enjoyed the peace and tranquillity, something he longed for more and more with age. As a young man he had been full on, in your face and obnoxious. Now despite his cold manner he longed for a quiet place to be still, to not have to think or fight anymore.

As he was crossing the courtyard Christian approached him, a solemn look on his face. His chest had been bandaged and he looked as if he had rested well, but Kasper was instantly put on edge by the grave look on his face.

"We need to talk," he said in a low whisper.

"Come with me," Kasper said and beckoned Christian to follow.

Christian followed Kasper until they reached a small yet ornate door in one of the courtyard walls. They found themselves in a vaulted ante-chamber through the centre of which ran a narrow stream of water along a gully. After a quick glance around the area Christian began.

"It's Indira, she tried to kill me."

Much to Christian's surprise Kasper did not react.

"Did you hear what I said?" he asked, a little taken aback.

"Yes."

Christian waited but when Kasper said nothing else he laughed scornfully, "What is going on here Kasper, are you sleeping with the devil? Have her womanly ways blinded you to her betrayal? Does she whisper sweet nothings to you at night when we all sleep?"

Kasper grabbed Christian by the collar and thrust him hard against the wall. Christian was not willing to be pushed around again and fought back with equal strength, throwing Kasper off and straightening his shirt.

"Correct me then, man! What is going on? Are you in love with the snake?" he wanted to shout but he settled for an angry tone.

"I know what she is, I have known all along, but we still need her. We need her to get through the Marshes and I need to know exactly what she knows and what the enemy has planned," replied Kasper, trying to keep his voice level.

Christian looked at him in disbelief, "And you kept this to yourself? I thought I was your friend, I thought you trusted me."

"I told you to keep an eye on her when we set out on this journey. I knew what she was back then and I wanted to keep her close, lure her in so I could keep an eye on her, learn what she knows and feed her false information."

"Kasper," growled Christian, "she tried to kill me and I'm sure she had something to do with the

Princess's fever. I overheard some of the monks talking as I was passing. They found something in her vomit, undigested herbs."

"I prepared that medicine myself," Kasper muttered.

"She must have tampered with it. If she's working for the Rebel King then she wants the Princess dead."

Kasper smacked the wall in temper; the sound reverberated down the passage way, bounding off the stone walls. He looked at his hand as he spoke, unable to look at Christian.

"I thought she was just after information, the location of the meeting place, the number of men we have," his voice was low and quiet.

"It seems you were wrong for once, Kasper."

Kasper looked up at Christian and knew that he was right.

"Does she know that the Princess has the willow bud?" asked Christian with concern.

"No, I told her it was moved long ago and that all that was sustaining the Princess was a piece of bark, which I had destroyed the moment she awoke. Sophia is good with sleight of hand, believe me," said Kasper, reassuringly.

Christian nodded in agreement.

"Play along for now, Christian; I know you two have never seen eye to eye, but just accept her excuses and lies. The time to expose her will come soon; until then we must make sure the Princess is never left unguarded, be that by you or I or a monk while we are here."

"I still don't feel happy, Kasper, Indira's sly, kill or be killed."

"Trust me, we will keep the Princess safe. And don't tell her, don't worry her."

Christian nodded reluctantly and placed his hand on Kasper's arm, "Now go bathe, believe me you will feel better for it."

"Indeed," said Kasper, placing his hand on Christian's who then turned and left, whereas Kasper headed deeper into the monastery's underground spring. He followed the little gully of water as it got steadily larger until he reached its source, a small stone fountain from which a little spout of water bubbled. In the room, next to the main chamber was a deep pool, carved into the snowy white stone floor, with seats hewn around the edge and a large plug in the middle. A large copper tap was poised over the edge, ready to gush forth life-giving water. Kasper gazed around, calmed by the simplicity of everything around him and the gentle sound of trickling water. This was the place he sought, one of peace and stillness, a place where he could just exist. He walked over to the pool and peered into it, then he turned the tap on and there was a gurgle and a glug then a torrent of water flowed into the pool, hitting the bottom with a splash. Kasper spotted a shelf heaped with towels and grabbed a couple before laying his two katana swords on the floor and slowly undressing. He removed his jacket and shirt, his arms aching as he did, then his boots and trousers as the pool slowly filled. It felt good to take off his clothes, like lifting off a heavy burden. He stood naked, watching the clean water rising, his bare skin tingling in the cold, still air of the chamber. He closed his eyes and let the stillness seep into his skin, deep into his flesh and into his tired bones. It had been a long journey before it had even begun.

Finally the water reached chest height and he turned the tap off. It continued to drip for a moment or two before the room was silent again. Kasper took a deep breath, bracing himself for the shock of the cold water and stepped down into the pool. The freezing water took his breath away and he exhaled hard, the cold stabbing painfully at his chest, yet he continued until he was totally submerged. From beneath the water he watched countless tiny bubbles rising to the surface, the cold penetrating deep into his aching muscles and torn flesh. He felt his lungs start to burn as his body cried out for oxygen but he resisted the urge to breathe, letting the water do its healing work. After a moment he burst up through the surface of the water and took a deep breath of sweet air, his body trembling from the cold, but it felt good. He felt refreshed and rejuvenated - one more plunge and he would be battle-ready once again. Taking another breath, he let the water rush over him, engulfing him in icy coldness. When he finally came up for air he could hear footsteps and voices. Quickly he climbed out of the pool and wrapped the coarse towel around his lower half just as Brother Icka appeared in the doorway followed by another monk who was helping the Princess walk.

Kasper felt his body grow tense and his guard went up. He quickly gathered his weapons and his clothes, not caring that they were becoming wet clutched to his dripping body. Standing motionless he waited for them to notice him, debating with himself whether to just leave discretely without speaking to the Princess, or to get dried and dressed then and there not caring who was watching. Right at this moment in time he wanted nothing more than to be alone and he felt angry that they had interrupted his solitude.

As the Princess entered, talking animatedly with Icka, the decision was made for him. There was no way to leave the room without being seen and as Emelda glanced up her eyes fell on Kasper and her conversation came to an abrupt halt. Her eyes widened in horror at the sight of him half naked and wet; hastily she averted her eyes.

"Forgive me, Sir," she said to the ground.

"I am sorry, Kasper I did not realise you were here," said Brother Icka apologetically, a flicker of a grin on his lips.

"I was just leaving," replied Kasper quickly and he began walking towards the exit.

"Please don't feel you have to rush off on my account," said Emelda as he approached, daring to glance up at him.

For a moment she could not take her eyes off him, deep concern in her eyes. His broad chest and strong arms were covered in the scars and wounds of countless battles. Most of the scars were old, but some were still red and angry, others had barely healed. She could now see the ornate tattoo penned in red ink that snaked up and down his left arm and she almost reached out to touch it as if it was a familiar action for her, but she caught herself.

"So much pain," she murmured, imagining how each injury had caused Kasper suffering, then she remembered who she was speaking to and looked away again quickly.

"It's all part of my duty; none of them have been fatal so there is no need for your concern," he said bluntly.

Brother Icka raised his eyebrows slightly but said nothing.

"If you will forgive the intrusion, the Princess ought to bathe before you leave and I believe you are planning to leave at sunrise?" said Icka.

Kasper nodded, "Providing the Princess is well enough."

"After bathing I'm sure she will be; now if you would excuse us we can begin."

But Kasper did not move, instead he pulled his trousers on underneath his towel and placed the rest of his clothes and swords on the floor.

"I will assist you, Princess," he said nonchalantly.

"But I...," she began to protest, her heart pounding in her chest and she could feel her face flushing with heat.

"Do you want all the men in the Kingdom to see you naked?" he asked with a sneer on his face.

"I don't think Brother Icka counts as all the men in the kingdom, plus I don't really want you to see me naked either," Emelda replied, meeting his gaze, and bristling at his tone.

He looked taken back for a second before regaining his composure, "I have no interest in you or your unimpressive body, who do you think changed your clothes and dressed you in that?" he pointed at her white robe, "there are no women here."

Emelda felt her cheeks burning even more, so much so she was sure she must have been scarlet, and she scowled at him, "How dare you!"

He shrugged and leant in close to her face, "Just be glad it wasn't Christian."

Emelda felt so angry she could have slapped the smug look off his face but she restrained herself and took a deep breath.   She hoped those scars had hurt him.

"I don't need you to undress me, I can do that on my own; in fact, I may only need your help getting out so you can wait outside until I call you."

"As you wish, Your Majesty," he said with a laugh.

Kasper picked up his clothes and pushed past Emelda and the monks. Emelda waited for him to leave the room before thanking the monks, who then left her alone. As Icka was leaving he turned to her and rested a hand on her shoulder.

"He has a good heart, but it has been a long time since he has let anyone see it. He changed more than most when he joined the King's Guard," said Icka quietly, shaking his old head, "I have never seen such a

101

dedicated man, but I don't believe he knows how to deal with his emotions, let alone express them."

"He was in love?" Emelda looked confused, unable to hide the surprise in her voice, "but he seems so cold, so unfeeling."

"He has spent the last decade in the King's Guard; it produces a certain type of person. Now, Your Majesty, please enjoy the water," he said bowing ever so slightly and turning to leave.

Brother Icka hadn't really answered her question, and as she watched him leave, she felt a thousand more questions on her lips, left there to remain unspoken. Nervously, Emelda carefully put weight on her ankle and found it was much more bearable than it had been even an hour ago. She walked gingerly over to the edge of the pool and peered in. The water was deep, still and clear. Glancing over her shoulder to make sure Kasper was not watching she pulled the gown over her head and sat down on the edge of the pool. She dipped a toe in and withdrew it again quickly, the cold water sending shivers up and down her spine and making her skin prickle. Taking a deep breath, she slid herself into the water; it was so cold she couldn't stop herself crying out.

"Princess!" came Kasper's voice from outside the doorway and a second later he appeared.

"Get out!" she shouted at him, hastily covering her small breasts with her hands even though she was beneath the edge of the pool. Kasper rapidly withdrew from the room.

"It was cold," she called out to him, but he remained silent. She could hear him shifting around outside the door and Emelda took his silence to mean that he was satisfied with her answer, but just to make sure she wouldn't be caught off guard again, she grabbed her gown and pulled it back over her head and down into the water.

The cold water was biting and it stung her flesh like a thousand needles but she made herself endure it. Gritting her teeth against the cold she submerged herself, letting her mind drift back to London as she floated in the freezing water. She tried to remember the streets, the names of the bars and shops, her shop, but she couldn't. Her life in the other world was becoming more and more like a distant dream, except for Nicholas - for some reason his face remained as clear as day. Her thoughts turned to this world, her world. She pictured the faces of her mother and father, kind and smiling, the way she remembered them when she was a child. Her older brother's face, stern and just, his familiar crown of red hair and piercing green eyes a mirror of her own. Luca. His name came to her in a rush, then all she could see was blood. Blood all over his bedroom, as if an animal had been brutally slaughtered; the blood seemed to be seeping out of the very walls, in through the windows and dripping from the ceiling. She looked down at her hands, and to her horror they too were covered in blood. Desperately she tried to wipe them on her clothes but the blood wouldn't wipe away - instead it seemed to exude from the very pores of her skin like sweat. She looked up from her hands, her eyes searching around the room for her brother's body but she couldn't see it. She called out his name and cold water filled her mouth and she began to choke.

She wrenched open her eyes as she felt strong hands lift her under her arms and out of the water. As she coughed and spluttered, desperately gasping for oxygen, Emelda felt a rough towel being draped over her body and heard her own name being called.

"Luca," she whispered staring up at the white ceiling.

Kasper's face loomed over her but his eyes were tightly shut. Emelda looked up at him, puzzled.

"You were under the water far too long, what were you thinking?" he exclaimed angrily, getting up and picking up another towel.

Emelda sat up clutching the towel to her chest; she looked up at Kasper, his face turned away from her, a towel in his outstretched hand.

"I was remembering," replied Emelda quietly, taking the towel and the hand underneath she pulled herself to her feet, "I was remembering my brother's death. It keeps coming back to me like a nightmare."

She saw Kasper's shoulders drop a little; without another word, he disappeared out of the room and returned with a neatly folded pile of clothes, which he placed in front of her before turning away again. She hurriedly got dressed as he began to speak.

"You found the murder scene, no sign of Luca but enough blood to convince everyone he couldn't have survived. A week later they found a body in the woods surrounding the castle. It was the rainy season and the corpse had rotted badly, been gnawed on by animals, as well as being horribly mutilated, but it wore your brother's clothes and your brother's rings. It also had a birthmark on its chest just like Luca and that was enough for your parents. I was young at the time but I remember the whole kingdom mourning for the dead prince; everyone wore black for what seemed like an eternity and out of that tragedy the King's Guard was formed in earnest."

"And that's when you joined?" asked Emelda, curious to know more after everything Icka had whispered to her.

Kasper hesitated, remembering his rebellious youth, "I joined a few years after, when the Rebel King was first at large. When they hid you."

Emelda wasn't content with his answer, "How old were you?"

"Eighteen," he said carelessly,

"That was ten years ago?" She looked at him hard, "You're younger than I thought."

"Thanks," Kasper felt a little insulted but he carried on anyway, "It wasn't the life my father wanted for me but I was too hard-headed to listen to anyone. Are you dressed yet?"

Kasper finished the conversation and turned to face the Princess.

"I need a little assistance; my wrist is still a little weak at that angle," she turned away from him and lifted her damp hair from the back of her neck.

Slowly and gently Kasper did up the fastening at the back of her neck before stepping away and admiring the gentle slope of her shoulders and the soft hair that graced the nape of her neck. Blinking slowly, he forced himself to speak.

"Why can't women learn to dress themselves," he muttered more to himself than to Emelda.

He placed the damp towels in a heap by the door and led the way out, not waiting to see if Emelda was following him. Surprised at the renewed strength she felt coursing through her whole body she followed silently behind Kasper with new hope in her heart.

Chapter 9

Indira and Christian had finished eating by the time Kasper and the Princess joined them. It had been a slightly awkward dinner, with neither saying very much, their mutual dislike and suspicion tainting the atmosphere. As the other two entered Christian felt a sense of relief and relaxed a little, smiling at Emelda in his usual way. Indira watched them, observing their body language to see whether the dynamics of their relationship had changed at all. Kasper and the Princess had spent a long time together and it seemed that he had seen or heard no one else while she was indisposed, much to Indira's chagrin. She was relieved to see that there were no sideways glances or subtle smiles. Kasper's face was still hard and cold, so much so that she sometimes thought him utterly emotionless, except when they were alone and his face would soften and he would touch her hand carelessly. Much to her own dismay and better judgement her body longed for him; his gentle words and whispered sweet nothings evoked a deep lust in her soul that she fought hard to control so as not to betray herself. There had been several moments when she had thought about abandoning her mission and asking him to leave with her, to let this damn world go to rot, Princess and all, and although he had never kissed her, never touched more than her hand, she often imagined the feel of his body and the passion that lay behind his eyes.

Indira's feelings towards the Princess were dark; there was something about Emelda that was captivating and she couldn't deny that her face was striking, which made her hate her all the more. There was something that drew people to Emelda that Indira did not have, and she was the only person she had ever seen Kasper look at the way he did, with a distant longing. He did not look at her like that.

She bowed her head slightly as the Princess approached so that she could swallow the bitter jealousy, her face returning to normal as she looked up.

"Kasper, may we speak?" she asked before he could sit down. He nodded, and without excusing themselves the two left the room. Emelda sat down next to Christian; she watched them go, her eyes trailing after them.

"How are you feeling, Princess?" he asked her.

"Better, in fact I feel the best I have yet," she smiled at him, unable to take her eyes off the closed door through which Kasper and Indira had just disappeared.

Christian looked from her face to the door and back again. He knew the look of a confused heart all too well. He was about to speak when a monk appeared carrying food and drink for Emelda; he placed it in front of her and bowed deeply before leaving. She called out her thanks to him as he left.

"Honestly, Princess it is nothing; Kasper isn't that kind of man," he tried to reassure her as he stabbed a potato with her fork for her.

"We are all human," she said looking down at her plate, as she moved the potato around a bit, then sat back heavily in her chair.

"Let me tell you something, Princess, Kasper is not a ladies' man. I've known him about ten years, and to begin with he talked of a woman, a lover maybe, only referred to as 'her'; but after a while that stopped too. He doesn't even seem to notice other women."

"'Her'?"

"I wish I knew, I guess I never will. I'll ask him if you like?" He grinned at Emelda.

She looked at him, but there was a distance in her eyes, a loneliness that he could do nothing about. Suddenly she snapped out of it, pushing her chair hard back from the table and making it screech across the stone floor. Christian winced, looking up at her in surprise.

"No, thank you, his business is nothing to do with me, nor do I care who he pours his affections on. In case you have forgotten I have a Prince, your brother, waiting for me. Why would I have any interest in who Kasper shares a bed with? Now I am going to rest before we leave," she glanced up at the door one last time before turning on the spot and heading for the exit.

Christian, shocked at her outburst, barely had time to stand before she was gone. He stood in the empty room, wondering whether to go after the Princess. He sat down in his seat and folded his hands behind his head, deciding it was best to let her have some space.

Emelda wandered the maze of intricate passageways and rooms that made up the monastery. She couldn't go back to her room; there was no way she could lie down and sleep. Her heart was beating too hard and there was too much churning going on inside her belly for sleep; her head whirled with confusion. Who was Kasper? One minute he was cold and distant, then the next he was kind and gentle, and there was something about him that seemed so familiar. But no sooner had she seen the other side of him it was gone, and she was nothing but a mission to him. He infuriated her.

She walked quickly, her footsteps echoing down the corridors, running her fingers along the rough walls until her finger nails bled. She scarcely noticed, and the pain couldn't distract her from the jumble of emotions she felt. Hitting a dead end with nothing but a closed door, she clutched at her chest and pounded the wall.

"Foolish girl," she cried, "foolish, foolish!"

Much to her horror the door opened and Brother Icka stood in the doorway. Emelda stepped back, her hand clasped to her mouth, then she dropped to her knees grabbing Brother Icka's hands and holding them tightly in her own.

"Please forgive me, Brother, I have disturbed your peace and that of the whole monastery. Please forgive me after all that you have done for me," she pleaded, her face hot with anger and embarrassment.

"Stand up, your Majesty. You are no fool; it is the sound of heartache in your voice and the look of sadness on your face that worries me more than the noise. Please, your Majesty, come in; I had been meaning to seek you out one last time before you left," he said to her with kindness in his old eyes. He helped her to her feet and took her hand; he took the sleeve of his gown and gently wiped away the blood from her hands.

She clasped his hands in hers. "Brother, I am so confused; just as I start to feel as if I belong I'm reminded that I'm on my own, that I don't really know anyone, although they all presume to know me. I had a life, I've lived a life, I am not a child anymore. And to make it worse I'm forgetting all of that, the people I once loved, the people who knew me," said Emelda, a tremor in her voice.

109

"No one expects it all to come back straight away, Princess, you are allowed to take your time, don't let anyone tell you otherwise. Enjoy remembering and experiencing things as if they were new to you," he comforted her, "Now come in, come in."

Taking her gently by the hand he led her into the room. Inside there was a large desk with hundreds of drawers of different shapes and sizes, each one with its own unique little handle. The walls themselves were hidden by shelves and shelves of books, more than one could read in a lifetime even if they never slept. It smelt familiar and melancholy at the same time. Her mind wandered back to her father's library, sitting on his lap and listening to stories. She remembered her brother bursting in on them once, anger all over his face, spitting his words like acid. According to Luca the King spent too much time with her, spoilt her, when he had more pressing matters to attend to, matters that included himself. It was the first time she had remembered Luca with such anger in his eyes, but now she could see him like that she struggled to remember him any other way. Always angry, always bitter, always rebuking their father for the way he ran the Kingdom.

"Just one moment," said Icka, interrupting her daydream as he flicked through a large set of keys with the dexterity of a younger man, until finally he found the one he was after. "Here we go," he said, pushing the key into one of the locked drawers. He reached in and pulled out a second key, smaller than the first but similar in design, then he began hunting through the rows of books until he found a small green leather-bound book with no title but just the initials 'S' and 'L' embossed on the spine in gold. He pulled the book out and handed it to Emelda. She flicked curiously through the pages, but much to her disappointment every single page was blank. She started to speak but Icka held up his hand to silence her and gently took the book from her hands - he turned the book over and revealed a crest embossed in gold.

"The sun and the lion," whispered Emelda, reaching for the book, "my father's crest."

Seeing the crest, she felt a part of her father had come back to her and she pressed the book to her breast, wondering what was going to come next. Brother Icka then pushed the key into a small keyhole cleverly disguised in the rays of the sun on the crest, and the pictures began to move. The lion opened its jaws wide enough to engulf the sun, its mane turning into golden flames. Icka let her watch, then removed the key and placed the book back on its shelf. There was a loud grinding and whirring and the bookcase itself began to move. It shifted back, slowly slotting neatly behind one of its fellow shelves and revealing a twisting flight of narrow steps.

Emelda stood wide-eyed in amazement as Brother Icka beamed at her in delight. He began to descend, beckoning her to follow him, and she obeyed dutifully. It was only a short flight of steps but it was dark and cold, the only light coming from a small lamp. After several twists and turns the staircase ended and they found themselves in a small room. Here Icka took a taper from his pocket and lit the wall lamps. The room slowly became illuminated, relinquishing the secrets it held.

In the very centre was a large stone slab, ornately carved with suns, lions and willow trees, all the symbols of her Kingdom; on top lay a sword and at its hilt a crown.

"These are yours, Your Majesty," said Icka.

Emelda stood in the dim light, unable to move, just staring at the beautiful items in front of her. She felt the hotness of tears and she let them fall, all the built-up emotions pouring out through her tears.

"Your father had these made for you just before he died. I think he knew he didn't have long left," said Icka gently.

"He died recently?" asked Emelda,

"A year or so ago. Many assumed he died when the castle collapsed, but he survived. Lord Hart found him cradling the Queen, sobbing like a child. He expected to die, he had passed on his legacy to you, but death cheated him, crippling him instead. He spent the best part of a decade rallying troops to fight for you, setting up safe areas for men to train in. There is a mighty army waiting for you," explained Icka, sadness creeping into his voice.

"Why haven't they attacked already?" asked Emelda.

"They need you, he couldn't have led them into battle, he could barely move from his bed. They need the willow bud, the power of life over death, to win against the resounding evil of the Rebel King. I hear reports that his eyes bleed in battle with his fury."

A vision of the boy with bleeding eyes froze Emelda to the spot; she felt her skin go clammy and her palms sweat. She shook her head, no, not now. She forced herself to move towards the slab and admire the objects upon it. She lifted her hand and ran her finger along the flat of the blade. It was beautifully crafted, ornate and strong, with a sun engraved into the hilt, its rays running down the blade. She picked it up carefully, it fitted her hand perfectly, it was light yet sharper than any blade she had ever seen. Memories of practising sword fighting with wooden swords came flooding back to her - she must have been twelve or thirteen and her opponent, a boy, a year or so older than herself. He had pushed her back easily, a mischievous glint in his eye and a confident smile upon his lips. Despite her best efforts she had been no match for him, all she could do was attempt to parry his attacks, yielding to his swordsmanship.

Once after a succession of attacks she failed to dodge a blow and his blade caught her cheek. Instantly her hand went to her face and she dropped her weapon. Her eyes stung as she desperately fought back childish tears. There was a loud clatter as her opponent threw his weapon to the ground and dashed over to her, scooping her up in his strong arms and carrying her into the castle. She buried her face in his chest, warm and familiar. Now she breathed deeply, trying to identify the smell; it was something she had smelt recently, not just in her memories. The answer was so tantalisingly close but she couldn't put her finger on it, nor could she get clear view of his face, but it made her feel safe and secure. She wondered if it was Luca? But she wasn't sure. Then it hit her, the smell was lavender, but where had she smelt it recently?

Her thoughts were interrupted by Brother Icka's gentle voice and his hand on her shoulder, "Your Majesty?"

"Sorry, the memories keep coming, some are so vivid it's like I'm there experiencing it all over again," she said, turning to face the monk, her sword still clutched tight in her hand.

"What did you see?" he asked curiously,

"A boy, almost a man, we were sword fighting and I got hurt," she raised one hand to her face without thinking, "and he looked after with me with such affection, I felt so safe. I couldn't see his face but it must have been my brother for him to care for me in such a way."

Her voice trailed off as Brother Icka watched her with unwavering eyes. Even as she said it Emelda began to doubt it had been her brother. She could only see the fire in Luca now and he had never had time for her; he would never have taught her to fight. No, now she was

113

sure the boy in her memory was not Luca, he was always too busy playing King, cold and unapproachable. He thought himself better than her and despised her for taking up the King's time. She recalled watching him spout judgement on a man caught stealing as he pushed his father for a harsher punishment, then openly disagreeing with the King's decision in front of the court. Her father had lost his temper and sent Luca away, Luca's face twisting into a bitter grimace full of malice and hate as he stormed out. No, the boy that had carried her close to his chest held none of that anger and hate, at least not at that time.

"If it wasn't Luca..." she muttered.

She looked at Brother Icka, who was in turn watching her intently. There was a slight smile on his lips enhanced by the wrinkles around his and mouth, and his grey eyes sparkled, but when she said nothing more he looked away sadly and reached for the crown.

"Please, Your Majesty, do me the honour of trying it on," he said, holding the little gold crown out to her, returning to his normal cheerful demeanour.

Emelda smiled and placed the sword back on the stone plinth, then she took the crown from his outstretched hand and carefully placed it on her head. Brother Icka stepped towards her and adjusted it slightly on her head before stepping back once more and taking a long look at her.

"How do I look?" she asked.

"Like your mother, like a Queen of St. Dores, you are utterly breath-taking," he grinned at her and bowed his head to her before reaching up and cupping her face in his hands, "we have waited many years for your return, sweet child, like all good things you were worth the wait. The people will follow you, have no fear, they will come like a moth to a flame."

His reassuring words filled her with strength and hope. She had wondered how the people would feel

114

about a Queen so out of touch with their world, their trials and tribulations but now she realised it didn't matter, for them she was the light in the darkness. A change was coming - she could feel it and she was the catalyst. Her hand automatically went to the little vial that should have been around her neck that contained the piece of the Great Willow. Brother Icka saw the panic in her eyes and reached inside his robes.

"Here, I told you I had kept it safe," he smiled, holding the vial out to her.

She grabbed it hastily, fastening it back around her neck where it belonged.

"Yes, thank you."

"I took the liberty of retrieving it from you when you first arrived; I couldn't take any chances that it might fall into the wrong hands."

"You don't trust your own monks?" asked Emelda, surprised.

"It's not them I am worried about."

Emelda looked confused, "Who, then?"

"My child, your fever was no accident. There was poison in your stomach, slow-acting so that your death would have looked like a fever caused by an infection from the bite on your ankle," revealed Icka.

"No, I don't believe you," she said, shaking her head vehemently.

He clasped her hands in his and looked into her eyes pleadingly, "Why would I lie?"

"Who are you worried about, then?"

"That I cannot tell you my Princess, but be on your guard. Trust no one, even those closest to you," warned Brother Icka, his face becoming serious. He pressed his lips to her hands then turned away. He took hold of her sword, placed it in its sheath on a decorated leather belt and tied it around her waist. The weight of it at her side felt comforting and familiar. Reaching up she removed her crown and looked at it, turning it over in her hands, the emeralds and diamonds gleaming in the lamplight.

"I'm not worthy of this yet," she said handing it back to Brother Icka, "please bring it to me when I am rightfully Queen, when I have honoured my father and mother and brought peace to my people. Only then can I wear it and be entitled to the respect it warrants."

Her voice rang out, echoing off the stone walls. She was filled with a new confidence; she could remember the feeling of determination and purpose that she had gone into the other world with, the love of her kingdom and her mother, father and brother and her hatred of all things dark. She remembered being taught to handle a blade, to be quick on her feet, to fire a bow and arrow, even to engage in hand to hand combat. Though she didn't remember her instructor she remembered his hard lessons and strict attitude, as well as her deep respect for him. She felt ready for anything.

"Brother Icka, thank you for everything, but now I really must rest before we go," she said, bowing.

"May I walk you to your room?" he asked.

"Thank you, but there is no need, Brother."

She bowed gracefully and he said nothing but bowed in return and gestured towards the steps. Emelda climbed the stairs renewed, she felt more like her old self now than she had only an hour before, as if there was a fire burning in her, driving her forward for the people of St. Dores, her people. This was who she was born to be - the thought of being Queen no longer filled her with dread, the true Princess Emelda had finally become the phoenix rising out of the ashes of her memories.

Leaving Brother Icka she strode confidently through the dimly lit stone passages, one hand on the hilt of her sword. Eventually she emerged from the half-light into the last rays of the setting sun. The light felt new and alive on her pale skin and she lifted her face to catch the last few rays of the sun. Arms spread wide she soaked up the warmth and light: she was the sun and lion, the light and the fury.

As she stood in the sun she felt someone watching. She gazed around at the empty courtyard, her eyes struggling a little in the half light. There was a movement to her right and she called out.

"Indira!"

Indira jumped down from the narrow ledge she was sitting on and came across the courtyard to face Emelda. She stood in front of the Princess, a mocking look on her face, not trying to hide her dislike.

"Are you feeling well now, Princess?" she said, sounding exasperated.

Emelda stared at her, her piercing green eyes boring into Indira with all her fury. She had no reason to hate her. Indira had done nothing to offend her that she knew of, but her unjustified hate and disrespect angered Emelda and her new-found confidence was not going to let it go. She stood up tall before laughing in her face.

"What's funny, Your Majesty?" Indira asked, looking confused.

"I pity you, Indira, the fact that you have to belittle me to boost your own self-esteem; your hate for me consumes you and what good does it do you? I have no idea why you are angry, or what I could have possibly done to you in the three short days I have known you but don't ever talk down to me again," replied Emelda, then she brought her face close to Indira's, "Don't forget who I am, I haven't."

She left Indira speechless and fuming, her face contorted with rage as her lips curled around the bitter words, "Trust me, I won't."

Kasper sat hidden in the shadows watching; a grin spread across his handsome face making it come alive again. He thought about leaving after Emelda did but something held him back and he waited to see what

Indira would do. She stood motionless for a while as the night drew in around her, before pulling herself together and using her skills to disappear into the night. Kasper knew what to look for when she became invisible, the glint of a belt, the flash of teeth, the moonlight reflecting in her eyes. With trained eyes, he followed her movements until she had jumped and climbed her way onto the top of the monastery and stood silently in the deepening night. He watched her put something to her lips, then look around impatiently. After a moment, a large black raven swooped down and landed on the arm she held out for it. She placed a small roll of paper into a container attached to its leg and then launched it into the air. She watched it go, then spun on the spot, her eyes searching the darkness for the spot where Kasper was hiding. Taking out a small blade she crept silently towards him. Kasper held his breath. She thrust the knife into the darkness and growled in annoyance, piercing nothing but the night. She listened to the sound of footsteps disappearing below her, the person's identity hidden by the darkness.

Emelda lay on her bed, her eyes tightly shut, trying to make herself go to sleep, but she couldn't get Brother Icka's words out of her head. 'Trust no one', 'no accident' - who was trying to kill her? She couldn't get the anger in Indira's face out of her head either. If anyone wanted to kill her she was sure she had seen enough hate in her eyes for her to be a contender, if not the only one. Women over time had done far worse for love. She could hear movement outside her door; maybe it was the person who wanted her dead? Slowly she opened her eyes and was overwhelmed by the thickness of the darkness. She waited a moment for her night vision to kick in before getting up, her knife in her hand, and walked over to the door. Hand on the door knob and heart in her mouth she swung it open, crying out, hoping to take her attacker by surprise.

In the dim light of the soft lamps she saw Christian jump in alarm, dodging her wild knife thrusts and pushing himself against the opposite wall so he was out of arm's length. He raised both hands in surrender.

"Easy, Princess, it's just me," he said.

Emelda felt the breath whoosh out of her lungs as she exhaled in relief.

"What are you doing outside my door? Shouldn't you be asleep?" she asked him.

"Kasper asked me to stand guard, that is my job after all. Neither of us wants anything untoward to happen to you," he smiled at her.

"Why, what might happen? What aren't you telling me, Christian?", suspicion creeping into her voice, Icka's words echoing in her head.

"Nothing, I'm just here to make sure it stays that way, your Majesty, now please go back to bed," he gently pushed the door open a little wider for her to turn around.

"No joke, no risqué comment?"

"Not tonight, Princess," he smiled at her, but she could tell he was worried.

"When will you sleep?"

"Kasper will take over soon, don't worry, one of us will be here to watch over you all night."

"And Indira?"

Christian hesitated, "She is organising the route down with the monks and making preparations. She is busy."

Emelda felt relieved, "Good night, Christian."

"Good night, Princess."

She went back into the room and closed the door behind her before slumping down on the bed. She hadn't bothered to get fully undressed and now her trousers were uncomfortable, so she quickly removed them and her bodice and climbed under the thick scratchy blankets, placing her knife under her pillow just in case.

119

Eyes shut tight she tried to remember the face of the boy in her dreams, hoping that sleep would bring him to her with clarity this time. Emelda woke once when Kasper came to relieve Christian. She heard Christian's footsteps leaving and after a moment the door to her room creaked open. She felt under her pillow for her knife in the darkness, her fingers quickly finding the cold of the blade and the wood of the handle. She held her breath, waiting for him, but he never came into the room; instead he stood in the doorway for a moment or two before shutting the door quietly again and taking up his post.

Chapter 10

When Kasper entered her room with the first wisps of morning light she was already up and dressed. She stood in the middle of the room adjusting her belt and sword.

"Morning, your Majesty," he said in his usual cold tone, "ready?"

"Indeed," she said striding towards him and out of the door, "let's waste no time."

Christian and Indira were waiting for them in the main courtyard, the few items they needed gathered at their feet. They were travelling light, carrying mainly water, some food and weapons. Christian asked if she had slept well and gave her a bag to carry; he chatted away in the way he always did. Emelda's eyes met Indira's who quickly looked away, keeping her distance and speaking only to Kasper in low whispers, which he indulged. She gave Christian the odd one-word answer, saving her silence only for Emelda.

It wasn't long before they were ready to go and Emelda looked around. Taking in the amazing building one last time, she thought to herself that she would return one day to really appreciate the beauty of the monastery. Brother Icka had come to see them off and it looked as if the entire population of the monastery had come with him. Emelda bent her head to receive Brother Icka's blessing, focusing on the soft words of his prayers and letting them wash over her and encourage her. He gently kissed her on the forehead, lifting her chin with his old hands.

"My Queen," he whispered so only she could hear, she clasped his hands in return and kissed them before saying her goodbyes.

One of the monks had volunteered to take them through the mountain passage and down the other side before the sun was too high in the sky. He alone carried a small lamp and a length of rope over his shoulder, striding ahead of them into the dark passage. They had decided to keep the party small so as not to draw any unwanted attention, having already been attacked twice. It was as if evil was following them, lurking in the shadows behind them, waiting for an opportunity to strike. The idea that someone was out to kill her made Emelda feel nervous and she felt she needed to be looking over her shoulder constantly.

The passage to the other side of the mountain was relatively direct, but as they emerged Emelda was filled with dread at the sight that stood before her. The other side of the mountain was steep and narrow; cautiously Emelda stepped towards the edge and peered over. Her stomach lurched, her throat caught and she took a deep breath, backing quickly away. She had never liked heights, but now was not the time to give way to irrational phobias. The monk turned to face them and removed the rope from his shoulder. He tied it tightly to his belt then passed it back to Emelda who did the same. Kasper followed her, then Indira and lastly Christian. Steadily they made their way down the path which twisted and turned as it snaked its way down the mountain. Loose rocks shifted underfoot making the journey painfully slow. After her experience on the Grey Man she held onto the rope with both hands, making sure she focused on where the monk ahead of her placed his feet and copying him.

They were halfway down before there was a sharp tug on the rope that jarred Emelda, making her stumble. She grabbed onto a thin shrub that was clinging to the side of the mountain and peered over her shoulder. The monk in front of her stopped as well, his voice low and worried in the early morning light.

"Your friend!"

Emelda could hear Christian's voice calling out for help, fear and desperation evident in his voice. Kasper was already heading back, pulling Emelda and the monk with him - they had no choice but to follow him.

"Christian, hold on!" he shouted, throwing himself onto the rocky ground.

In the light of the lamp Emelda could see Christian clinging to the edge of the sheer mountain path. There was fear in his eyes and he tried desperately to get a foothold, but the rock beneath his feet kept crumbling away and he couldn't find another handhold, his right hand dangling free. Emelda could see the end of his rope swinging beneath him and to her the ends looked frayed. Kasper lay on his stomach hanging over the edge and reached down, stretching as far as he could; his fingertips brushed Christian's, tantalizingly close. Panic gripped Emelda as she gazed down at him

"I can't hold on," cried Christian.

"No!" yelled Emelda, coming to her senses, and pulling her dagger from her thigh she sliced through the rope that attached her to the monk and flung herself to the ground next to Kasper, throwing the rope over the edge.

"Grab hold," she called out to Christian.

"I'll pull you over, Princess," he said, "I can't risk that."

"Maybe me but not all of us, come on!"

As she called out the small ledge Christian was holding started giving way, the rock breaking up beneath his fingers. She cried out to him as she watched him slip away.

"No!"

Then she felt the rope go taut, almost pulling her off the edge of the path. She braced herself, gripping the rope so hard her knuckles began to turn white. The coarse rope cut into her hands, but just as she felt it begin to slip, strong hands reached out and grabbed hold of the rope just in front of her hands, and another set of hands wrapped around her waist, anchoring her to the ground. She looked up and saw Kasper leaning over her, pulling hard and on her other side she saw the monk holding her steady. Between them they slowly managed to pull Christian up until Kasper could reach under his arms and lift him to safety. Once on firm ground Christian lay motionless, breathing heavily, eyes closed, his hand resting on his chest. In the lamplight Emelda watched his chest rise and fall steadily; she was overwhelmed with relief and she knelt at his side scooping up his hand in hers.

He opened his eyes and turned his head to look at her, "You shouldn't have risked your life for me, Princess."

"I didn't, I risked Kasper's," she laughed.

"But you cut your own rope," he insisted.

"I was still tied to Kasper," replied Emelda, "you would have taken both of us and that would have been the end of that."

"Hang on," interrupted Kasper, reaching for the rope that was still attached to Christian.

He lifted it up and in the morning light he examined the end. Tell-tale cut marks ran across the end of the rope, the ends fraying and broken.

"Where's...?" Kasper began but was interrupted by the sound of laboured footsteps approaching. Kasper stood up, throwing down the rope and drawing both katana swords from his back, he held the blades out in front of himself ready.

"Show yourself," he called out.

With slow, exaggerated steps Indira came into view, clutching her head and groaning. When she looked up and saw Christian lying on the ground a look of annoyance crossed her face, just a flicker that Kasper thought only he saw, before her expression changed to one of worry. She turned her gaze anxiously towards Kasper and hurried forward, the pain in her head seemingly forgotten.

"What happened?" she asked.

"Where were you?" he responded calmly, but he did not lower his weapon, his eyes fixed on Indira.

"I lost my footing, fell and bashed my head. I blacked out and when I woke up you were all gone. Christian, are you ok?" she seemed genuinely concerned.

Emelda wondered how much bile Indira had had to swallow to plaster that false concern over her face - if she was lying she was good. It made Emelda's blood boil that no one else seemed to see what a viper she was, what a traitor. Indira glanced over at her then stepped towards Kasper and after a moment of hesitation he replaced his katana and she drew herself into him. He recoiled a little, almost unconsciously, before pushing her back and raising a hand to her head to examine her. There was a small cut on her forehead and a dribble of blood oozed down her temple but it was insignificant, Kasper had had worse papercuts. Forcing himself to be pleasant to her he brushed the hair from her face and spoke softly to her.

"It will heal in due course," he said.

Indira caught Kasper's hand as he tried to withdraw, pressing it to her cheek. Her eyes met Emelda's over his shoulder, an unnerving glint in them and a cruel smile on her face. Kasper hurriedly removed his hand from her face and turned to help Christian to his feet, but Emelda and the monk were already assisting him. Christian caught Kasper's eye and he knew what he was trying to tell him without saying a thing. It was her, Indira.

Christian turned to Emelda and held her hands in his, a determined look on his normally carefree face.

"I owe you my life, Your Majesty," he said, looking into her eyes.

"Then it's a good thing that I have you to protect me, isn't it," she said with a gentle smile.

Kasper's chest tightened.

"And I shall protect your life with my very own; my life is yours even more so than it was before," Christian dropped to his knees and pressed his lips to her hands.

"Get up," Kasper muttered, "respect and honour doesn't suit you."

Christian got to his feet and drew close to Kasper, pulling him in close by his clothes so that his mouth was next to his ear.

"Get rid of her before it's too late," he whispered angrily.

Christian let go of Kasper roughly and walked away, a fierce look on his face, leaving Kasper standing alone with Indira.

"Let's get off this wretched mountain," Christian called out to the monk, putting himself between Kasper and Emelda.

As the morning sun filled the sky, melting away the early morning chill, they finally reached the bottom of the mountain. Here the monk prayed for Emelda before heading back up the mountain, his lamp swinging at his side. The sun was warm and uplifting but no one seemed happy. None of them spoke to each other, instead they began walking at a steady pace led by Kasper and Indira, Christian refusing to leave the Princess's side. On the horizon Emelda could see a vast vale of fog that refused to clear even when the sun reached its highest point in the sky. It was thick and deep and seemed to go on as far as the eye could see. Much to her dismay they seemed to be heading towards the impenetrable blanket of fog that rested on the horizon and beyond.

"What is it?" she asked Christian.

"Ah yes, the Marshes, not my favourite place I must admit, Princess," he replied, making her spirits sink a little more.

"We are going through it, then?" asked Emelda uneasily.

"Unfortunately, yes, to go around would cost us time we don't have."

"I see," she automatically put her hand to her sword.

"That is a beautiful blade," smiled Christian trying to lighten the mood a little.

Emelda looked down at her hand on the hilt, reassuring and firm at her side, "It was a gift from my father."

"He was a wise man - he would have chosen well, it will flow from you like an extension of your body. Do you know how to fight?"

"I believe I do," her thoughts went briefly to the boy, "but I may need a little refresher. It's been a long time since I sparred with anyone, but I know someone taught me once."

Kasper who was a little way in front of them clenched his hands into fists and quickened his pace, his eyes fixed on the mist that loomed ahead of them.

"I will spar with you, Your Majesty, it would be an honour," Christian said enthusiastically.

"But you mustn't hold back, I need to get back up to speed, I can't be a burden to anyone anymore," she grinned at him, "I can take it."

A mischievous look crossed Christian's face and he reached for her hand on the hilt of the sword, their fingers brushed momentarily and he laughed; Emelda's heart fluttered a little at the sound.

"I'm sure you can take it but I could never hurt someone so beautiful," his eyes were full of innuendo.

Emelda allowed herself a smile as she looked up into his blue eyes and charming face. At the same time Kasper glanced over his shoulder. He swallowed hard at seeing the look of affection on Emelda's face and her closeness to Christian as they walked. Neither noticed Kasper's eyes on them.

"Ah, Christian, you are so sweet and kind to me and for that I adore you. You are the one thing in this place that seems familiar to me, that reminds me of the world I left and my dear brother Nicholas. I never want to forget him even though I know I will. At least I can take comfort in the fact that if you are with me then so is he," said Emelda affectionately.

She felt her eyes go glassy but no tears fell, instead she took his hand in hers as they walked and whispered to him, "Thank you."

"Anything for you, Your Majesty," murmured Christian, his voice deep and serious.

Emelda gazed into his eyes and knew that he meant it; there was no frivolity, no sexual innuendo, all the childishness was gone from his face. This was the man he truly was when it mattered and she trusted him deeply despite the short time they had known each other.

She let go of his hand gently and they continued to walk in comfortable silence, trying to shake the overwhelming presence of the encroaching fog. It was bleak and grey like the countryside around them, void of life and unnaturally still. It worried Emelda that they had seen no one, that there were no dwellings, no signs of civilisation at all. It was like the earth before God had shaped it and brought all life into existence.

They felt the air temperature drop and the ground beneath their feet began to feel spongey, then fog seemed to engulf them. Kasper stopped just ahead of them and signalled for them to stop.

"We should rest before we go any deeper into the Marshes. None of us have eaten properly or rested since this morning, and Princess, you have only just recovered your strength," said Kasper.

"I am fine," replied Emelda, "don't stop on my account."

"Well, you may be fine but I am hungry, so sit down," ordered Kasper bluntly.

Glaring at him, Emelda went to sit with Christian who had perched himself on an old tree stump. He shifted to make room for her and opened his bag. The monks had kindly packed each of them a bag of food and water and both Christian and Kasper had offered to carry Emelda's, but she had politely refused. She could carry her own; she refused to be anybody's burden again. Being only a few years younger than Kasper and of a similar age to Christian she was their equal, if not their superior.

Christian shared out the bread and cured meat from his bag before taking some for himself and tucking in. After a few moments Emelda ventured the question she had been toying with for some time.

"What is so dangerous about the Marshes? I have a sickening feeling in the pit of my stomach; I am sure we scouted around it when the King sent me to the Grey Man to be hidden in the other world," she said.

Indira rolled her eyes at Kasper, and thinking Emelda hadn't seen she quickly pushed a look of indifference onto her face.

"There is a legend about the spirits of the Marsh, the souls of those sacrificed to the gods of old, luring weary travellers into the fog and drowning them. But of course there are no spirits here, just a rather foul band of thieves and criminals that have taken up residence since the legend began. They murder travellers and attack carriages that stray too close. It's a good hiding place and they are impossible to track unless you know the marshes well. You have as much chance of losing you way and drowning in the marsh as you do of being killed by the men and women in there," explained Indira.

"I'm sure I should have known that," said Emelda with anguish.

"It's ok, these things will come back to you, you will remember in time, as long as your core memories have returned the others are trifling," said Christian, kindly placing a hand on Emelda's shoulder.

"Stop touching the Princess!" shouted Kasper, unable to control himself any longer, "you forget yourself time and time again."

Christian stood up and Kasper rose to meet him, anger in his eyes.

"It is not I who has forgotten my place - you need to deal with the real issue here before it destroys us all," snarled Christian, his eye darting over Kasper's shoulder to where Indira sat. She now got up and pushed Kasper aside, fury burning in her golden eyes. Her hair swung behind her like a braided whip as she trembled with anger.

"How dare you speak to me like that, you foolish little boy," she cried, inches from his face.

"Enough!" shouted Emelda, her voice echoing and authoritative.

Breathing heavily neither Indira or Christian moved, anger bristling inside each of them. Kasper pulled Indira back and murmured something quietly to her, at which she nodded and Emelda gingerly pulled at Christian's arm until he too turned to face her, an uncharacteristically serious look on his fair face.

"If it wasn't for you, Princess," he murmured.

"Let's move on," said Kasper seriously, "Indira, we need you now more than ever."

His eyes met with Christian's and something passed between them, unspoken but understood.

"Very well," Indira said, spitting on the ground where Christian had been standing, "but if he gets lost in there I am not going back for him."

She picked up her bag and the others followed suit, Kasper grabbing Christian's arm and whispering angrily to him as he tried to go past. Emelda didn't hear what was said but Christian shrugged him off and Kasper walked away. Emelda held back a little with Christian before whispering to him.

"Why are we following her?"

"She knows the way," he replied.

"How?"

"She claims she escaped from here many years ago, but I am sure she was one of them," he grumbled, "just prepare yourself for something untoward to happen."

"Them?"

"Just stay close, do not leave my side or go near her," he instructed her.

His words worried her, there was something going on here and no one would tell her what, first Brother Icka, then Christian. She knew it had something to do with Indira - why did she seem to hate her so much? Whatever was happening between Indira and Kasper was nothing to do with her. Love made you do crazy things, even so, she wasn't sure that was all it was.

The heavy fog quickly wrapped itself around them, swallowing them whole. Indira had assured them, albeit via Kasper, that if they made good time they would be out the other side by nightfall and Emelda prayed earnestly that it would be so. She also pressed on them the need to be as silent as possible, blaming Christian for potentially giving them away already with his little outburst. The fog was suffocating and demoralizing and the smell of stagnant water and damp earth filled the cold air, adding to the depressing atmosphere. The fear of attack made them all, except Indira, anxious. The idea that there could be people less than two metres away and they had no way to tell except to listen made Emelda worry. Her reactions weren't as quick as the others, she would fall prey to a surprise attack easily. To make matters worse she had to concentrate hard on the ground underfoot which was water- logged and hard going, while Indira up ahead seemed to move nimbly between the pools of deep dark water. Following her shadowy form, they managed to keep their feet on dry land. It wasn't long before Emelda found herself getting tired, despite all her bold words to Kasper earlier, although she was following Indira's every step carefully not to land herself in a watery grave.

Indira stopped suddenly, raising her hand in a signal for everyone else to stop as well, and drew her weapon. The others drew theirs too and waited tentatively. Emelda held her sword, reassuringly heavy, and prepared to fight. Christian's words echoed in her head; this was the something untoward, the darkness that seemed to follow them like a shadow, relentlessly hounding them. Emelda thought she heard movement to her right, then again to her left. Quickly Kasper and Christian surrounded her, creating a shield with their bodies. Indira, however, kept her distance, her bow drawn, the taut string creaking in her hands.

Indira turned on the spot and shot an arrow into the fog. This was followed by a thud and a groan and the body of a woman came into view cutting a path through the fog, her hands clutching Indira's arrow which protruded from her chest. The men drew a little closer to her as silence fell again. All Emelda could hear was the slightly elevated breathing of her protectors and her heart that pounded so loudly in her ears she was sure that the men and women waiting in the fog for her could hear it, a clear signal.

There was a noise to her right and she felt Kasper shift a little in front her, her breath moving the hairs on the back on his head he was so close, then the silence was shattered by the cry of attack and out of the fog came a wave of men and women waving their weapons wildly. The onslaught was hard and vicious, coming from all sides and unrelenting, the attackers disappearing in and out of the fog skilfully using it as cover. Christian and Kasper stood firm, not letting a single blade stroke come close, yet as hard as they tried to stay close to the Princess, there was a gap emerging between the three of them. Emelda turned her sword over in her hands, they were so sweaty she wondered if the blade would slide out of them if she tried to swing it. From somewhere deep in the fog she could hear the twang of Indira's arrows, but she couldn't see her.

Without warning Indira appeared out of the fog, grabbed Emelda by the arm and pulled her into the fog after her. She felt Kasper's fingers brush hers as she was quickly engulfed, and barely managed to call out before she could no longer see Kasper or Christian. She heard the men cry out to her but very quickly they were consumed by the fog, their voices drowned out by the clash of metal on metal. Gripping her sword tightly she called out to Indira.

"Get off me!" she shouted angrily, but Indira didn't answer, instead she held on harder, grinning over her shoulder at Emelda.

The look on her face filled Emelda with dread and terror; it sent a chill down her spine and she felt her skin prickle all over. Digging her heels in she pulled Indira to a stop. Indira looked surprised by Emelda's unusual strength. She tried to twist her arm free, but Indira dug her nails in, tearing through her clothes and breaking the skin on her forearm. She winced in pain as Indira twisted her wrist, invoking her old injury.

"Let me go!" cried Emelda, lifting her sword with her other hand and bringing the hilt down as hard as she could onto Indira's wrist.

Indira screamed as Emelda felt her sword shatter bone. Indira immediately let go of Emelda's wrist, her eyes full of pain and hatred.

"All yours!" she shouted seemingly to empty space, before glaring at Emelda and disappearing into fog clutching her broken wrist.

Emelda was left alone, clasping her sword desperately with both hands, the damp fog pressing in on her with its cold, clammy hands. She heard the call of a raven and the beating of its wings. She peered into the fog, trying to see if anyone was there, but no one came, even the sound of fighting was barely audible in the still air, all she could hear was her own ragged breath. As she stood waiting for death or rescue, unsure which would find her first, she tried to remember everything she had been taught about sword fighting. She had never been in a real fight. She had never killed a man. She didn't want to start now but she knew she would have to. The feeling of Indira's bones through her sword was the closest she had got to harming anyone. She imaged cutting through bones, puncturing organs, a sea of warm blood trickling down her sword. Fear of the unknown made her chest tight and she twitched at every noise.

The waiting was intolerable, worse than any fate that might await her. Movement behind her startled her into action and she spun round to face it. A dark figure loomed out of the shadows and she braced herself, heart racing, mind spinning. She saw a flash of steel and her body moved before she had time to think about reacting. She felt her blade hit something hard, as steel met steel.

It sent shock waves down her arm but she managed to stay on her feet and parry another attack. A man came into view, a nasty grin on his blood-thirsty face. Seeing Emelda was on the back foot he quickly came at her again, raising his sword and bringing it down towards her. Instinctively she caught the blade against her sword and shoved him back. Surprised at her strength he stumbled back and Emelda took the advantage, leaping towards him and swinging her sword hard at his chest. A line of deep crimson blossomed from his torso and he dropped his sword to clutch at it, but Emelda wasn't finished. Pressing forwards, she plunged her sword into his neck. He dropped to his knees, blood gurgling up out of his mouth and spilling from his wounds. Emelda breathed, heavily unable to take her eyes off his lifeless form.

It was only a moment before another shadow approached through the fog, then another and another until she was surrounded. Taking a deep breath Emelda forced the panic back down into her stomach and readied herself - at least she would die fighting. But instead of attacking, the man in front of her dropped to the ground, blood dribbling from the corner of his mouth.

"What...?" murmured Emelda, still holding her ground.

Then silently the second and third man too fell to the ground dead, her silent saviour still concealed in the fog. Emelda gripped her sword a little tighter as a cloaked figure came into view. Though she couldn't see his face, he filled her with terror and she began to step away as he approached. From beneath his hood she could make out a twisted smile surrounded by scarred, angry skin.

"Princess," he whispered.

Lifting his sword above his head he came at her. Her reactions were just about quick enough to get her sword in front of her face, but he was so strong and his blade so heavy that her arms almost buckled under the weight, the two blades almost brushing her nose. She stepped back trying to get out from under his blade, but he just pushed harder, forcing her to the ground. He swung at her again and this time she managed to roll out of the way, dropping her sword in the process. With a malicious grin, he raised his sword one last time, preparing to make his death blow. Emelda could do nothing but stare up into his crimson eyes waiting for death to come. Her hand went to her neck and she pulled out the little vial; she wished she had managed to get the willow to the encampment. A tear ran down her face at her own failure.

"Sorry," she murmured.

Time seemed to slow down as she watched the sword coming down toward her. At the last moment she raised her hand, holding the willow as if it would protect her. From nowhere a blinding blue light surrounded her throwing the man back, his sword flying out of his hands and landing somewhere out of sight. Emelda stumbled to her feet in shock; the man was lying some distance away clutching his head. She looked from the vial to the man then back again. Thrusting it back into her shirt she quickly located her sword and began to run, not caring where it took her as long as it was away from him.

She ran and ran until she could see figures in the fog ahead of her, weapons ready and making their way slowly in her direction. She stopped and squinted in their direction, trying to make them out but the fog, thick and heavy, obscured every detail. Emelda swallowed hard, pushing her hair wet with sweat from her face, torn between turning and running back into the enveloping fog or waiting, hoping it was Kasper and Christian. She readied her sword and stood her ground, heart in her mouth, she prayed it was not Indira or her attacker. As she lifted her sword ready to take the offensive the anxious faces of Kasper and Christian emerged out of the fog. They were blood-spattered and weary but as they caught sight of her the relief in their eyes was all too clear. Kasper's face, however, almost instantly turned from relief to anger.

"What happened?" he asked in a low voice.

"Indira," Emelda managed to reply, "and there was a man."

It was clear that Kasper's anger was not directed at her but it still scared her.

"A man?" he asked.

"There were others at first, but then one man, he killed all the others, then he attacked me. Tall, cloaked, his face looked scarred," she told him, "and his eyes, like fire."

"It can't be," murmured Kasper, looking out into the fog.

"Are you ok?" asked Christian kindly.

Emelda nodded, despite being so close to death just moments ago, "The light stopped him."

"I did wonder what that was," replied Christian.

"The willow, somehow..." wondered Emelda.

There was movement behind them and Kasper grabbed Emelda by the hand, "Don't leave my side. Let's go."

"What about Indira? We don't know the way," said Emelda.

"Forget her," Kasper retorted.

Emelda wanted to question him further but he was already ploughing into the fog, with Christian giving her a weary look and following close behind. They walked as fast as they could, still trying to avoid the inky pools of water that covered the marsh, Kasper keeping a tight hold on Emelda's hand with one hand and one of his katana in the other. Barely able to keep up with Kasper's pace, her feet slipped on the wet ground and she struggled to catch her breath, but they dared not stop. The threat of more attackers was constantly at the back of their minds and any noise made Emelda twitch nervously, craning around to see where it was coming from.

Pushing on through the endless fog Emelda felt her legs turn to lead and her ankle began to ache; her spirits took a dip as she hung off Kasper's hand, unsure of where they were going. She was sure she would never see the sun again, for all she knew they were going around in circles. She had no idea how Kasper knew where he was going but he seemed confident about the direction they were headed. The fog was so thick and oppressive it seemed to suck all the light out of the air, the afternoon sun barely more than a dim glow in the grey sky. Emelda felt tired and depressed - she tugged at Kasper's hand, trying to slow him down.

"I can't go on, I don't want to go on," she moaned giving in to the sinking feeling in her stomach, "we are lost."

"Keep your voice down," growled Kasper, hauling her along behind him.

Christian took hold of her other hand.

"Come on, Princess," he encouraged her.

"I'm so tired," she murmured.

She was barely able to keep her eyes open, everything grew fuzzy and her feet started to stumble over the soft ground. She half walked and was half dragged through the last of the marshland, the fog slowly withdrawing its thin, cold fingers as the murky shapes of trees and bushes started to emerge out of the gloom.

She could hear the voices of Kasper and Christian either side of her encouraging her to keep going and somehow she forced her feet to move, despite her body crying out at her to stop. As the fog dispersed she took a deep breath of clean, fresh air and felt relief sweeping over her. Dropping to her knees, unable to go on she felt Kasper and Christian haul to her feet and virtually carry her further out of the fog. They carried her for at least half an hour before they let her rest, lying her carefully on the ground. Kasper took a bottle from his medicine bag and carefully poured a little of its contents into her parted lips. The bitter taste revived her; she coughed and spluttered as it burnt its way down her throat, heaving as it hit her stomach.

She sat herself up, eyes wide open, "What was that?"

"A restorative liquid, bitter but effective," answered Kasper, "it should sustain you for a while. Using the willow took up all your strength."

Christian pulled out his water bottle and offered it to her. She took it a long gulp, gratefully savouring the cool and thirst-quenching relief to her parched throat.

"Thank you," she said looking from one to the other, "thank you."

"Let's put some more distance between us and the marsh," said Kasper, helping her to her feet but still not letting go of her hand. She tried to shake it free, feeling a little uncomfortable at his proximity, but he only held it tighter.

"I told you not to leave my side, didn't I? Nothing has changed - we are not out of danger yet," he said bluntly.

Despite his protectiveness, Emelda found herself scowling at him.

"I like it about as much as you," he complained.

Lacking the energy to argue with him, Emelda gave in and remained silent. The mild afternoon sun was warm and comforting like a long-lost friend and Emelda lifted her face up to feel the rays on her skin. The day's journey through the marsh and the power of the willow had sapped her of her energy and by the time the sun was beginning to drop down to meet the horizon she was struggling to put one foot in front of the other again. Kasper felt her slow down, her grip on his hand loosening a little. At that moment he realised how tightly he had been holding her hand, his need to have her near and safe subconsciously conveyed by that one simple, instinctive action. He glanced at her over his shoulder as she trailed along like a child, her head down staring at her feet, and he was instantly transported back to his youth. He felt her soft hand in his, his other covering her sparkling green eyes as he led her into her room on her birthday. He recalled the glorious smile on her face as he revealed his gift to her, a room filled with her favourite flowers.

It was a memory he had almost forgotten and for a moment it stopped him in his tracks; he felt a sharp stab of emotion in his chest and took a deep breath. That was the moment when he had realised just what he was feeling, when he had gone out of his way to give another person joy and happiness with nothing but her smile as his reward. It had been all for her. Yet she didn't remember him and maybe she never would. His face hardened and the emptiness that had consumed him for so long returned.

"Kasper?" said Emelda, confused by his sudden stop.

He said nothing and continued to walk, purposefully letting go of her hand. He could not allow himself to be weak, not after he had already given her up, not when they were so close to the end of their journey.

Emelda stood alone for a moment gazing down at her own outstretched hand, the warmth of Kasper's hand already fading. A mixture of emotions left her feeling alone and confused; one minute he was demanding that she be by his side, the next he was pushing her as far away as he could. She was unsure whether she wanted him or hated him, or if there was even a difference. Her legs would no longer carry her forward and her whole body ached in protest, as if all her strength had left with his touch. He had been driving her forward and now that he was gone she was left cold and abandoned. Her chest ached as she let her hand drop to her side and she forced her legs to move. Kasper was already a little way ahead, but Christian was still close behind her.

"Princess?" he asked, placing a strong warm hand on her shoulder.

She looked up him, her eyes filled with sadness but she managed a smile.

"I am so very tired, can we rest soon?" she inquired quietly.

"Of course, your Majesty," replied Christian, "But just a little further, the more distance we put between us and the marshes the better."

Emelda nodded silently and started to walk. She wasn't sure how she made her body obey her for the next hour but somehow it did and she followed Kasper with Christian at her side. The sparse grey woodland soon gave way to open fields that looked like they had once been ploughed and tended but now lay barren and abandoned. Not even the weeds dared to grow in the empty soil. Farmers' cottages and herdsmen's huts scattered the landscape, those too left to fall into ruin. It was a sad sight that met Emelda's tired eyes, the emptiness of her kingdom and the starvation of her people.

As the last rays of the sun began to fade Kasper called them to a stop outside an abandoned herdsman's hut and, sword raised, he cautiously swung open the dilapidated door. There wasn't even the flutter of wings or the scurry of tiny claws to greet them, just silence and darkness. Emelda gazed back towards the marshes, but all that could be seen now was a faint line of trees that indicated the end of the bordering woodland they had just crossed. The thought of that place and that man still made Emelda shudder and she quickly turned away again to watch Kasper enter the hut. His tall form was instantly swallowed by the darkness but a second later his strong, cold face appeared and he beckoned them in.

The hut was bare, save for a scattering of dry leaves that Kasper had hastily swept into a corner and a fire pit encircled with large stones, but it was dry for the most part and a shelter from the chilling night wind.

"I will go collect some firewood, Christian you start making camp," ordered Kasper authoritatively and left the hut.

Christian dashed after him, catching him by the arm just out of ear shot of the Princess.

"What is going on? What about Indira? I didn't want to ask in front of the Princess," frowned Christian.

"Let it go for now, please," said Kasper pulling away.

"I warned you, back at the monastery," continued Christian.

"I said let it go, we will talk later," growled Kasper walking away.

Shaking his head Christian returned to the hut and to Emelda. Once Kasper had left, Emelda crumpled to the floor, the last of her strength leaving her in a sudden rush. Shaking a little she pulled her knees to her chest and hugged them; she was so disappointed in herself, she wasn't stronger, she was once again a burden. She had felt so confident, so determined and now the wind had been knocked out of her sails and she was frightened again.

"Your Majesty," murmured Christian, kneeling at her side as he wrapped a blanket around her shoulders and placed a hand on hers.

She looked up into his boyish face and tried to smile, but it was no use, she was defeated.

"Will they ever stop coming?" she asked him, "the people that want to kill me?"

Christian stopped smiling and looked sadly at her, "Not until you stop the Rebel King once and for all, but until then we won't let anyone harm you."

"What about Indira? Is she working for him? For the Rebel King? Brother Icka told me not to trust anyone.

I'm so naïve, so foolish," she could feel tears creeping into her voice.

"Indira tricked us all, Your Majesty, please don't think like that."

"Maybe I spent too long asleep, maybe I spent too long in that place, with those people..." she trailed off, unable to remember their names or faces anymore.

"Princess ..."

"It's infuriating not being completely part of this world or the other. I don't know where to go or who to trust. I was filled with such purpose back at the monastery but now I am drained. Maybe I was wrong, maybe I can't do this."

"It will be ok. Just wait until you see how many people have gathered under your name, just wait until they see your face. That is all they need, they have been subdued long enough, your name has run through them like a river washing away their fears and filling them with confidence. Your name is power, it is sweet like honey on the lips of the oppressed. The reason that so many have come to kill you is because you are a threat to the Rebel King and he is scared; his reign is coming to an end. You and that tiny bud will be the end of him," Christian's voice was confident and steady, his words bold and uplifting.

"Thank you Christian, your confidence gives me strength."

Emelda felt a glimmer of hope; she could do this, she was born to do this. It was her destiny. She couldn't ignore the danger that her future would hold but neither could she ignore the light in Christian's eyes as he spoke of change, of the new things to come. Something still niggled at her, the boy from her dreams and her brother; she was sure they were not one and the same but she knew there was something important about both of them, yet what that was evaded her.

Just then a shadow blocked the slice of moonlight that illuminated the little hut. Christian stood, his sword drawn, but he quickly dropped his guard as the sullen face of Kasper appeared out of the night. He tossed the large bundle of firewood he had collected to the floor and began gathering up the dry leaves from the corners of the hut to make a fire. Emelda remained huddled on the floor watching Kasper as he quickly conjured the leaves into flames and placed some of the wood on top. Soon a fire roared in the middle of the hut, smoke drifting up through the small hole in the roof.

The warmth of the fire soon filled the small room, the flames casting shadows across the tired faces of the company. They ate what little they had with them, assured by Kasper that they weren't far from a small town at the edge of St. Dores. The meagre meal of dried meat, dried fruit and flat bread was like a feast to Emelda's growling stomach; she hadn't realised just how hungry she was. Yet what she longed for most was hot food to warm her to the core, followed by cakes and steaming custard. Her mouth watered at the idea of the sweet things she had enjoyed when she was last in the castle, chocolate sponges and fruit-studded buns ... she recalled sneaking into the kitchens with a young boy and stealing sweets being prepared for the evening's feasting. A gentle smile played across her face and she laughed quietly to herself, pulling her blanket closer round her shoulders - at a time like this when she stood on the brink of her destiny all she could think of was cake. Neither of the men seemed to notice her stifled laugh as she gazed around the room, each face was lost in its own thoughts. Christian was sharpening his blade and Kasper was sitting, gazing out of the doorway.

Her belly full and suddenly overcome with tiredness again, Emelda excused herself quietly and shuffled into a space a little way from the fire. She removed her cloak and bundled it up to make a pillow and then wrapped the blanket tightly around herself. Despite the hardness of the floor she found sleep soon washed over her, a sweet relief from the reality of the world, a dark oblivion. The others soon followed suit, Kasper volunteering to take first watch. After being attacked so frequently over the past few days they were on highest alert; they had also decided on a cover story for when they reached the town. Emelda would wear her headscarf all the time they were in public and they would say they were soldiers headed for the castle if anyone asked. Emelda knew she didn't really fit that description; she was more like a victor's prize or a spoil of war but not a soldier.

As the deepest part of the night fell black and cold, Emelda stirred a little - in her dreams she heard the creak of a door. A moment later she was awake and Kasper was gone. Knowing that if she woke Christian he would stop her, she snuck out of the open door, trying desperately not to make a sound. She slipped out into the night and stopped, waiting for her eyes to adjust to the darkness, then she strained desperately, looking for Kasper. He was nowhere to be seen in front of the hut so she skirted around to the back and began to walk into the inkiness, the cold night air capturing her breath in faint clouds. She glanced over her shoulder at the hut, small and hunched in the dark landscape; a thin trail of smoke from the fire wafted out of the roof and she wondered why she had left its side. She turned back around and walked a little further, away from the hut. As she climbed over a large grassy mound she spotted a figure in the darkness, a woman with golden hair. She ducked behind the mound, pressing her body flat against it as she peered over the top.

Indira stood in the darkness gazing into the sky, apparently waiting. It was then that Emelda saw another figure approaching her silently from behind.

"Kasper," she gasped, the monk's warning running through her mind. Surely he was not a traitor, he could not betray her, not now.

There was a thud and the raven that Indira had been using to send a message back to the Rebel King fell out of the sky; it twitched for a moment before falling still. She tried to turn around, a grin on her face - he was here, the one she had been waiting for, but she wasn't fast enough. Her good arm was already pinned to her back and the sharp point of a blade was unmistakable under her ribs; it pricked her every time she took a breath.

"How dare you come back?" whispered a familiar voice.

Kasper's breath caressed Indira's neck, playing with the wisps of hair that escaped her braids. She struggled a little but he only held her tighter; with one arm out of action she was at his mercy and it excited her. She had longed for a moment when he would draw her this close, when his lips would brush the delicate skin on her neck, his body pressed hard against hers. It was a shame about the blade. She had been swept away on a wave of emotions ever since she had met him; his cold aloofness just made him more alluring, she like to be treated mean. She had thought when the moment came that she would be able to convince him to change sides and take her as a lover - that was until she had met the Princess. The moment Kasper had seen Emelda she had known that his heart was hers, yet still she had pressed herself on him, enjoying the flickers of envy and sadness in the Princess's eyes. Her heart lied to her as it wondered if maybe there was still a chance to convince him of her love for him. She felt a moment of pleasure tainted by sadness as the warmth of his cheek pressed against her and his soft dark hair fell on her face. He held her tightly in a deadly lover's embrace, exerting a little pressure on the blade between her ribs so she couldn't relax.

"Did you think I wouldn't kill you if you came back?" he snarled into her ear.

She remained silent. She knew he would kill her if she didn't do something. She thought of all those moments of intimacy, all those gentle words and the briefest of touches; they had been the deepest of lies but she couldn't stop her body longing for him even now. For a moment the girl inside her wanted to ask if he felt anything for her, but it was quickly subdued by the woman she was, the woman who fought and killed to keep herself alive.

"Just do it," she murmured, her voice soft and seductive.

With her injured arm she reached for his belt and pulled him even closer to herself so the blade pushed hard against her flesh.

"Tell me one thing, is Matthias alive?" he asked,

"Very much so! It's not only your Princess with a piece of that tree," she exclaimed, turning her head abruptly and forcing her voluptuous lips against his.

Emelda watched as a clenching tightness gripped her chest and she felt she could hardly breathe. She watched them pressed together in a tight embrace, desperate not to believe what she was seeing, not after everything that had happened, yet she saw Kasper's eyes sparkle in the darkness, filled with passion. Although she had seen the way Indira had poured herself all over Kasper and the gentle looks that he had given her that were so different to the cold hard judgements that he directed her way, she couldn't believe that after Indira had tried to kill both her and Christian that he would go back to her. Emelda knew it was Kasper's duty to protect her, but clearly he had chosen to love Indira. She wanted to turn away but she couldn't tear her eyes away from the private moment that she had interrupted. Heart in her mouth she saw Indira's lips press against Kasper's. She didn't wait to see his reaction, instead she turned and ran, her hand over her mouth stifling her sobs. She threw herself down next to Christian, who woke but seeing her feigning sleep let her be. He sat up and gathering his sword, stepped into the doorway to see if he could see Kasper; he was sure he must be nearby. He called out into the darkness but worryingly there was no reply. He couldn't leave the Princess so he would have to wait until morning to go looking for Kasper.

Emelda lay with her back to the door, cursing her foolish heart. Despite his coldness and his arrogance there was something about Kasper that still made her heart pound like no one else had done before. He was so familiar and reassuring for some unknown reason, yet a total stranger to her. She had hoped his coldness was a front, a cover for love lost and hearts broken. Now she would never know, she would never let herself. She dismissed the flashes of kindness and concern that he had shown her as his duty and let her heart harden towards him.

Kasper pushed Indira hard in the back, knocking her to the ground, a disgusted look on his face. She knelt on the ground, the wind knocked out of her. She coughed as she tried to get up. Kasper was temporarily distracted by a noise in the distance and Indira took her opportunity to escape from him but he was too quick; he grabbed her long braids and pulled hard, exposing her soft vulnerable neck.

"You disgust me," he whispered coldly and pushed the knife against her throat.

A drop of blood oozed from her neck as the knife sliced into her flesh, but now that Indira's hands were free she fumbled in her cloak, her fingers quickly finding the small blade she concealed there. With all her strength she pushed herself into him, then swung hard at him with her blade making contact with his shoulder and making him stumble back. Kasper dropped the knife in surprise, his hand going to his shoulder. Indira hurriedly scrambled to her feet and ran, merging herself into the night as she did.

Kasper cursed as he held his shoulder and pulled the blade out, watching Indira disappear into the darkness. He thought about chasing after her, but it was pointless - she was gone and he was injured. The night was her playing field; she was skilled at hiding and stalking, moving like a shadow. He knew she would come back to haunt him and the sooner he got to the next town the better. There were worse things than Indira - Matthias was alive. He had wondered when Emelda had said a strange man had attacked her in the marshes but he had prayed he was wrong.

Kneeling down on the ground he picked up his blade and cleaned it then returned it to its place on his belt along with Indira's small blade. As he made his way back to the hut, he thought about the last time he had seen Matthias. It was several years into the fighting. The Rebel King was getting stronger and stronger, sending more and more assassins to find the Princess' sedated body, to kill her and retrieve the willow bud. Christian, his father and himself had successfully managed to keep most of them at bay, not letting them get further than the Monastery. But one man had managed it, one man had killed his father and pushed them to their limits. Matthias had somehow found a way around the mountain range that held the monastery and they had clashed on the very mountain where Emelda's body lay hidden. Kasper's father had been the first to fight and die for the Princess; brave and true he was no match for the young Matthias who was vicious and bloodthirsty with no concern for his own injuries, fighting on despite being torn to ribbons by Lord Hart's blade. There had

149

come a moment where Matthias had had Kasper pinned to the ground, Christian was unconscious nearby and his father was lying dead in a pool of his own blood. He had slashed at Kasper's face like a wild animal, madness in his snake eyes. Kasper with the last of his strength had managed to force his thumb into his eyes, get free and kick him hard in the back, sending him falling to his death over the edge of the mountain. He had stood gazing down, watching with his uninjured eye, until Matthias hit the ground, a mangled mess of a man, stone cold dead. Or so he had thought.

Kasper had been left with the thin scar across his left eye that split his eyebrow in two, yet luckily hadn't affected his vision, and a gaping hole in his life where his father had been. He had felt the loss of his father for a long time; it encouraged the bitterness and solitude he had resigned himself to. From that time on he spoke only to his Captain and Christian, keeping himself to himself, never parted from the little black bag with its glowing contents, which his father had given to him moments before they were attacked.

Reaching the hut, he scanned the horizon looking for any sign of Indira, but there was no one there. She would not return, at least not tonight and probably not alone. It appeared that Emelda had already encountered Matthias in the marshes and may have slowed him down, though with whatever small part of the willow he appeared to have, he was seemingly indestructible - he would find them eventually.

Kasper had objected initially to Indira's involvement in the mission to bring the Princess back; she hadn't been part of the King's Guard for long and although she was a solitary soul like him she seemed discontented with her solitude, unlike Kasper, who relished it. It was as if there was conflict in her soul and now Kasper knew exactly why; she was rotten to the core, a traitor from the start yet torn between him and her allegiances. He was glad he had kept her close, but clearly not close enough, as she had attempted to take the Princess's life at least once and was now feeding Matthias information and he was none the wiser about the Rebel King's plans. Kasper felt angry at his incompetence; Emelda should never have come to any harm for the sake of information, but he had been blinded by his need to know everything, to be in control. He should have killed Indira days ago instead of forcing himself to be kind to her, even affectionate, especially every time she belittled the Princess and he had wanted to wipe every smug smirk off her face with his fist.

By the time he had sat down at the fireside the pain in his shoulder had dulled to an ache and the bleeding had stopped. Christian was sitting staring at the dying flames, his face wrought with worry.

"Where have you been?" he said angrily, trying to keep his voice quiet so as not to wake Emelda.

"Indira," he murmured.

"She hurt you," replied Christian, sitting next to Kasper and reaching for his shoulder.

Kasper shrugged away from his touch, "You were right, I should have killed her as soon as you told me she had attacked you. I put you and the Princess in danger for the sake of information I never got."

"Kasper," Christian said softly.

"I'm sorry," the words barely escaped his proud lips.

Christian resisted the urge to make him speak up. Instead he nodded, and holding his tongue he grabbed the medical bag and pulled out a stream of bandages. Kasper removed his shirt and washed the wound then let Christian dress it. They spoke in hushed voices about the future, about the men and women across the country that had gathered in secret, waiting for a messenger to bring them news of the location to which the Princess was being brought. Kasper himself had only received the location from Brother Icka at the monastery.

Christian reassured Kasper that they had needed Indira to help them cross the marsh, that it would have taken them longer than a day without her. Kasper told him he would rather have walked for three days around the marsh had he known what had been waiting for them within the fog. He had been gripped with fear when Indira had stolen the Princess away from them in the fog, turning into a madman, hacking and slashing at anything that moved until he could get a clear path after them.

After a while they sat in silence watching the fire, Kasper still shirtless, enjoying the warmth of the fire on his bare skin. Kasper let his eyes wander over to the Princess who looked peaceful and gentle, her chest rising and falling with the normal rhythms of sleep. They used to sneak out in the dead of the night when they were young, light fires and sit together talking for hours, the glow of the firelight illuminating her sweet face. He would have given anything to be back by the fire of their youth now listening to her joys and desires, her worries and fears. His sweet Princess, his one and only. Christian caught him watching her but said nothing.

"You should sleep, there are a few more hours until the dawn," whispered Christian.

"I don't think I can," replied Kasper.

"Try, please."

Kasper nodded and Emelda felt the warmth of his body as he lay down next to her, close but not touching. She had been awake since Kasper had returned but in her anger and sorrow she had remained motionless, pretending to be asleep and praying that she would actually drift off again. But sleep had eluded her, her body was stiff and tense and she couldn't make it relax. She had thought about turning over and speaking to the men, but then she heard Kasper undressing and the quiet whispers of their intimate, inaudible conversation that she couldn't bring herself to interrupt. She wasn't sure what she would have said to Kasper anyway, not after what she had seen. Instead she shut her eyes tightly, flushed with embarrassment at the idea of him being half naked within touching distance despite having her back to him. She had experience of men in the other world, had seen them naked, touched their skin and felt their lips on hers but here it was different. None of those feelings, those memories seemed like they were really hers; here she was clean and untouched. Her skin was untainted by the hands of those men, she was whole, complete and innocent. It embarrassed her and made her feel childish, a side of herself she did not want Kasper or anyone else to see. She was a woman, a Queen, not a child.

Chapter 11

She must have fallen asleep, as when Emelda woke the morning sun was pouring in through the hut door, a thin slice of light warming her face. Kasper was nowhere to be seen but Christian was quietly gathering their belongings, getting ready to leave. He looked up as she began to stir, a tired smile on his face. She rubbed her eyes and stretched her back, uncomfortable from the hard stone floor.

"I hope I didn't wake you, Your Majesty?" he said, "Please have something to eat."

He offered her the same flat bread and fruit that they had eaten the night before; she took them and thanked him, looking at them carefully for a moment before speaking.

"Where is Kasper?"

"He needed some fresh air, Princess, he won't be long."

"It doesn't matter."

Emelda began eating breakfast and Christian gathered up her blanket for her, packing it neatly in her bag.

"I heard you last night," she breathed, barely letting the words escape her lips.

Christian stopped in his tracks and looked down at her, his eyes a mixture of sadness and anger, but he quickly looked away again, running his hand through his blonde hair.

"I'm sorry, and so is Kasper, but I'm not sure you will get him to say it again," said Christian quietly.

"He knew all along," it was a statement more than a question, "yet he was...with her."

"Princess, it's not what you think, it wasn't like that, believe me," said Christian trying to defend Kasper.

"It looked like that to me last night."

"Pardon?" Christian looked confused.

Emelda didn't say anything else - she had let the hurt she was feeling get the better of her tongue and she instantly regretted it. If Kasper had known that Indira was a traitor all along then surely he wasn't fraternising with her last night; there must be some other explanation, but now she had sown the seeds of poison she was no better than Indira.

"I wonder if anything he told me wasn't a lie," murmured Christian, anger in his voice.

"No Christian, I'm sorry I shouldn't have said anything, I must have got it wrong," said Emelda, trying to backtrack but it was no good. Christian kicked Kasper's neatly packed bag and the contents split out over the floor. Emelda quickly bent down to pick them up.

"Don't," said Christian, quietly but forcefully.

"Christian, I'm sorry, please."

But he didn't listen, instead he started pacing the hut like a caged animal.

"He put you in danger, not just for information but for his own lust," he was almost shouting and Emelda tried to put a hand on his shoulder in the same way he did to her when she was upset but he shook her off.

She stepped back from him a little and he realised what he had said. He turned towards her and quickly scooped up her hands in his.

"I'm sorry, but I don't like being lied to. He was irresponsible, careless and all for..." began Christian.

"For what?" came a cold, hard voice, cutting across them like a knife.

Kasper stood in the doorway, blocking the morning light, his face stern and unfeeling as always. He approached them and Emelda recoiled a little. How could she even look at him after last night and after what she had just told Christian? She turned away, unable to look him in the eye.

"You lied to me, I thought you were playing her to get information!" said Christian angrily, "You let her near the Princess just to slake your own lust."

"It was a ruse and I don't need to explain myself to either of you," said Kasper bluntly, turning his back and bending down to collect up his belongings.

Kasper's emotionless dismissal only angered Christian further. He grabbed Kasper's injured shoulder and hauled him to his feet before swinging his fist hard into the side of Kasper's face. Kasper braced himself as Christian's fist made contact with his jaw, he felt his teeth clatter together and pain shot through the side of his face. Kasper took it, knowing that although he had never had any inclination towards Indira, he had let his own need to control everything get in the way of his duty to the Princess, so he deserved Christian's rage.

Christian slung his bag over his shoulder and turned to Emelda.

"I'll be outside," he said, pushing past Kasper and leaving the hut.

A painful silence fell over the room and Kasper looked up at Emelda as if he was about to speak, but she stopped him.

"I don't need to know, or want to, just take me to my fiancé and my people," she said coldly before she, too, left the hut.

Kasper was left alone to gather up his belongings, the pain in his face nothing compared to the pain of her words in his chest.

Outside Christian leant against the wall of the hut gazing at the morning sun. The glowing light made his hair look like gold and his blue eyes shone more brilliantly than ever. He looked down at her, a little surprised to see her watching him so intently.

"Shall we?" she said, wrapping a long cotton scarf around her head to partly conceal her face.

"Yes, Your Majesty, let's get you home," he replied as Kasper emerged from the hut, wiping the blood from his lips, a bruise already forming on his face.

Kasper's heart felt heavy but he fixed his face into its usual hard expression and followed behind the Princess and Christian, keeping his distance but still close. As they walked in silence Kasper thought about the previous night's events. He could still feel Indira's lips on his own and it disgusted him. He wiped his mouth again with the back of his hand. He had washed briefly but she had left a bitter taste in his mouth that he couldn't get rid of. He had known who she was yet he had failed to get any real information, putting everyone in danger, and now the one man he called a friend believed him to be a liar, and worse still the Princess was repulsed by him. Her rejection hurt more than his own disappointment in himself and he fought to keep his composure, reverting to the cold stranger he was so used to being. He walked steadily, head bowed, oblivious to the passing countryside, the small farms with lights in their windows and the line of houses scattered across the horizon that grew steadily wider.

Christian and Emelda said very little to each other, the atmosphere tense and heavy. Emelda kept her eyes firmly fixed on the small houses on the horizon, the idea of a hot meal and a soft bed propelling her forward. She didn't dare look back at Kasper; she knew if she did she wouldn't be able to keep her heart from breaking, she was barely holding on as it was. She knew her resolve would falter and she could not let that happen; whatever it was that had drawn her to him, the feelings of familiarity and importance, was shunted to the back of her mind and she focused on the steady pounding of her feet on the hard, earthen path. Just as she had been regaining her confidence, her purpose, it was once again on the brink of being shattered around her like glass.

It took the best part of a day to get across country to the town of Brushmire, and it was late afternoon by the time the mud under their feet became a solid stone road. Small houses lined the edge of the road, some in a state of disrepair, others occupied but barely standing, like a mouthful of crooked teeth. People wandered through the streets and Emelda felt overjoyed to see them going about their business, paying them no more attention than any other traveller. A few eyebrows were raised at the array of weapons they carried with them, but the whispers of the Princess's coming must have reached the town as others were also sitting outside their houses sharpening swords, or polishing armour. Brushmire usually kept itself to itself, paying the crippling taxes when they were demanded by the Rebel King as well as half of their monthly food harvest, and they were for the most part left alone. But now there was a different atmosphere in the town, a buzz like an electrical current that brought colour back to the bleak landscape.

The townspeople were stirred up and alive again as they dashed back and forth, carrying all manner of things: quivers full of arrows, swords or armour that clattered and clanged as they walked. Many carried domestic goods: baskets of bread still warm from the baker's oven, apples shiny and red, and smoked fish.

Emelda glanced around with a smile on her face; it was so good to see people with friendly faces, people other than Kasper and Christian that weren't trying to kill her. She watched a man rolling a heavy wooden barrel up the street, sweating with the exertion. As she watched, his hands on the barrel slipped and he lost his footing. The barrel slipped from his grasp and tumbled down the street towards Emelda, who stood frozen to the spot. It hurtled towards her, gathering speed as it went, racketing down the busy street, people dodging left and right, crying out to each other. She felt a hand around her waist pulling her out of the way as it took off from the ground and landed, smashing into hundreds of shards of wood right where she had been standing. The contents washed back down the street, the smell of good wine filling the air. Emelda tensed as she realised it was Kasper who had rescued her and she was still pressed against his chest, his arm holding her closely. Wrenching herself free she brushed off her clothes and turned away from him, mumbling her thanks. Kasper let his arm drop limply to his side and waited in silence beside her as Christian, who had been forced to the other side of the street to avoid the barrel, made his way over to them, dodging a woman carrying a sack of apples as large as herself.

"Something has changed, what's happening?" he asked Kasper.

"They know the Princess is coming, they are holding a feast before they send their sons and daughters into battle," replied Kasper.

He looked around at the people marching by, many were carrying trays of home-cooked food and all were heading for the town centre, chatting excitedly amongst themselves. A group of children ambled by and Emelda tapped one on the shoulder. He stopped and looked up at her, a quizzical look on his young face.

"Can I help you, miss?" he asked politely.

"Where are you going?" she asked.

"The great feast, miss, everyone is going," then he lowered his voice and cupped his mouth with his hand, "The Princess has awakened!"

Emelda smiled down at him from behind her scarf, hoping her eyes would convey her joy at his words. He stood on the spot looking up at her, his eyes darting from her face and back to his friends.

"Do you have something else to say?" asked Kasper impatiently.

"You have pretty eyes, miss, just like how my Mumma described the Princess, are you a Princess miss?" he asked shyly.

Emelda laughed, "No, I am no one. Run along."

The boy turned and scampered off after his friends, laughing and fighting with them. Kasper turned to face the others, a look of concern on his face.

"Let's get off the streets, quickly," he said, "I didn't think eyes like yours would be that memorable."

He turned away but Emelda stopped him, infuriated. She pulled him round to face her - after his betrayal, after his arrogance, she couldn't hold her tongue any longer.

"How dare you speak to me like that! You are as bad as Indira with your bitter remarks. I don't understand after all the times you showed me so much care and tenderness, how sometimes you can be so hateful and cold. I don't know how anyone, even Indira, could have loved you, I doubt you even feel love."

Her emotions and her anger overflowed as her voice shook with rage. Kasper smiled at the passion in her eyes and grabbed her arm. Emelda twisted away instinctively, still in his grip and not taking her eyes off his. His eyes were so striking, a deep, gleaming ebony

160

that burnt into her like fire. Kasper longed to kiss her, to take her into his arms and still the beating of his heart, but out of the corner of his eye he saw Christian's hand go to the hilt of his sword and people had started to stare. He let go of her arm with force and turned away, unable to look at her any longer.

"We need somewhere to stay," he muttered, heading out into the crowds.

Christian quickly caught up with Kasper, gesturing for Emelda, who had reached the opposite side of the street a short distance away, to hang back. He pulled hard on Kasper's arm and he stopped, shaking Christian's hand off angrily. Emelda watched and waited, the noise of the crowds drowning out what they were saying. After a fraught exchange, Christian gesticulating wildly, Kasper finally grabbed him by the shoulders and said something to him calmly. Emelda saw all the anger drain out of Christian's face to be replaced by sadness, and he stopped fighting Kasper. Instead he placed a reassuring hand on Kasper's arm, glancing over in her direction.

Christian beckoned her and she made her way over cautiously, wondering what on earth Kasper could have said to calm the fire in Christian's eyes, until she was standing before the two men, brothers again. She looked at them expectantly.

"Please, Princess..." began Christian.

"I can speak for myself," interrupted Kasper, "forgive me, Princess, I should not have spoken to you like that, or treated you the way I have. I have something I need to work out and it should not affect the way I treat you."

"Very well," Emelda said through gritted teeth, swallowing the last of her anger. She, too, had an issue that she needed to work out and she was as guilty as he was of hiding behind harsh words.

As Kasper walked ahead of them Emelda lowered her voice so that only Christian could hear her, "He must be a very good friend for you to trust him again after everything he's done; forgive me if I am not so quick to follow suit. It's a good thing I trust you, Christian."

Christian paused momentarily and looked her directly in the eyes, "Believe me it was a revelation. I wouldn't ever have guessed he felt so..."

Christian stopped himself midsentence, "You should really hear it from him. It's not my place."

They continued up the street until they came to the town square, where a long table lay, heaving under the weight of countless dishes of food; wine and beer flowed from large wooden barrels and many people were already seated at the table, laughing and drinking. Large decorations adorned the table and bunting in a rich green and gold, the King's colours, hung from the surrounding shops and buildings. The square was lit by rows of candles down the centre of the tables and in all the windows of the buildings: it was a magical sight. Emelda's eyes widened in amazement; all of this was because of her, because these people on the very edge of her Kingdom had heard of her return and were overjoyed. They believed in her and her power to bring change. Her heart swelled with pride. She was their hope and their new beginning and she was determined to be just that.

Kasper led them down a side street to an inn that was tucked out of the way and quiet. A portly man with a flushed face greeted them warmly.

"Have you come for the celebrations?" he asked, "I hear people from some of the smaller villages have come to join us in our festivities."

"No, two rooms please," replied Kasper in his usual abrupt manner.

The innkeeper looked a little offended, but glanced down at his ledger and ran his finger carefully down the page, then flicked it over and scratched his head.

"I have two rooms but they are not next to each other," he said.

"That will have to do," sighed Kasper.

The man looked at him with disdain then turned to get the keys from a small cabinet behind the counter. Kasper paid for one night, an evening meal and breakfast, and enquired as to where they could get horses for the following day. The man was helpful but curt and before long they were being shown to their rooms by the innkeeper's wife, who was a slight woman in comparison to her husband. As she turned to leave, Emelda placed a hand on hers.

"Is it not dangerous to celebrate so openly?" she asked.

The woman laughed, but there was a sadness in her eyes, "What have we got to lose? The Rebel King knows the Princess is coming, this may be the last chance we get to celebrate."

The rooms were small and clean, each containing a small double bed, a chest of drawers and a small china washbasin. Unlit hearths sat piled high with kindling and logs stacked neatly to one side. Emelda was shown to her room first then the men were taken to theirs after reassuring the Princess that one of them would be back shortly to check on her.

Sitting down heavily on the bed Emelda was overcome with exhaustion; she slipped off her boots, rubbing her wounded ankle as she did, then fell back onto the soft sheets. The bed was firm but comfortable, the sheets washed and fresh and, glad of a moment to herself, Emelda closed her eyes just for a moment.

She must have fallen asleep as she was woken what seemed like a minute later by a loud knock on the door. Rubbing her eyes, she hastily sat up and smoothed down her clothes and hair before jumping up and opening the door.

"Your Majesty," whispered Christian.

"Come in," she beckoned.

"Did you sleep well?" he asked, entering the room and shutting the door behind him. He was carrying a large box.

"Is it that obvious?" she said, running her hand through her hair.

"I came to check on you earlier but you were asleep. I've been sitting outside - I thought you could do with a rest," he smiled, "I have something for you."

Christian presented the box to her with a grin, "I hope you like it."

"Thank you, Christian."

Emelda grinned as she took the box from him eagerly and lifted the lid. Inside was a parcel carefully wrapped in pink tissue paper. She lifted it out and gently ran her fingers over it until she found an opening. With a light touch she pulled back the paper, careful not to tear it, to reveal soft folds of forest green fabric. A gentle gasp escaped her lips as she let the rest of the paper fall away, lifting the fabric up it tumbled down like a waterfall to reveal its full glory. Emelda held a stunning green dress by the shoulders and admired it. It was embroidered with leaves and flowers in a light-catching golden thread; she had never seen anything to beautiful. She pored over the delicate pattern and felt the satisfying weight of it in her hands, rich and costly, before laying it gently on the bed and running her hands over the soft velvety fabric.

"It's beautiful," she breathed, "Thank you."

"Don't thank me," he smiled, "Kasper chose it."

Emelda looked up from the dress at him in disbelief; she couldn't imagine Kasper in a clothing shop picking out fabrics and styles. He would have looked so out of place.

164

"Who would have thought he would have such good taste!" she said, raising her eyebrows in surprise.

"He's a good man, Your Majesty, he's just difficult. He lost the woman he loved and his father in almost the same breath, he wasn't the same after that. Dedicated himself to the King's Guard and closed himself off to everyone else," Christian ran his hand through his golden hair, "it may be hard to believe but he does care."

"He has a funny way of showing it," replied Emelda dismissively, but there was no malice or dislike in her voice, as careless as the words were meant to be - the wind had been sucked out of her sails.

"I know, after pushing down his emotions for so long he doesn't know what to do with them when they resurface. He resorts to the only thing he knows, arrogance and sarcasm, he stops anyone getting close."

Emelda frowned a little, "But you are friends!"

"I'm persuasive and persistent; we were in it together from the beginning so I knew he would have to let me in at some point," laughed Christian, "no one can resist my charms. Not even Kasper!"

"I see," replied Emelda.

"He cares for you more than you know, Princess, but he would never admit it to you."

There was another knock at the door and when Christian opened it a maid stood carrying a small metal bath tub which she handed to Christian before disappearing again.

"Kasper took the liberty of sorting out a bath for you; we won't be stopping at another town after this, we are taking back roads the rest of the way." he told her, "I will leave you to it. We eat soon so don't be long."

Christian placed the bath in front of the fire and left. Once she was alone Emelda sat on the edge of the bed looking down at Kasper's gift. She was so confused; her feelings for Kasper were growing stronger and stronger, but she wasn't quite sure what they were just yet. One minute she hated and distrusted him, and the next moment her heart pounded out his name. No matter how hard she tried to convince herself that he was bitter and arrogant, that she disliked him, her heart shouted otherwise. She couldn't work out why, either, it was more than just the last few days that they had spent together that had caused feelings like these. She felt like she was missing out on a whole lifetime of feelings, as if a huge part of her life had been torn out. She stroked the dress, then looked down at her filthy clothes. She knew they needed a good wash, but she would never have dared ask for more, let alone anything so beautiful. She tried to imagine Kasper choosing it for her, asking the shop assistant to hold it up so he could see it, imagining her in it. The last thought made her blush.

Another knock on the door made her stand up quickly, and half expecting Kasper to come in she waited nervously, but it was only the maid and the owner's wife, each carrying two large buckets of steaming water. They carried them over to the bath and carefully poured them in, then the owner's wife left and the maid put up a screen around the bath.

"Sir asked me to assist you," she said in a quiet voice.

"Thank you - I will call you when I require assistance," replied Emelda, disappearing behind the screen.

"Throw your clothes over, miss, and I will see it that they are washed and ready for you in the morning," said the maid.

Quickly Emelda removed her clothes and hung them on the screen for the waiting maid. They disappeared and as she climbed into the hot water she heard the maid leave. The heat soaked into her body, warming her to the core; it felt so good, as if all the bad things that had happened were floating away. As she slid deeper into the water she realised that this was the first time in days she had really felt warm, and she relished it. After the sting of the heat had subsided a little she closed her eyes and submerged herself. For a moment her mind returned to that morning in the bath, when she had thought she was being drowned, and she almost breathed in a lungful of water. She pushed herself back up to the surface and took a deep breath; it was then she noticed a bar of soap on a little dish attached to the edge of the bath. She reached for it and brought it up to her nose, inhaling deeply. It smelt of lavender and olive oil, a fragrance so familiar and emotive that she held it too her nose for some time . . . it smelt like home, safety, more than that it reminded her of someone she knew well, someone she was intimate with, someone who made her heart beat hard against her ribs, who made her skin tingle and her eyes light up. But who? She simply couldn't remember and it infuriated her. How could she have forgotten someone so important to her?

Slowly she began to wash her tired body and hair, hoping that having the scent on her skin, engulfing herself in it, would help her remember the person who meant so much to her. She heard a knock on the door and it opened.

"Are you ready, miss?" came a quiet voice from beyond the screen.

"One moment, please," she called back.

Emelda disappeared under the water and then emerged to find that a towel had appeared on the top of the screen. She climbed out and dried herself off. She took a moment to examine her body. It seemed more familiar to her now than the squatter, fuller form that she had owned in her other life. She was not disappointed with the taller, firmer body she now had, but she had always been proud of her curves before, thinking of herself as womanly and feminine. Now things were different - she felt her figure was a little more boyish, but she wasn't displeased.

She emerged from behind the screen wrapped in the towel to find the maid beginning to unbutton the back of the dress; next to it was a set of clean underwear. Emelda stood watching her, her long hair slicked to her back and dripping onto the floor.

"Please, miss, let me dry your hair or you will catch a cold," the maid said kindly, before disappearing behind the screen and retrieving a second towel.

Emelda put her underwear on and then sat down on the bed in front of the maid, who gently started drying her hair. Once she was done she took Emelda by the hands and helped her to her feet. Warm and tired, she let the maid dress her and arrange her hair with delicate, deft hands, and as the light outside her window faded she found herself looking in the mirror at a completely different person. The dress fitted like a glove, cut in just the right way to make the most of her figure, yet it was dignified and modest. She ran her hands over the soft contours of her body and smiled. This was what it was like to feel like a Queen; it sent shivers down her spine as she gazed at her reflection. She turned to thank the maid but she had already gone, leaving as quietly as she had come.

For a moment Emelda was lost in thought and gazing around the room she wasn't sure what to do with herself, then her eyes fell on the box the dress had come in. At the very bottom, left unnoticed was a smaller box. Emelda reached in and picked it up, opening it slowly. Inside was a beautiful silver hairpin adorned with a single emerald set in silver leaves, simple yet breath-taking. She stood staring down at the beautiful hairpin, her heart full of joy at such a lovely gift. Gingerly she turned to the mirror and placed it in her hair then she stood back and admired it. One day her head would be adorned with a crown full of glittering emeralds and diamonds - this was a small glimmer of her future. Her fingers went once more to the hairpin, she felt the sharp contours of the emerald, the soft sweeping silver of the leaves so delicate and weightless. She was so busy admiring herself in the mirror, she didn't notice the door of her room opening until it was too late.

She spun on the spot. To her horror Kasper stood in the doorway, dressed in black as usual but looking clean and fresh. She could see that he still wore his katana strapped to his back as if he was unable to relax for even a moment. There was a surprised look on his face, his lips parted as if he was about to speak but the words had dissolved on his tongue like sugar.

"Kasper..." the word escaped her lips like a faint whisper before she regained her composure, "how dare you enter without knocking?"

"Princess," he murmured, a deep well of emotion flowing up and out of his soul at the sight of her, he couldn't hold it back any longer.

Pushing the door shut he strode across the room and pulled her forcefully into his arms. She made a half-hearted attempt to protest but he silenced her with his lips, gently at first but when she didn't refuse him he became more passionate, entwining his tongue with hers. She could feel everything he had been holding back, flowing out of him like a rushing river from his soul into hers. His hands found their way around her waist and into her hair, cupping her face tenderly. He pulled her closer still into the warmth of his body, the faint smell of lavender caressing her senses as she let herself melt into him. The hairpin clattered to the floor as she succumbed to his embrace. Her arms were around him drawing him into her, her heart beating hard against his strong chest.

Then it happened, she remembered. It hit her like a sheet of ice, stinging every part of her body. Kasper, protector, friend, lover. She closed her eyes slowly and opened them again, his face millimetres from hers - he was her everything, her purpose and meaning. How could she have forgotten him for so long? She remembered him. The boy in her dreams, her childhood friend and confidant, the young man who taught her to handle a sword, who filled her bedchamber with her favourite flowers on her birthday every year. He was the young man who had tenderly taken her hand on the day she left and placed a lingering kiss on it as her eyes filled with tears. He had sworn to protect her, to wait for her, and she had imagined his kiss upon her lips for the entire journey to the Grey Man, her adolescent heart full of love for him. He was the man who was cold and indifferent towards her yet had carried her up the mountain to keep her from harm, who had protected her, killed for her, would die for her. The boy and the man were one and the same.

"Kasper," she whispered pulling away so that her mouth lingered next to his ear, barely able to say his name.

Her heart overflowed into her eyes, so many memories, so many feelings. She reached up and brushed the hair from his face so that she could look at him with new eyes, but all she saw was Indira. Her lips on his, his hands on her skin, her voice in his ear. She pushed him away roughly, not caring if he saw the tears that had begun to well up in her eyes. She let them fall - she didn't have the strength to hold them back, not for him. She breathed heavily, her chest rising and falling as if she had run a marathon.

"I can taste her!" she spat at him, her voice trembling with emotion.

Kasper looked confused as Emelda pushed past him and disappeared out of the door. He listened to her feet pounding on the stairs and he felt as if his heart was being stamped on with each footfall. He knew he should follow her but he could not make his body obey him. If he moved the gentle warmth of her body and the smell of her skin that was imprinted on him would disappear all the quicker and he would be left cold and alone again. As he stood motionless his gaze fell on his own reflection; he almost didn't recognise the man staring back at him, much as Emelda hadn't herself. He touched the scar across his left eye, remembering his father with a heavy heart and wishing he was still here. He stared hard at the face, his dark eyes taking himself in, once cold and emotionless but now tainted with sadness. Where had his youth gone? When had he become this man, battle-worn and tired? He ran his hands over his face, it was rough and unshaven, stark like the empty earth that covered St. Dores, barren and hard. Yet when he thought about Emelda he felt alive again, he was eighteen again, her love coursing through his veins. She may have loved him then, but there was no way she could love him now.

His eyes turned to the floor where she had stood and he spotted the hairpin that he had bought for her, dropped in their fleeting moment of passion. He bent down and picked it up, placing it carefully in its box. She was a Princess, a Queen, and who was he, no one important, just a soldier, a protector, a fool.

He thought of her face as she had pushed him away, the tears that had fallen, tears that were because of him, her words echoing in his ears.

'I can taste her.'

Slowly he turned and made his way towards the open door, contemplating what she had said. He knew Christian was waiting in the bar down below so he let his feet take him quietly out of the room, closing the door behind himself with a little clunk. It was true he had been blunt and dismissive with Emelda but he hadn't known how to act around her, afraid to let the emotions get the better of him. He had been devastated when she didn't remember him and distance had seemed like the best option. Then it struck him as he reached the top of the stairs, Indira, the noise in the distance, the opportunity she took to escape . . . they had been watched.

"No," he murmured, the words barely making it past his lips, so faint, so filled with sadness.

Kasper realised what it must have looked like to Emelda. She wouldn't have seen the blade pushed hard against Indira's ribs, or seen the look of disgust on his face. There was an unpleasant tight feeling in his chest as he rushed down the stairs; he had to get to Emelda and explain the misunderstanding. It also explained why Christian had been so angry at him when all had seemed forgiven. Losing all normal composure, he barrelled down the last few steps and into the bar. People mulled about drinking and smoking; a hazy cloud of smoke distorted the air filling Kasper's senses with the smell of tobacco and alcohol. He scanned the room desperately looking for Christian and Emelda, but they were nowhere to be seen. He crossed the inn in several strides and swung open the door.

The chilled evening air flooded in, refreshing and sharp; Kasper breathed in deeply and dived out into the square nearly knocking over a young woman carrying a basket of bread. She called out after him but either he didn't hear or he chose to ignore her, his eyes searching the festive scene that lay before him. Men and women sat in rows at the long table, some eating, some drinking, others deep in jovial conversation. Some danced in front of a band that was elevated on a wooden stage, all bathed in the soft glow of lamplight. Each face was alive and upbeat, the sounds of laughter and joy echoing off the very stones the town was made of.

But Kasper could not see the Princess anywhere and his pulse started to quicken, the sound of his own heart beat thumping in his ears - then something caught his eye. Across the street in a side alley, Kasper could see a pool of dark liquid glistening in the cold, silvery moonlight. His feet could not take him fast enough, but as he reached the alley he pressed himself tight to the wall and pulled out his katana. Cautiously, heart racing, he peered around the corner. Nausea swelled in his stomach as his eyes fell on the slumped body of Christian, barely propped against the wall, blood soaking through his clothes and covering the ground around him. His weapon was some distance away but in one hand he clutched a small knife; the other was pressed limply against his stomach and his eyes closed in pain, his face grey. As Kasper rounded the corner Christian opened his eyes and feebly lifted his knife, but seeing his friend in the moonlight he let the blade fall from his hand as if he had been holding on for him.

"It's not all my blood," he said, laughing gently, fresh blood blossoming from between his fingers as Kasper knelt beside him.

"She's wounded... she won't have gotten far...hurry," coughed Christian.

"I'll be back for you," said Kasper, knowing all too well that he would not see his friend alive again.

Christian nodded and closed his eyes with a pained smile, "Ok, I'll just wait here for you."

Kasper placed a hand on his shoulder and stood up. He could see a trail of blood splattered on the ground and he gave chase, his heart pounding with every step, until he turned a corner and his heart stopped.

Before him stood Indira, backed into a dead-end. She held the Princess in front of her, close to her body. Her sword was pressed against Emelda's throat so hard that it had drawn a thin line of blood across her ivory skin, making it hard for her to swallow. He could see the panic in Emelda's eyes, but she was keeping it contained, remaining calm and still.

"Let her go!" he called out, his voice low, his black eyes furious.

Indira laughed and Emelda winced at the cruel sound, the sharp blade stinging against the soft skin of her throat. Her voice was loud in Emelda's ears but Indira's breathing was laboured; Christian had managed to deal a death blow before he had succumbed to the wound in his side.

"What do you want?" Kasper said through gritted teeth. If Emelda had not been trapped between them he wouldn't have had a second thought about slicing Indira's head clean from her body.

"The willow, where is it?" Indira said, trying not to let the pain creep into her voice but Emelda could hear it in her shallow breathing.

"She doesn't have it," he called out.

Kasper's eyes met Emelda's and he begged her forgiveness, longing to speak to her, to tell her not to worry, that she would be ok. He would have given anything to be the one with a blade to his throat, not her.

"I know that, you fool," sneered Indira.

Kasper implored "I have it, let her go."

"I don't believe you, show me," ordered Indira.

Kasper reached inside his cloak and took out a small black cloth bag; reaching inside he pulled out a small piece of wood that glowed faintly, then he quickly thrust it back inside the bag. Emelda looked confused - that was not the willow, yes, it had the same dim glow but that was not it.

"Smaller than I expected, drop your weapons on the ground and kick them away. Then bring me the willow," she told him.

"Very well," he said taking a step towards her.

"Stay back," she warned, pushing the blade against Emelda's throat, making her gag.

Kasper dropped his katana one after the other and they clattered loudly in the quiet alley, the sound of the festivities carried to them on the wind. Then he took his

174

knife from his belt and kicked it aside and advanced slowly toward Indira and Emelda. He came within two paces of them and Indira called for him to stop.

"That's close enough, pass the willow to her," she said.

But instead of stopping he took another step and instinctively Indira stepped back. Emelda heard Indira's boot scrape the wall behind them. She wondered why Kasper was backing an angry woman with nothing left to lose even further into a corner. Then she realised what he was doing; he could tell Indira was injured but now that he was closer he could hear the rattle in her chest and her laboured breathing. Christian had plunged his blade deep into Indira's chest and slowly blood was filling up her lungs. She was drowning her in her own blood and Kasper could hear it.

He passed the willow to Emelda who in turn handed it to Indira, fumbling it as she did so. Indira's eyes moved for a split second from Kasper to the willow and that was all it took for Kasper to leap forward and grab hold of the hand that held the blade to Emelda's throat and wrench it back. There was a loud pop as Indira's shoulder was ripped from its socket. Kasper's other hand went straight to her throat as Emelda dropped to her knees and crawled away, clutching at her neck.

"I told you I would kill you if you came back," he murmured, his face close to hers.

With one quick practised movement he snapped Indira's neck and let her body slump to the floor with a sickening thud. He turned away and pulled Emelda to her feet, embracing her tightly against his chest so that she would not see the gruesome scene that lay before them, and she let herself be held by him. Relief washed over her in waves that made her tremble and he held her tighter. After a moment, he released her a little and held her face in his large hands, looking down into her eyes.

"I'm sorry," he said.

She shook her head and looked away, unable to meet his intense gaze. With a sudden urgency, she pulled his hands from her face.

"Christian!"

Saying nothing more she turned and rushed back down the alley to where Christian was still propped against the wall. Kasper quickly retrieved the piece of willow, put it his little black bag and followed her. Emelda flung herself on the ground next to Christian and clasped his hand in hers. It was cold and bloody, she knew that he was dead but still she called out to him. Cupping his face in her hands she tilted his face up towards hers and called his name desperately, over and over again. Gradually her voice grew quieter and quieter until it was no longer words, but a gentle moan that escaped her lips. She kissed Christian's forehead, lingering there for some time, letting her tears fall onto his sweet face. She felt as if the air was being choked from her lungs, as if Indira's blade had truly sliced through her throat.

It wasn't until Kasper placed a hand on her shoulder that she let go of Christian carefully, and after taking one last long look at him she stood up. She turned to face Kasper, tears continuing to fall freely down her face. Kasper made to wipe them away but she caught his hand.

"Let them fall, I am not ashamed, they are for him," she said softly.

He let his hand fall to his side and he looked at her, bathed in the soft, silvery moonlight. Her dress was covered in blood, her hair had come undone and twisting locks fell around her face and neck. Despite the sadness in her eyes she was beautiful but Kasper had to resist the urge to reach out and touch her.

"You could have prevented this," she said, her voice little more than a whisper.

"Princess, I..."

"No, he's dead because of you!" she cried.

She let all her anger and sorrow pour out, reaching up and pounding on Kasper's chest with both fists as tears ran down her face. He didn't try to stop her, taking all her anger and pain until finally she fell against him, drained and empty.

"I have never, I would never. Not with Indira, not with anyone," he said quietly into her hair and he held her to him. She remained silent in his arms for some time, feeling nothing, numb.

When she finally spoke, it was barely more than a whisper, as she murmured into his chest, "You should have killed her sooner."

"I know."

Kasper released her from his embrace and ran his hand through his hair, gazing down at his friend's blood-soaked body.

"What now?" she said.

"We don't have time to bury him," he said, with regret.

"But we can't just leave him here," she replied.

"There isn't time, we need to move on."

"Not without burying him," she argued.

Fresh tears blossomed from Emelda's eyes leaving tracks down her blood-spattered face. She tasted them, salty in the corner of her mouth, and they moistened her dry lips. She fixed Kasper with her fiercest stare.

"Not without burying him," she repeated, the idea of just leaving his body here was abhorrent to her.

Kasper opened his mouth to argue but the look of sadness mixed with determination on her face made him hesitate and he merely nodded. Kneeling down beside Christian he took his own cloak from his shoulders and draped it over the body.

"Wait here in the shadows, I will bring the horses and our bags. You will be safe for now," Kasper told her, heading back towards the inn.

Emelda sat staring at Christian's body, trying to will him back to life. Maybe if enough tears fell, or she prayed hard enough he would move, he would speak to her in his kind voice. Her chest ached with grief as she sighed heavily.

It felt like an eternity before Emelda heard the sound of the horses and Kasper reappeared. He looked down at Christian half expecting him to have moved but he was exactly where he had left him. Christian was not a small man and for a moment Kasper, feeling weakened by his loss, wondered if he was going to be able to lift him. With a deep breath he gathered Christian into his arms, the body still warm as he cradled it close to his chest. The familiar metallic smell of blood drifted up to his mouth and nose, so much so he could taste it. Kasper was no stranger to death and gore; he was usually the cause of it, but this time it was different, the same as when his father had died. He could barely look at the body in his arms. Christian had been like a brother to him, a close friend despite Kasper's bad attitude; he hadn't deserved to die like this, without seeing the light, without tasting freedom.

Emelda watched Kasper struggling with his emotions but remained silent, unsure what to say and unable to be his comfort. Her head was still reeling after the night's events and it wasn't over yet. Her hands trembled as she bent down to pick up Christian's sword; it was heavy and caked in blood, some Indira's, some Christian's. The blade was cold and weighty, lifeless in her hands. Christian had moved with grace and agility, his golden hair falling around his sweet boyish face; now he was still and cold like his blade. Emelda cast a brief look over her shoulder in the direction of Indira's corpse, the fingertips of her lifeless hand protruded from around the corner. She took hold of the horse's reins and followed Kasper who had already started riding, his shoulders slumped as he held his friend close to his chest.

Caught up in the tantalizing fantasy of freedom, none of the local people had seen them leave town; no one knew that the very Princess they were raising their glasses to had been amongst them briefly. The village was still caught up in its celebrations, all too aware that the end of the night was coming, dawn would finally break and loved ones would don their weapons and their armour and head for the Southern Woods, on the doorstep of the once grand castle Dores. But it would be an end to the suffering and toil; with the willow growing in the soil again the land would become fertile, the animals would return and their children and grandchildren would once more be safe.

Kasper and Emelda rode in silence, each consumed by their own grief. Emelda wanted to comfort him, but she wasn't sure what to say, she wanted to carry Christian with Kasper but she knew it was a burden too heavy for her. Eventually Kasper turned off the path and out into the hills until he found a spot he deemed acceptable. By the time they came to a stop Emelda's tears had dried on her face, but she still felt numb, her heart heavy and her body weak.

Emelda left the horses tied to a small bush and watched as Kasper carefully placed Christian's body on the ground as if he were only sleeping and looked down at his friend. Emelda stood, staring down at Christian, looking but not seeing, until with a deep sigh Kasper dropped to his knees and pulled his knife from his belt and began to dig, but the ground was so cold and hard that the knife made slow laborious progress. In his frustration he flung the knife to the ground and began clawing at the earth with his bare hands until his fingers bled, yet he carried on letting the pain wash over him, a punishment for letting his emotions take hold. If he hadn't kissed Emelda then they would have all been together when Indira had attacked, and Christian would not have died alone in that dismal alley. Kasper cried out and pounded the ground like an animal, warm blood running down his arms and dripping into the shallow grave.

Emelda watched, although she didn't want to. She couldn't speak, couldn't move, all she could do was stare, fists clenched and stomach churning, fixed to the spot; she felt her throat close as she swallowed hard, trying not to cry again. Things could go one of two ways now - she could let the unnerving fear that gripped her consume her, turning on her heels and running, or she could take a deep breath and carry on. She didn't think Kasper would notice if she ran now, he was so consumed by his task and his grief he wouldn't have noticed even if the sky had fallen down. She tore her eyes from the sorry scene and looked out towards the horizon, the sun slowly crowning it with soft pale light. Go, run, her mind told her, but her heart kept her steadfast.

"I can't," she murmured, yet it would be so easy.

Emelda let out a gentle sob and Kasper froze, so consumed in his task he had almost forgotten she was there. His grief had blinkered him to everything else, pain and misery holding him captive. Slowly he turned to face her, the morning sun starting to rise behind her; his brow was dripping with sweat and his face covered in blood and dirt.

"Princess," he whispered.

She shook her head; his kindness would only bring on the tears she had fought so hard to control. In that moment she made her decision. Wiping her face, she went and knelt at Christian's side; between them they carefully lifted the body into the shallow grave. Kasper went to remove his cloak but Emelda stopped him; she wanted to remember Christian's face sweet and smiling, not blood-spattered and contorted with pain. She could still feel his hand pulling her out of the way as Indira had appeared before them out in the street and lunged for her. She would never forget the sight of Indira's blade darting through the darkness at her, and Christian using his body as a shield, taking the blade meant for her. He had staggered back, one hand at his side, then lifting his sword he had given such a mighty roar as he swung at Indira with all his strength before dropping to his knees, blood pooling around him. Emelda recalled his outstretched hand as Indira had dragged her away by her hair, her blade pressed to her throat. Even in death Christian was beautiful.

Emelda threw the first handful of dirt over Christian's body and prayed for his soul, then they both began piling on the earth until they stood breathing heavily before a small mound of freshly dug soil. They stood together, so close yet not touching each other, waiting for the other to speak. Eventually Kasper broke the silence, his voice quiet and hard.

"Let us be on our way. I need to get you to the encampment, he must not have died in vain."

"Yes," murmured Emelda, covering her face and vowing to herself she would come back and give Christian the honourable burial he deserved.

They returned to the horses and without a backwards glance they rode towards Castle Dores, a tiny dark silhouette on the horizon.

Chapter 12

In the grey light of the dawn Indira's body slowly
turned cold, her dead eyes staring unseeing into the
hazy sky. The sound of gentle, practised footsteps
approached the bloody scene and Matthias gazed down
at Indira. He reached down and carefully closed her eyes
before searching her body. He cursed as he came up
empty-handed. He laid his hand upon Indira's face and
after a moment, a faint blue light emanated from the
ring on his middle finger. He closed his own eyes and
watched as Indira's dying moments projected out of the
ring, hazy and muffled. The last thing he saw was
Kasper's face, full of hatred and anger. He removed his
hand and smiled. He knew Kasper's smell, he could find
him, and now he was sure it was the Princess he had met
in the Marshes, he knew her face. He stood up and
looked up into the sky expectantly. A large black raven
swooped down and landed on the ground before him,
eyeing first him then Indira's corpse as it hopped from
foot to foot. He knelt and tied the ring to the raven's foot
- a message for the Rebel King, he had caught up with
the Princess at last - before it hopped over to the body

and began pecking at it. He got up and walked calmly away from the grisly scene.

The midday sun was bright and warmer than usual, but Emelda felt cold. Her body ached and she struggled not to slouch in her saddle. They had ridden hard through the dawn and the morning, skirting the towns and villages that might have offered them relief and respite from weary, jarred bones. Maybe Kasper was punishing himself or both of them for what had happened, for he had pushed them hard, barely speaking a word to her since they had left. His cold temperament had returned along with his distance from her, as well as a grim look of determination on his handsome face.

As they rode Emelda could not help but glance over at him, remembering more and more of him. Like a sweet intoxication his memory flowed through her veins and filled her with such a mixture of emotions she could barely contain them; joy and excitement, passion and sorrow, a deep longing for him, but most of all love, deep and unfaltering. Maybe once it had been the lustful passionate love of youth but after all this time, after all that had happened it had become something new, something deep and strong, ingrained into her very soul. She was convinced he felt something for her, but with what intensity she was unsure, all she knew was that since his touch she was hungry for more of him. Yet despite his proximity he was a million miles away, unreachable and lost to her. With a heavy heart Emelda fixed her eyes on the road ahead and prepared herself for what lay before her.

It was early afternoon when they finally stopped to eat something and rest the horses. A small stream wound its way through the bare trees and they tethered the horses close to it so that they could drink. Emelda sat opposite Kasper, unable to think of anything to say.

There was so much between them left unsaid, yet Kasper just sat gazing down at his cured meat and bread disinterestedly. Occasionally he would glance up at the castle in the distance, looming ever closer. It sat proud at the top of a hill, surrounded by woods to the south and hills and valleys to the north. Emelda gazed up at the sky - the dark silhouette of a raven circled above them. Her heart beat quickly as she took a deep breath, determined to break the suffocating silence, when Kasper suddenly jumped up and grabbed her wrist, pulling her to her feet. Her eyes widened at his sudden touch and she dared not breathe.

"Run, get to your horse and go," he said urgently, releasing her and drawing both katana, "now!"

Emelda glanced over her shoulder in the direction Kasper was looking and froze with terror. A tall man in a black cloak was walking slowly towards them, the same man who had attacked her with such glee back in the Marshes. She turned and ran, glancing back over her shoulder to see Kasper readying himself. Reaching the horses, she fumbled with the reins, her hands shaking with fear as she tried to loosen them from the tree they were tied to. She heard Kasper's voice behind her and she turned to look. The man had dropped his hood to reveal a mangled face, freshly burnt and scarred, what was left of his mouth twisted into a cruel smile.

"Matthias," said Kasper, "I thought you were dead."

A thin voice replied, more of a hiss than words, "Never assume anything."

His eyes looked past Kasper to Emelda, their eyes met, the same eyes that had shaken her to her to her very soul deep in the marshes. There was something so evil in his eyes that Emelda couldn't tear her gaze away from them.

Kasper let out a terrifying roar and charged at the disfigured man, the full force of his rage and fury bearing down on him. Matthias didn't flinch - instead he threw his cloak back and produced his own sword, long and glinting in the sun. There was a deafening clash as the blades met with equal force. Emelda could not take her eyes off them as they tussled back and forth, an evenly matched pair, neither of them giving up ground. It was as if they were performing a deadly dance, they moved so quickly, the sun flashing off their swords. Yet for a split-second Kasper faltered, his arm still weak from Indira's blade. Although he corrected his step in the blink of an eye, Matthias noticed and barrelled into him, using the hilt of his sword to smash against his shoulder. Kasper's swords flew from his hands and landed with a thud some distance away.

"No!" cried Emelda.

Matthias looked up at her and a frightening look came over his face. He took advantage of Kasper's lapse and pounded the hilt of his sword into the side of his head. Kasper dropped to the ground, his head spinning as he fought to stay conscious. He attempted to get up, but Matthias was quickly upon him, forcing him back down with his foot on his head.

He let out a cruel laugh. "So this is your dear Princess, I believe we have met before, these beautiful burns are your handiwork," he cackled, then he bent down to speak to Kasper, "I told you I'd kill her and you'd get to watch."

He pushed his own blade down through Kasper's jacket, pinning him to the ground. He smiled as Kasper grabbed the blade, crying out in pain.

"Run," shouted Kasper, "run, Emelda, run!"

Kasper pulled desperately at the blade. Blood dripped down his arm as he struggled, the sight of Matthias taking one of his own katana and advancing on Emelda driving him through the pain. There was no longer time for her to run, she hadn't gone when he had first spotted Matthias and now there was no hope of her out-running him. He knew that but still he cried out to her. If he didn't get to her then she was dead and all the hopes of St. Dores along with her. He couldn't bear to lose her again; the thought was more painful than the blade pinning him to the ground and slicing deep into his hand.

Emelda's heart raced, she knew Matthias would simply cut her down as she fled. She could feel the sweat gathering on her face and body, her breathing was fast and panicked. Adrenaline flooded her body, making her tremble. Her last protector lay trapped by his own blade, her own death approaching her with a terrible grin on its face. She would be dead before she could reach Kasper. Tears welled up in her eyes at her hopeless situation and her vision clouded.

'No,' she thought, 'I have not come all this way just to die.'

With a speed she didn't know she had she pulled her sword from its sheath and countered Matthias' attack. It was as if she was watching herself from outside her own body as she swung at him, pushing him back. Matthias, caught off guard, stumbled back, a surprised look on his face, but it was only for a moment.

"Oh, I do like a woman with a bit of fight in her," he grinned.

He launched himself towards her, a crazed look on his mutilated face. Emelda reacted, swinging her sword to meet his. But his strength was immense and he pushed her down, leaning over her like some monstrous beast. He pushed her hard and she hit the ground, dropping her sword. He bent down and placed his foot heavily on her chest, crushing the breath out of her lungs. She struggled under the weight, trying to push his boot off. He bent down, his face close to hers and tore the scarf from her face. She stopped struggling, her fingers reaching for the small blade on her belt.

"That's a good girl, lie still while I kill you," he whispered to her.

He drew closer still until she could feel his hot, sour breath on her neck and the wet sound of his lips, then his tongue ran up her neck to her ear lobe and she took her chance. Suddenly he drew back, a startled look came over his face and he toppled back, dropping his sword. Emelda's blade protruded from his thigh, a stream of blood pouring out. As he bent to pull it out, he made a sickening, gurgling sound and as he straightened up Emelda saw the tip of a sword jutting out of his chest. He grabbed the blade, before dropped to his knees and landing face first on the ground. Behind him stood Kasper, breathing heavily and clutching his bloody hand to his shoulder, his face wrought with pain and relief. Emelda scrambled to her feet and dashed over to him, but he shrugged her away.

"We need to keep moving," he said through gritted teeth.

"But your shoulder, your hand," she reached for him but he moved away from her touch.

"It doesn't matter," he cut across her.

He walked towards the horses and gathered up the reins. Silently she took them from him but did not climb on.

"Get on," he ordered.

"Let me dress your shoulder and take a look at your hand first."

"We don't have time."

"Enough," she said loudly and she tore the hem of her dress, her heart breaking a little at the piece of beautiful fabric in her hand.

Roles reversed, Emelda took Kasper's hand and led him to a dry patch of grass away from Matthias' bleeding corpse, where he reluctantly sat down and let her undo his shirt and pull back the collar. Her fingers were soft and gentle and he closed his eyes as she cleaned the wound. He was memorising the feel of her fingers on his skin, knowing full well it would be the last time. She looked at his face, it was so still, so sad, she wondered what he was thinking. He opened his eyes and she quickly turned back to the job at hand, tying the fabric tightly over the wound. She pulled his shirt back and did it up again before tending to his hand in the same manner, then fashioned a sling with yet more of her treasured dress. Quietly she got up and climbed onto her horse.

He opened his eyes, disappointed not to see her face so close to his, and stood up, heading for Matthias' body. For a moment he searched the corpse until he spotted Matthias' ring. His head pounded as he reached down and pulled it off his finger. It had the same blue glow that his little piece of dried willow bark did. Kasper was certain that now Matthias was without the ring, this would be the last time he would have to kill him.

"You could have used the willow," Kasper told her.

"I didn't think, it happened so fast, I'm sorry."

There was a lump in Emelda's throat as she watched Kasper grimace in pain as he heaved himself onto his horse; she longed to reach out to him but his hard eyes told her no. Maybe if she had remembered what power she had in the little bud around her neck this could have all been avoided. There was already a deep bruise forming on his face and a thin cut had oozed a trickle of now-dried blood down the side of his face. She knew she should have cleaned that too, but she wasn't able to bring herself to touch his face and it was too late now.

They rode in slow, agonizing silence, not stopping even when darkness fell. Kasper would stop regularly, turning his head as he listened for a moment before carrying on. Emelda watched the colour drain from his face as the blood continued to seep from the wound. He struggled to hold the reins and keep pressure on his shoulder.

As the next day dawned a cold morning light bathed the two riders in an ethereal glow, revealing Kasper's slumped form swaying unsteadily in the saddle. He had tied the reins around his waist and was grasping the saddle with the hand of his good arm. Emelda pulled her horse in close and called out to him, reaching for his reins.

"Kasper," she said yanking his horse closer to hers.

He looked up at her glassy-eyed and squinted at her as if he didn't recognise her. Then he shook his head and pulled the reins out of her hand.

"I'm ok," he muttered.

"No, you are not, you've lost a lot of blood and that knock to the head must have done more damage than I thought," she argued with him, "we need to stop, you need to rest."

"No," he said angrily, "we've got this far, we can't stop now."

She pushed her horse on crossly, widening the gap between them. She knew she shouldn't leave his side but his stubborn attitude angered her; he was going to die trying to get her to the encampment. She could still hear Kasper's horse trotting along behind her so she carried on a little way ahead, the scraggy line of trees, which signified the start of the Southern Woods, growing steadily taller. Encouraged, she pushed harder until she could see thin lines of smoke rising above the tree tops. She was turning to point them out to Kasper when she heard a groan and saw Kasper sliding from his horse. Immediately she reined her horse in hard and spurred it on, reaching him just as he lost his balance and fell. She caught him with one hand, barely keeping her seat in the saddle under his weight and pushed him back onto his horse, then she grabbed his reins and

189

brought both horses to a stop. She tied the reins together and clambered onto Kasper's horse behind him, reaching round him for his reins.

"Hold on, we're nearly there," she whispered in his ear, "just hold on, I will get you home."

She could just about see around him as he slumped against her and she kicked the horse into a gallop. He was heavy on her arms but she ignored the numbing ache and pressed on, her horse galloping and sweating alongside them.

She rode for what seemed like an eternity before they reached the edge of the wood where Emelda stopped, unsure of what to do next. She gazed up at the great withered trees, bleak and dying like everything else in her kingdom. What now? She had made it this far - her army was waiting for her somewhere within those trees but she had no way of knowing where or how to get to them. There was a noise to her right and she drew her sword, the horse moving anxiously beneath her and took a deep breath.

Three soldiers carrying shields with the royal crest emerged cautiously from the trees, swords raised ready for an attack. The moment they laid eyes on Kasper clutched to her chest, she saw the amazement in their faces and they dropped to their knees, heads bowed low. Overcome with relief she let her arm drop limply to her side, her sword suddenly a dead weight in her hand.

"Quick," she called out to them, "he needs help."

They scrambled to their feet and dashed over to where she still sat upon her horse, cradling Kasper against her chest. Their roles had been reversed, she was protecting him now and she would do so at all costs. The men quickly lifted Kasper from the horse and two of them carried him off into the woods. Emelda watched them go, her heart in her mouth, she closed her eyes and looked down at the soldier who was still beside her. She felt tired, so very tired, and now that she knew Kasper was going to get the help he needed, all the emotions and pain she had been ignoring flooded her body and she felt herself crumble.

"Your Majesty, let's get you home," said the remaining soldier, and he took hold of the horse's bridle and led the Princess proudly into the woods.

Chapter 13

Kasper had felt hands lifting him away from Emelda, tearing him from her warmth. He had tried to call out to her, to hold onto her but his body had refused to obey him. He had watched through a disorientating blur as she had gotten smaller and smaller, her lone figure astride her horse. How much a Queen she was already, he had thought, before he finally succumbed to his injuries and the darkness swallowed her up. She was there in the darkness as well; her sweet, laughing voice spoke to him, whispering all the things he wanted to hear, all the things he knew he would never hear from her lips, and he let himself be lulled into oblivion, this reality more alluring than the one he had left behind.

As Emelda was led on horseback through the thick woods, the trees seemed to tug and pull at her hair and clothes but the soldier in front seemed unaffected by the clawing branches. She tried to ignore them, gazing ahead, trying to catch a glimpse of the soldiers carrying Kasper, but she could see nothing but spindly trees. Yet as she strained to see she started to notice leaf buds sprouting on the barren branches, some even unfurling into sweet green leaves. Up ahead the trees were bare yet as she spun in her saddle to look over her shoulder, she could see that the trees that had reached out to her, that had touched her were starting to come back to life. Behind her was a trail of green that left her in awe.

"The trees," she murmured.

"They know who you are, Your Majesty," said the soldier, he looked up at her briefly before casting his eyes back towards his path through the wood, "they sense the presence of the Willow, of life renewed."

Emelda sat back in her saddle, allowing the trees to touch her, no longer feeling that they were pulling at her but instead caressing her. She closed her eyes, swaying gently with the steps of her horse; she thought of Kasper and prayed she had gotten him here in time. When she opened her eyes they had come to a stop in front of a row of thin trees, through which she could make out people moving around.

"Excuse me, Your Majesty, but the encampment is on the other side of these trees," the soldier told her, "are you ready, Princess?"

Emelda reached up and felt her hair; most of it had escaped its trappings and she carefully released the rest, letting it flow down her back in a torrent of fiery red waves. Then she reached into her bag and pulled out the little box that Kasper had given her. She opened it, took out the hair pin and admired it briefly before twisting a little of the hair at one side of her face back behind her ear and fixing it with the pin. Now she had a little of him with her she could face the unknown; the weight of it in her hair quelled her nervous heart as she ran her hands over her face. She could feel the dirt and blood encrusted on her face - there was no way she could enter the encampment looking like this.

"Do you have some water, sir?" she asked.

"Only what is in my flask, Your Majesty," the soldier said, reaching to his belt and handing her a small hip flask of water.

She was about to pour some into her hands when she noticed they, too, were equally as dirty, she would only smear her face with more grime. She tore at the hem of her dress again, her heart breaking a little more at the destruction of Kasper's beautiful gift to her, and handed it to the bewildered looking soldier.

"Please clean my face," she instructed, climbing down from her horse so that they stood eye to eye.

The soldier passed the reins to her and took the water; with careful hands, he gently wiped the dirt from her skin. He washed away the mask of filth that she was hidden behind, leaving her fresh-faced and exposed. As she climbed back onto her horse she took a deep breath, the reality of the situation sinking in. Just beyond those trees was an army of men and women waiting for her, knowing that she would bring them freedom and new life; all their hopes were pinned on her. Such expectancy, such responsibility that for a moment she wanted to turn and run again, but then she thought of Kasper and of Christian. She held the reins tightly, her hands trembling a little; she looked down at them and berated herself for being nervous, for ever having contemplated leaving. Good men had died for her and after all that she had been through this was the easy bit, these people wanted her, longed for her, needed her.

"I'm ready," she said in a voice louder than she had intended.

The soldier nodded and headed for a gap in the trees large enough for her and her horse to pass through. Before her lay a large clearing covered with a sea of tents. She could hear the clang of hammers on metal, smell the blacksmiths' fires and the horses. She gazed around at the men and women scattered everywhere, some dashing back and forth, others cooking over large, roaring fires, young boys turning large spits of crackling meat. Some sat around talking, comparing weapons or sparring. At first no one noticed her, just another soldier, another horse, and then one of the children tripped in front of her horse, dropping his bucket of water. It splashed up her horse's legs and snaked through the withered, well-trodden grass. The young boy cowered before her, expecting a beating but when it didn't come he dared to look up at her. She had dismounted and stood before him holding out the bucket to him, the sun crowning her in light and a gentle smile on her face. The boy took one look at her and dropped to his knees, pressing his face to the ground. By this time others had stopped what they were doing and were staring.

A strange hush fell over the encampment as Emelda glanced around; she could see the surprise and amazement on people's faces and it took a moment for those nearest to realise what they were witnessing, but before long they, too, had dropped to their knees. Others sensing something was happening began to crowd around her, but when they saw her face, men and women on their knees before a Princess, they too fell to the ground, heads bowed. It was as if a wave of honour was washing over the camp - as far as she could see there was nothing but bowed heads.

"Lead the way, Sir," she said taking the reins from the soldier and urging him on.

They walked slowly and steadily through the crowds, faces glancing up at her in awe, as if they couldn't believe what they were seeing. She had actually come, she was really here, freedom was tangible, they could smell it in the air like a sweet aroma. She could hear a buzz following her as those she passed got up from their knees and began talking excitedly amongst themselves. Desperately hunting for any sign of Kasper, Emelda's eye was drawn to a large tent in the middle of the encampment adorned with her royal crest, the lion and the sun, and her guide was leading her straight towards it. Next to it was a second, slightly smaller tent, which too was adorned with a crest, but not one she immediately recognised. An elegant white stag stood proudly in the centre of a wreath of oak leaves, its antlers flashing with brilliant gold thread. The white stag, mighty and beautiful - she immediately thought of Christian and her heart wrenched inside her chest. This must be his brother's tent, Eric Grey, the rightful son, but not the worthiest. She blinked back tears and pushed on, fixing her eyes on the tent ahead. As they approached the tent the soldier gave a short whistle and a boy came running out of the crowd and led the horse away.

"Let me announce you, Your Majesty, the last of your father's men await you inside," the soldier told her.

She heard the voices inside go silent as the solider cleared his throat and announced her arrival. She glanced over her shoulder at the crowd that had amassed behind her, and that was when she noticed the grass where she had walked was alive and green. Before she had a chance to look closely at the ground the door of the tent was thrown back by two men dressed in royal colours and she entered to face her destiny.

Kasper lay in darkness; he felt cold but at least the pain was gone. He couldn't see or feel anything and he strained to hear his Princess's voice that was once so clear. Little did he know that, as insurance, Matthias had laced his blade with a strong poison, which now coursed its way through Kasper's weakened body, pulling him down into oblivion.

Emelda entered the tent, unsure of what to expect. She was greeted by twenty men on their knees; most

196

were older in years but some were still young and vibrant. The thinkers and the fighters she thought to herself, as they slowly rose to their feet. She took a few steps towards them and curtseyed slightly, very aware of her dishevelled state.

"Your Majesty," said the oldest man, his greying hair still thick upon his head, "you do not know the joy we feel at your arrival."

She gazed around the room at the serious faces that stared back at her and wondered where the joy was. She couldn't feel it in here; it had been left outside wafting through the air. She hoped it reached Kasper wherever he was. She nodded her head at the man.

"Let us introduce ourselves," he said kindly, "My name is Lord Wolf, Jonathan Wolf. We are the King's Guard, old and new alike."

She slowly made her way along the line of men, each taking her hand and kissing it respectfully. She thought of Christian, how he should have been among them, pressing her hand to his sweet lips, and smiled to herself; he would have called these men uptight, unappreciative of beauty. The names and faces flowed over her in a wave of sounds that meant nothing to her, as hard as she tried to focus on them, to log them in her mind. By the time she came to the last man, tall and sharp-faced, she couldn't remember a single name. Lord Wolf approached her again.

"Your Majesty, you must be exhausted and we will leave you to wash and rest, but first I must know what of those we sent to escort you here?" he asked her, concern in his dark eyes.

Emelda took a deep breath, looking around the room at the expectant faces, "It is a long story, kind sir, but I will tell you in short. Dear Christian was killed at the hand of Indira who was a traitor, a vicious snake in the grass hidden amongst you. She in turn was felled by Kasper, who now is being tended to somewhere in this encampment. He suffered greatly at the hand of Matthias, sent by the Rebel King to kill me and take the Willow."

As she spoke she noticed the sharp-faced man shift a little, his eyes flickering back and forth towards the door. As she finished speaking there was an outbreak of noise as the men exclaimed their grief and horror at her brief outline of events. Out of the corner of her eye she saw the sharp-faced man edge towards the door. He pulled it back and she saw a fleeting glimpse of a black wing.

"You!" she called out to him authoritatively, taking herself by surprise, and a hush fell over the men.

Emelda strode over to him and he quickly dropped the tent door. She bent down and picked up a sleek, black feather that had drifted gently to the floor. She held it up for them all to see.

"Explain this!" she said.

The man looked amused and laughed softly, "It is but a feather, Your Majesty."

"The last time I saw the raven this feather comes from I was in the presence of an assassin, so I ask you again, explain this?"

With quick movements, he pulled out a short sword and thrust it at her heart. Emelda braced herself but the burning pain never came. Instead the man dropped to his knees, blood spurting from between his lips. Lord Wolf stood between her and the man, his sword still raised in his hand, blood running down the blade. He turned to the rest of the men and gave them a fierce look.

"If anyone else has designs on the Princess's life I suggest you show yourself now so that I can kill you cleanly in private rather than hanging you in front of the whole army as an example of what we do to traitors!" he said in a low, menacing voice.

There was nothing but silence in response to his challenge. Emelda looked around the room; all the men met her eye then bowed their heads in allegiance to her. There was some movement at the door and one of the guards peered out to speak to whoever was outside. He soon came up to Lord Wolf and murmured something to him.

"His Majesty, Prince Eric, wishes to make your acquaintance, Princess," he told her as the guard waited dutifully at Wolf's side for her response.

"I am not ready to meet him, I need to wash and change my clothes. And I must ask after Kasper; he was not in a good way when your men took him away," she replied.

"Of course, Your Majesty," said Lord Wolf, ushering the guard away, "please ready yourself and I personally will find out what has become of Lord Kasper."

"Lord..."Emelda murmured under her breath.

Lord Wolf clapped his hands and the men made their way out to be replaced by a selection of women. She gazed around the spacious tent, her eyes falling on the vast table in the centre, covered with maps and battle plans. Apart from the table the main compartment was relatively empty, save for a few chairs and chests. She was ushered into a smaller compartment off the back of the tent; here she found a bed, a large metal bath, shelves of books and a wardrobe packed with beautiful dresses all made for her. Several women began filling the bathtub with buckets of water, whilst others started undressing her, all of them heads bowed, none of them daring to meet her eye. She was helped into the bath and washed by one of the women rather publicly. Although the heat of the water felt good on her tired body she was acutely aware of the number of women still in the room who had all now seen her naked.

She thought of Kasper. She wanted to be near him now, to find out how he was, to see him again.

"Enough," she murmured as one of the women poured more water down her back.

"Pardon, your Majesty?" the woman responded.

"Enough, I said." Emelda angrily climbed out of the bath.

The women clambered to help her but she pushed them away, getting out herself and standing naked in the middle of the room. A woman approached her with a towel and attempted to dry her but Emelda snatched it away from her.

"I am a Princess, not a child," she said crossly.

The women quickly backed away but did not leave the room. Instead they stood at the edge of the room, eyes staring down at the floor. Emelda dried herself whilst she looked around at them all.

"You," she said, pointing at a woman of a similar age to herself with rich dark hair. She looked up with eyes of deep earth.

"Your Highness?" she asked nervously.

"The others can go; I only need one woman to help me," she said dismissing the rest of the women who obediently left, curtseying as they went.

"Come here," said Emelda, her voice softer, kinder, "What is your name?"

"Jena, Your Majesty," she replied, her eyes still on the floor.

"Please look at me when you speak to me, I am woman just like you," she said, lifting Jena's chin with one hand.

The girl looked up at her nervously. Emelda felt she could have drowned in the deep darkness of her eyes, there was a distinct sadness in them. She was not sure what had drawn her to Jena, but she was pleased with her choice.

"Please choose me a dress, Jena, I am feeling a little lost," said Emelda with kindness in her voice.

"Yes, Your Majesty."

Jena scuttled off towards the wardrobe and quietly leafed through the dresses. Emelda watched as her hands paused over the more extravagant dresses before settling on something more conservative and simple. Emelda was impressed with Jena's choice, an elegant gown made of pale blue like the cloudless sky, trimmed with cream the colour of clouds. It was exactly what Emelda herself would have chosen, reserved and dignified. Standing naked in the middle of the room she waited for Jena to dress her, her skin prickling a little with the cold but she ignored it. She could think of nothing else but finding out how Kasper was, and at every sound outside her tent she pricked up her ears, turning her head towards the door in hope of news of him. Jena carefully led her towards a dressing table. Gazing at herself in the mirror Emelda let Jena brush her damp hair, twisting it up into knots on her head and pinning it there. She handed Jena the hairpin that Kasper had given her and she arranged it so that it was on show, shining brightly on top of her crown of amber hair.

Finally, Jena stepped away from the Princess and curtseyed low, "I am finished, Your Majesty, can I do anything else for you?"

"No, thank you, Jena, please leave me but don't go too far away. I would like to have you near if I need you," she replied.

"Of course, Your Majesty, I will be in the servants' tents."

Jena curtseyed again and hurried off, as if she was desperate to escape her Princess's presence. Left alone in the tent, Emelda sat in front of the mirror and stared at her reflection. It stared back at her, her eyes unseeing and unfocused. Tears gathered in the corners of her eyes and she buried her head in her hands, letting the tears fall. She felt as if she needed to cry all her tears now, to get them all out before she became Queen, before she had to be regal and dignified. There was a loud cough outside her door and a man's voice called out to her.

"Your Majesty," called Lord Wolf, "I have located Lord Kasper, would you like me to take you to him?"

Emelda jumped to her feet and quickly wiped her face, glancing in the mirror to see if it was obvious she had been crying; the tears had already dried on her face, the glassiness gone from her eyes. She reached for her ragged old cloak and fumbled inside it for the willow bud before stuffing it between her breasts. She dashed across the room and flung back the tent door. Lord Wolf quickly bowed, surprised at her sudden appearance.

"Please," she begged him, "As fast as you can."

Lord Wolf led her out of the tent into the encampment. As they passed, people stopped what they were doing and bowed to her; it made Emelda feel a little awkward but she knew she had to get used to it. She had a sudden thought that hadn't crossed her mind before - she had been so focused on getting there and remembering who she was that she had never thought about dying out on the battlefield. She had always thought that once she had made it to the encampment she would be safe - her mind hadn't drifted much beyond that. She had assumed Kasper and Christian would be there to guide her. Her heart sinking a little she looked over at Lord Wolf; his aged face was lined with worry, it did not bode well. After a short walk they arrived at a large tent, open at the sides, row upon row of beds filling the ground beneath its canvas roof.

"This way, Your Majesty," said Wolf, beckoning her to follow him.

She hurried after him into a small private room at the back of the infirmary tent. There he was, lying still on a bed, the blankets pulled up to his bare chest. Emelda rushed over to him, placing her hand gingerly on his cheek as if he would wake at her slightest touch. But Kasper didn't stir, his skin cold and clammy to the touch. It felt as if death had a hold on him, the atmosphere in the room heavy and still, and she felt as if she was struggling to breathe. His wound had been cleaned and bound and his face washed. His chest rose and fell gently but slowly, as if he was just taking enough air to keep himself on this plane of existence.

"Kasper," murmured Emelda.

Her fingers traced the red tattoo on his arm, all the way down to his fingertips, the hands that had held her just that once, now cold and lifeless. She reached up and brushed a stray hair from his face, then bent down and placed the briefest of kisses upon his forehead. She pulled away, hoping that it would be like all the fairy tales she had seen, the power of true love's kiss rekindling a fading heart, but he lay there as motionless as before.

She felt a hand on her shoulder and she turned to see Lord Wolf looking down at her sadly.

"The physician believes there must have been poison on the blade; a wound such as the one he sustained should not have brought him so close to death," he told her.

"Poison?"

"Yes, they have done all they can for him but they are not sure what is keeping him alive still, any other man would be dead by now."

Emelda looked back down at Kasper and stroked his face one more time.

"I could use the willow," said Emelda, but Lord Wolf stopped her.

"Your Majesty, it is not an unlimited resource, not yet, he would not want you to waste it on him. I'm sorry but we must go back to your tent, there is much we need to organise," said Lord Wolf, "we are hoping to attack at dawn. We have waited so long and the men are eager to get the battle underway."

"Very well," said Emelda, tearing her eyes away from Kasper, "but I am to be informed if there is any change in his condition."

"I will inform the nurses; you will be the first to know, Princess."

She nodded and took one last lingering look at Kasper before bowing out of the tent door that Wolf held open for her. As they walked back across the encampment to the main tent, Emelda felt everyone's eyes watching her expectantly and she tried to look confident as she walked next to Wolf but inside she was shaking. Lord Wolf paused at the entrance to the tent and turned to speak to her.

"Whatever feelings you may have for Lord Kasper you should lay to rest, Your Majesty, you have a duty to perform," he told her, kindly but authoritatively.

"I am well aware of my duty, Sir," she replied holding her head up and looking him in the eye.

"I have called for Prince Eric, he will be here shortly. We will allow you some time to be acquainted and then we must begin organising ourselves for war."

"Very well."

The last thing Emelda wanted to do was meet Prince Eric, although she was sure he was a gentleman. Maybe he was even as nervous as her at the prospect of an arranged marriage, but her heart only wanted Kasper no matter what her head said. Then there was Christian, how was she supposed to tell Prince Eric his brother was dead? She pushed past Wolf into the tent and he followed her.

"Does he know about Christian?" asked Emelda quietly.

"He has been informed, you do not need to worry about that now."

Emelda nodded but it did not make her feel any easier.

"Send for Jena, please, Lord Wolf," she ordered him and he bowed before dipping out of the tent.

The girl appeared a moment later, head bowed in a curtsey, "Your Majesty."

"I wish to have you with me when Prince Eric comes, another woman in the midst of so many men." Emelda saw Jena's eyes widen a little before she composed herself and smiled gently at her.

"Of course, Your Majesty," she replied.

Emelda reached out for her hand and she looked surprised, but did not pull away.

"You know this game better than me at the moment; I'm a little out of practise, shall we say. Prompt me if I make an error, be my guardian angel, will you?" she asked Jena.

Jena smiled up at her, there was still sadness behind her smile, a sadness that Emelda knew all too well, of broken hearts and forbidden love, but she nodded and placed her hand on top of Emelda's.

"Of course, Your Majesty, anything you need."

There was a loud cough from outside the tent and Jena jumped into position just behind Emelda, yet she did not let go of her hand. Emelda clasped her little hand tightly in her own and took a deep breath, trying to push the unhappiness out of her own eyes.

"Come," she called out.

Lord Wolf entered, followed by a tall man dressed in a soft grey military-looking uniform, a fancy sword hanging at his side, that swayed gently as he walked.

"Your Majesty, may I introduce His Royal Highness, Prince Eric Grey," announced Wolf.

Prince Eric stepped forward and bowed, whilst Emelda curtseyed to him. He stepped a little closer and took her hand in his, placing a soft kiss upon the back of it.

"I am honoured to finally meet you, Your Majesty, you are more beautiful than I could have imagined," he spoke softly to her, his voice soothing and calm; if he was sad about his brother's death he hid it well.

He was as handsome as Christian had said, if not more so and Emelda was a little breathless for a moment. His hair was indeed like silver and it seemed to shine even though there was no natural light inside the tent; his blue-grey eyes traced the features of her face in a pleasing way. As he looked up from her hand to her face he caught sight of Jena behind her and Emelda saw recognition followed by surprise cross his angelic face, but he quickly hid it, a picture of serenity and beauty once more. Emelda felt Jena squeeze her hand gently and shuffle a little behind her. Emelda smiled knowingly.

"Shall we take a little walk, Prince Eric? Get to know each other before the horrid business of war starts," she asked him, looping her arm through his, "You may wait for us here Jena, Lord Wolf."

Both parties opened their mouths as if they wanted to speak and Emelda did not miss the longing in Jena's eyes.

"I would enjoy that very much, your Majesty, shall we?" he replied, pulling back the tent door so that she did not have to duck her head to get out. He glanced tentatively back at the young woman they had left behind before disappearing with Emelda.

They strode arm in arm for some time as Prince Eric gave her a tour of the encampment, his lovely voice explaining everything in fascinating detail, and for some time Emelda was captivated. A life with him would have been sweet and pleasurable; she would have been happy to wake up to his face every morning had her heart not belonged to someone else, and if she was not mistaken his, too, was taken. Every time she looked up at him she wished he was Kasper; she felt as if she was betraying both Eric and Kasper, cheating both them and herself into unhappiness. They finally reached a quiet corner of the encampment where they could just see her old home, her father's castle, through the dense forest. It wasn't as she remembered it, white and beautiful, with tall bastions topped by flags showing the lion and the sun flying proudly at each corner of the curtain wall.

Now the castle was blackened with fire damage, crumbling in places and swarming with soldiers clad in black armour, like a plague of shiny dark beetles. Emelda let go of Prince Eric's arm and gazed at the castle, once so full of happy memories, memories of her mother and her father, of Luca, of Kasper and childish innocence. Her heart beat hard in her chest as she turned to face the Prince, who was watching her in silence. She looked at him nervously, unsure how to begin.

"Your Majesty? Are you ok?" he asked her, taking her hand in his as she placed her hand on top of his and looked up into his eyes.

"My heart belongs to another," she said quietly.

He did not let go of her hands but she did detect a little relief on his face.

"And I believe yours does too," she ventured.

He gently removed his hands from hers and ran one through his hair, turned away and looked out towards the forsaken castle. The afternoon sun bathed him in a hazy light, making him seem all the more angelic.

"What makes you say that?" he finally said, regaining his composure.

"I saw it in your eyes and hers, I saw the same sadness I see in myself," Emelda replied.

He shook his head, his hand still in his hair; it came slowly down to his chin and he rubbed it thoughtfully.

"You can tell that much from someone's eyes?" he asked her, and she nodded, "I guess if we are to be married we should start our life together in honesty."

He paused.

"Yes, I am in love with another, I am totally lost, I don't know what to do with myself," he admitted, "I came here prepared to fall in love with you and while I waited my heart was stolen by another. They say love can be a whirlwind."

Emelda saw the heartbreak on his face, torn between love and duty. Ultimately they would have to forsake their lovers and marry to unite the two kingdoms; this was not a fairy tale.

"I understand with all my soul. A life with you would be most pleasant I am sure but I could never truly give you my heart as hard as I would try, it will always belong to another," she confided in him.

"But we must marry for the sake of the kingdoms, for unity and prosperity, Princess,"

"No, we don't have to," she said boldly, "I am to be Queen, I have no father pushing me into marriage, I can and I will make my own decisions. I will not force you to love me. We can make an alliance without a marriage bed if you are willing?"

He nodded, surprised at her boldness.

"We are a new generation, old blood renewed, change is good, believe me. All it takes is for the two of us to be absolute, to be united in our decision not to be united," she smiled at him, feeling empowered.

Her fire was contagious and Prince Eric swept her into his arms, placing a tender kiss on her surprised lips, quite forgetting himself. Emelda broke free, taken aback but smiling.

"Forgive me," he murmured, "I just wanted to know what such courage tasted like."

They walked back to the tent, deciding not to cause anymore chaos by announcing their broken engagement. Jena was nowhere to be seen when they entered the tent but Lord Wolf had been joined by the rest of the King's Guard and they were poring over the battle plans spread across the table. They all looked up when they entered and Emelda saw Eric's eyes wander the room in hope of seeing Jena; there was a fleeting look of disappointment when she was not there.

Emelda touched his arm gently and leaned in close to him so only he could hear her, "I will send her to you when they are gone."

He smiled and touched her hand.

"Come now, there will be time for the whisperings of sweet nothings once the war is won," said a large man with a chest like a barrel, "Maximus Bigge, Your Majesty, at your service."

Emelda and Eric instantly separated themselves from each other and took their positions at either end of the table. The discussions went on and on as dusk began to fall, and Emelda stifled a quiet yawn. None of this meant much to her; it was a man's game, her role was simple: ride up and down in front of her army as they waited for the signal to charge, declaiming some rousing speech to encourage them. She would show them the willow bud, then keep it safe, along with several specially selected men ordered to guard her with their lives. She would wear all the trappings of a warrior Queen but she would be waiting in relative safety for the fight to be over, for her castle to be stormed and the Rebel King defeated.

Her stomach turned when she was told that Kasper was supposed to be one of the men protecting her, but as he was indisposed Maximus would take his place. As the night drew in and servants carrying food and wine entered the tent, the discussions finally came to a close and Emelda was allowed to retire to her quarters attached to the main tent. She found Jena, sitting in an armchair, her eyes heavy with sleep. She quickly jumped up as Emelda entered, begging her forgiveness for her laziness, her eyes cast down towards the floor. Emelda reached for her chin and lifted it so that her eyes met her own. Then she took her hands in hers.

"Go to him, tonight he is all yours and every other should you want it," she grinned at Jena.

There was a moment of confusion in the girl's eyes before she realised what Emelda was saying to her. She stood before the Princess wide-eyed and unbelieving. The future Queen was telling her to go and be with her future King.

"Your Majesty, I don't understand," she stammered.

"Understand this, it is not my place to steal love from where it has already taken root," said Emelda softly.

"But the union, the kingdom..."

"We will find another way, we are all adults here, not children with hands to be held. Now go to him, he is waiting for you."

Jena nodded, kissing Emelda's hands over and over again, tears of joy running down her face. She was about to turn and leave when Emelda caught hold of her wrist.

"Tell no one of this yet - you must be sworn to secrecy until the battle in won and I am on the throne."

Jena nodded and Emelda wiped the tears from her face.

"I have an idea," she said, pulling her over to the wardrobe, "choose one and I will dress you."

"I can't, Your Majesty you have already been so kind to me, I am indebted to you," Jena replied, shaking her head, "You are a Princess and I am no one."

"Please, I insist, it's an order," smiled Emelda.

210

Hesitantly Jena stepped towards the wardrobe, her hand drifting gently over the soft fabric. She paused over one or two and then turned to Emelda.

"Would you choose for me, Your Majesty?" She asked.

Emelda nodded and pulled out a dress of deep red trimmed with gold. This was the one. Jena looked at it wide-eyed, unable to stop the smile spreading across her face. She kissed Emelda again and thanked her effusively, before Emelda began undressing her a little clumsily and helping her into the new dress. It fitted as beautifully as if it had been made for Jena, and with her dark hair flowing down her back she was sent off into the night, wrapped in her servant's cloak. Emelda watched her go with a mixture of joy and sorrow in her chest; at least their love would be fulfilled tonight. In the midst of all the talk of fighting something golden and new still bloomed. She undressed and climbed into bed, suddenly realising how tired she was. Her limbs felt heavy and stiff and she shivered as she pulled the covers up around her neck and wondered whether to blow out the little lamp that barely lit the room. After staring at it for a moment she decided to let it burn out on its own, feeling a little apprehensive of the darkness.

Emelda dreamt again that night, the same dream she always had, but this time she could see Kasper's face, young and handsome, a daring grin on it as he took her hand in his. Then he changed as the blood poured from his eyes, his nose, his mouth, except it was no longer Kasper. His hair had turned to auburn and his face was sharper, less refined. Emelda woke to the sound of shouting. Thinking it was her own she tried to close her mouth to stop the noise but it had no effect. It took a moment before she was awake enough to realise it was coming from outside. Someone was calling her name and it took her a moment to respond.

211

"Your Majesty!" cried Lord Wolf, as he burst into her tent. Hurriedly she pulled her sheets up to her chin.

"What is going on, sir?" she asked, a little angered at his rude entrance.

"Can you not smell it, Your Majesty? The encampment is on fire!"

It was then that Emelda could smell the fire on the wind, the deep stench of burning canvas and wood. In the lamplight Wolf's worried face had aged another ten years. Emelda grabbed her lamp and lit it from his, then he left the room to allow her to dress hurriedly, gathering up her hair pin and her sword.

"Come now, Princess we must get you to safety, hurry."

Holding her skirts and hairpin in one hand and her sword in the other she hurried after Lord Wolf. The sight outside her tent took her breath away and for a moment she was paralyzed with fear. The flames were everywhere, licking at every tent and every workshop. People ran to and fro throwing buckets of water on the burning buildings. The heat was intense and brutal and the smoke was thick. A rushing wind was carrying the flames further still, despite the villager's best efforts. They were losing the battle before they had even begun.

"Princess!"

Lord Wolf urgently tugged at Emelda, putting one arm around her shoulders and guiding her through the flames. As they ran Emelda could hear the wretched screams of men and women trapped inside their tents, as they burnt alive. Pushed on by Lord Wolf there was nothing she could do to help them, though she wanted to desperately. Wolf's arm around her was firm and unmoving, forcing her through the inferno and out into the clear night air to a clearing on the edge of the camp which the fire had not reached. Men and women were gathered there, looks of horror on all their faces. Some wailed and sobbed, reaching desperately out towards the flames, others craned over the heads of the crowd to see if their loved ones had escaped. Others sat on the ground, their heads in their hands, unable to watch all theirs hopes shattered.

Emelda stood still, unable to speak or move, watching the flames grow taller and taller, devouring everything that they touched. Then in a moment of clarity Kasper's face came to mind.

"No," she cried, turning to Lord Wolf, "Kasper, someone must save him!"

She made to dash into the flames but Lord Wolf held her fast. She struggled against him with all her might, thrashing and wailing to get free.

"Your Majesty there is nothing you can do, you must stay safe, you must stay alive," he insisted.

Finally Wolf loosened his grip and she dropped to the ground, exhausted and trembling. This was not how it was supposed to end, not in flames, not in clouds of smoke, and this was not how she was going to let it end. With all her strength, she pushed herself to her feet and ran back into the fire. Lord Wolf was not fast enough and she could hear him calling out to her as she ran, her bare feet pounding on the ground. She prayed he would not be stupid enough to follow her. As she paused, gazing around at the fiery scene she realised that she didn't know where she was going. Men were running past, trying to escape the flames, not noticing her in a desperate attempt to save their own lives. She shielded her face from the flames as they leapt towards and pushed on, a terrible realisation dawning on her that she would surely die here lost in this fiery maze. Then she heard her name and two shadows loomed towards her out of the smoke.

"Prince Eric," she coughed.

"What are you doing?" he cried over the roar of the fire. He had his arm around Jena who was coughing badly.

"Looking for the infirmary."

"There's no time, you need to get out before you are burnt alive." Prince Eric tried to get hold of her hand but she pulled away.

"I must get to him," she said.

"I understand, but not you, Princess. You must not die, not now. Take Jena, get out of here - I will go back," he pushed Jena gently towards Emelda and ran back into the flames.

"Eric," Jena called after him, "Eric!"

But he was gone, his tall frame swallowed by the smoke. He had trusted Emelda with his most precious possession and now she must trust him with hers. She turned and led Jena back the way she had come, but they made slow progress. Dodging the vigorous flames and falling debris, their lungs become more and more clogged with smoke. Emelda tore the sleeve off her dress and ripped it in two, covering her mouth with one piece and handing the other to Jena, before taking her by the hand and ushering her on.

As they emerged out of the smoke into the cold night air Emelda threw down the rag and breathed in deeply. She coughed hard, so much so that she thought she was going to be sick. She could taste the smoke in her mouth, bitter and nasty; it made her throat feel dry and sore, as if it was closing. Lord Wolf came running over to them and gathered them both under his arms; more of the King's Guard who had managed to get out joined him, practically carrying the two of them as far away from the flames as they could. Emelda felt herself go limp in the men's arms, her body worn out and beaten; she tried to fight them but she couldn't find the energy.

"Prince Eric, Kasper," she managed to cough, her voice hoarse.

"Get the Princess some water," called out one of the other men and almost immediately a man appeared with a flask of water.

214

They passed it to her and she drank from it greedily before passing it to Jena who didn't take it. She sat motionless, staring into the flames, her eyes wide in horror.

"Drink," said Emelda, pushing the flask towards her again. Jena seemed to snap out of her trance and finally took the water from Emelda's outstretched hand.

She took a small sip before handing it back. Emelda encouraged her to drink more and slowly she took another mouthful. There was nothing that she could say to console her; she didn't know if they would see Kasper or Eric again and suddenly she felt selfish. She had promised Jena that she was not someone to steal love away but she had done just that, sending Eric back into the flames, when he could have been here with them now, his arm around Jena's shoulders, whispering gentle words of comfort in her ear and kissing her sooty face.

Emelda looked away from Jena's staring eyes and shuffled a little closer, putting her arm around her and pulling her towards her. She wanted to tell her how sorry she was, but the words would not come, maybe because her throat was so tight from the smoke or because her own apprehension and fear were choking her, holding her voice back. Instead they watched as the smoke rose into the blue-black sky, and waited in silence as those around them hurried back and forth with more water amidst all the panic. A little pool of serenity in the middle of the chaos, time seeming to stand still for the two women as they waited, their hearts almost bursting. Neither moved nor spoke, not daring to break the bubble of silence they had formed around themselves. If no one disturbed them then maybe the sorrow would not become real, would not drag them down into the depths of harrowing grief.

Eventually people stopped appearing out of the smoke although the fire raged on, making its way across the encampment. Lord Wolf approached the two women, unsure of what to say to them. All he knew was that people were starting to worry about the Princess and she needed to redeem a little of her royal countenance. He placed a hand on the Princess's shoulder and knelt down next to her.

"Your Majesty, you need to come with me, please," he said softly.

"No," she said shrugging his hand away, "not until Prince Eric returns."

"Princess, I think it unlikely that he has survived."

Emelda looked at him with anger in her eyes, "I have not given up hope and neither should you."

"But Your Majesty…" Wolf was interrupted by a cry from Jena.

Emelda turned away from Wolf and gazed in the direction that Jena was staring. Sure enough the tall figure of a man was slowly emerging from the flames. He was carrying the limp form of another man in his arms - his step was laboured and unsteady but he carried on, determined.

"Quick!" cried Emelda as loudly as she could, but her voice was still trapped in her throat.

Lord Wolf stood up and bellowed to his men as he himself dashed toward the fire, as finally Prince Eric emerged, carrying Kasper's lifeless body as if it were a most precious thing. Lord Wolf tried to take Kasper from him but he would not let him, allowing himself to be half carried out of the suffocating smoke. Coughing and spluttering they made their way over to Emelda and Jena who had gotten to their feet, their eyes wide in amazement. Emelda's heart was in her mouth as Eric laid Kasper at her feet. She mouthed 'thank you' to him as she immediately fell to Kasper's side, feeling for a pulse. Nothing. No pulse, no breath. She cried out and pounded the ground, her grief welling up inside her like a raging volcano. She felt hands on her shoulders trying to pull her away but she threw them off, thrashing around like a wild animal. She couldn't hear or see anything, it was all a blur except for Kasper's still, dead face. Then like a faint breeze there came a quiet voice in her ear and she fell still, straining to hear it.

"The willow, life renewed," came the sweet, gentle voice. Emelda looked round to see where the voice was coming from and her eyes met Jena's.

Jena was kneeling at her side her arm around her shoulders yet Emelda hadn't felt it until now. Eric stood over her protectively, watching them like a guardian angel making sure that no one else approached them.

"Your Majesty I beg you not to use it," urged Lord Wolf, but Emelda ignored him.

"Go on, Your Majesty," said Jena, her voice no more than a whisper.

"It's Emelda," she whispered in reply, pulling the little vial from between her breasts.

As she turned it over in her hands, it emitted a faint glow that seemed stronger than before. She looked up at Jena who looked back at her encouragingly.

"What now?" Emelda asked.

"I don't know, Your Majesty," she replied, shaking her head sadly.

Caught by an idea Emelda reached for her sword. She took the lid off the vial and carefully took the little twig and its bud out of the water it was stored in. Then she rubbed it against the sharp of her sword, taking a thin slither of the bark from the delicate twig. She ground it up between her teeth, then placed it back in the vial with the water, swirling it around so that liquid was speckled with bits of bark. Out of the corner of her eye she could see Prince Eric place a firm hand on Lord Wolf's chest, as she carefully lifted Kasper's head so that she could get the water into his mouth, and with her

217

thumb over the top of the vial she pushed it between his closed lips. She watched as, despite her best efforts, the water trickled back out of his mouth and onto the ground.

"Come on," she whispered, cradling his head to her chest, her tears falling onto his face.

In the darkness Kasper heard her voice, quiet at first and filled with such sorrow, but as he listened it got louder and louder. He tried to move towards it but he was still unable to move. Instead he let it wash over him, pulling him back from the brink of nothingness.

There was a moment of stillness, of great silence when Emelda though she had lost it all, when she wondered how she would go on, when she wondered if every moment of time without him would pass as slowly as this one. But as she cradled his head to her chest she felt a great surge run through Kasper's body which was emitting a brilliant blue light - he shook and trembled and she held on to him as tight as she could. Then it stopped and he took in a deep lungful of air before the light faded and he fell still again, his chest gently rising and falling in a steady, strong rhythm. Cautiously Emelda relinquished her grip on Kasper and looked down at his face, the grey pallor of his skin slowly ebbing away and the colour returning to his slightly parted lips. Tears fell like rain from her eyes and she didn't care who saw; she cried with joy, with relief, with sorrow at the devastation around her. Her tears ran off Kasper's face and onto the dry ground, washing the soot off his face until his skin was marbled with saltiness and dirt. As her tears fell so did Heaven's, great heavy drops of sweet cold rain that quenched the fires as if they were nothing but lit matches.

"Emelda," whispered Jena, who was still at her side, "let them take him now, he needs to get out of the rain, he will be ok."

Emelda looked up and saw that Lord Wolf and several of the King's Guard had now been allowed by Prince Eric to come a little closer. They were carrying a stretcher as well as more blankets and water for herself and the others. She nodded, and watched as they gently placed Kasper on the stretcher and carried him off to a hastily erected shelter. She stood up, letting the rain wash over her until she was cold and sodden, her hair plastered to her face, her clothes stuck to her skin. She closed her eyes and took a deep breath, inhaling the smell of damp earth and to her surprise she found herself laughing, a wide grin on her face. She turned her face skyward and opened her mouth, letting the rain fall on her tongue.

"Thank you," she whispered.

She felt someone at her side reach up and take hold of her hand. Opening her eyes she saw Prince Eric; he too was soaked to the skin but was smiling his radiant smile.

"Look at your Princess now, even her tears have the power to bring the rain to save us from the fire that was set to destroy us," he called out over the drum of the rain, "look up to the sky and feel the rain on your faces, then bow to her."

His words stirred movement in the awestruck crowd who had been watching Emelda the entire time; they automatically began falling to their knees, crying out their love of the Princess, their thanks and admiration. Emelda felt her heart brimming with joy as she gripped Eric's hand; she turned to him and returned his smile.

"Come, let's see what the fire has left us," she said, and hand in hand they turned and walked into the ruins of the encampment.

Chapter 14

After an initial scouting of the encampment it appeared that the damage was great. The fire had spread through most of it; although the forges and armouries on the eastern edge of the camp had survived mostly intact, the main tent, where Emelda had been staying, and the cookhouse, the infirmary and the supply tents had been lost, as well as most of the beds, blankets and many of the horses. All the sleeping quarters were gone and the smell of damp, burnt flesh hung in the air, stinging Emelda's nose. Lord Wolf and his men had done what they could to erect as many tents and shelters as possible, but although the driving rain had put out the fire, it had also caused everything to be soaked through. Emelda stood in the makeshift main tent in front of a large charred table, looking around at the tired yet determined faces of her men, the first light of dawn casting grey shadows over them all.

"I say we go now," said one of the men, who was named Edwards. He was young and feisty, there was fire in his eyes.

"We need to regroup, gather ourselves, find out what is left. We should wait," replied Wolf.

"No, we have the element of surprise, they will not be expecting us to attack after they set that fire, they will think us all dead!"

"You are young and reckless, we are not ready!" shouted Wolf, bashing the table. Shards of burnt wood fell to the ground covering it like blackened snow.

"We have been ready for weeks," shouted the young man.

Wolf was about to argue when Emelda cleared her throat loudly and held up her hands in a sign for quiet. Both men held their tongues as she nodded at them in recognition of their silence before speaking.

"The forges and the armouries survived, yes?" she asked calmly.

"Yes, Your Majesty, but..." Emelda held up her hand to silence Wolf and he fell quiet.

"Are the men ready to fight? Are they willing?" She directed her question at Edwards.

"Yes, I believe so, Your Majesty, just say the word," he was almost jumping at her words.

There was a loud cough from the tent door and a man peered in.

"Well?" asked Emelda.

"Lord Chen and Lord Aryan have arrived, Your Majesty, they requested your presence," he reported.

"That settles it then, I think we should attack, and soon; they will think us weakened but we will show the Rebel King that we are not. We may have to fight harder - we may have to sacrifice more but a change is coming, I can feel it, I know it in my heart. The Rebel King's days are numbered; it is time to put an end to his reign of terror and oppression. We will be free once more!" Emelda's voice grew with confidence as she spoke, the faces around the table hanging on her every word.

There was a moment in which Emelda held her breath, nervous about whether she had said the right thing, made the right decision, but suddenly the men erupted in cheers and cries. The fight had begun in their hearts, stirred by their Princess - now they had to take it onto the battlefield. All around her became a hive of activity as the men and women prepared for battle in the foggy, morning light.

Emelda emerged from the tent, her heart pounding hard in her chest, and was immediately confronted by Lord Chen and Lord Aryan. They stood proudly before their banners, their armies stretching out as far she could see amongst the tattered encampment.

"You have arrived at a time when we need you most, my heart is glad to see you Lord Chen, Lord Aryan," she said.

"We are honoured to take this opportunity to fight alongside you, Your Majesty, and to secure peace for both your lands and ours - too long have we been distant from each other," said Lord Aryan, his dark eyes sparkling.

"As are we, Your Majesty," said Lord Chen in a quiet voice, running his fingers over his goatee.

"We plan to attack immediately, my Lords. Please ready your men and join us on the battlefield. Please take anything you need from the encampment," she told them.

They nodded to her and turned to address their men. She waited for a moment, watching with admiration as Lord Aryan and Lord Chen rallied their armies for the attack.

Then she began making her way through the camp in her dirty, torn dress, her hair hanging loose down her back. She saw men being dressed in armour, swords being fitted, bowmen jamming their quivers full of arrows. She marvelled at the size of the bows the men wielded and size of the arms they used to fire the arrows.

She watched as the horses, too, were dressed in armour and adorned with her father's green and gold colours. It was a sight that made her chest swell with pride and she felt confident in her armies' skill and strength; she felt sure there was no way they could lose. They all wanted it so much, surely good always triumphed over evil? And she had experienced so much evil it must be time for good to pull through.

Emelda's thoughts and wanderings were interrupted as Jena appeared at her side.

"They are ready for you to dress, Your Majesty. The troops are gathering to move out and you need to be ready to give a speech before they go into battle."

Emelda nodded, she hadn't yet reached the quickly assembled infirmary, which she doubted was battle-ready. She hadn't seen Kasper, not since they rushed him away after the fire. Sadly, she followed Jena back to her makeshift tent. She stood arms out as Jena undressed her, peeling her damp clothes from her cool skin, and held up a dress that had been made for her to wear under her armour.

"I am to wear a dress under my battle gear, how will I move?" she asked Jena quizzically,

"Your Majesty..."

"Emelda."

"Emelda, you are not to fight, you must stay here safe."

"How can I do that when we need every man and woman we have? A single person may be enough to turn the tables, Jena."

"But..."

"No, fetch me some trousers and a shirt and give me that dress, I have an idea."

Obediently Jena handed Emelda the dress and disappeared out of the tent. Emelda took her knife and began to carefully unpick the seam that held the bodice to the skirts, then she removed the sleeves, trimming off the loose threads as she went. When Jena returned with a pair of narrow-legged trousers and a shirt Emelda was holding up the bodice of the dress, devoid of skirts and sleeves. She turned as she heard Jena enter and smiled at her.

"What do you think? It's a little untidy but no one will see under the breastplate," she said with a grin.

Jena helped Emelda with her clothes and armour, pinned her hair up and was arranging her precious hairpin in it when Lord Wolf called out from outside the tent.

"Your Majesty, the men are virtually ready, they await your face and your encouragement before they go into battle," he called to her.

"Come in, Lord Wolf," Emelda called back to him and he entered the tent.

"Your Majesty, that is not the outfit I was expecting to see you in," he said, a little surprised.

"How can I fight in a dress?" she asked him.

"You are not expected to fight, we can't risk your life out there."

"But what if we lose? What difference will it make then if I am dead or alive? You need all the swords you can get."

"No, Your Majesty, I will not allow it. It is my duty to protect you; Lord Kasper would say the same."

Emelda made to protest and then held her tongue. There was no point arguing with him, she would have to take the matter into her own hands.

"Let us go to the front, Princess, the men are waiting," said Lord Wolf, thinking he had won this argument.

Emelda and Jena followed him out of the tent before Emelda turned to Jena, and after kissing her on the forehead gave her a little shove back into the tent. Jena was about to argue but the fierce determination in the Princess's eyes made her bite her tongue. Instead she stood at the door of the tent watching the Princess and Lord Wolf disappear into the now eerily quiet encampment, prayers of victory and protection already on her lips. Emelda looked up at Wolf as they walked - he was a brave, courageous man and she knew he only had her best interests and those of her people at heart but she still felt anger towards him at his instant dismissal of her help in battle. She cleared her throat as they walked, clasping her hands together in front of her, unsure what to do with them.

"Lord Wolf," she said, "tell me about him, tell me about Lord Kasper. He never let on that he was more than a soldier."

Wolf looked down at her knowingly. He could see the desire in her eyes at the mention of Kasper's name; she did a poor job of hiding it. He felt her plight though, forced to marry another when your heart and body is longing for someone else. Time dulled the ache, but it never truly left. It wouldn't hurt to indulge her questions; she was already a prisoner to her love. Knowledge of her lover wouldn't make it and easier or harder for her to let him go.

"Lord Kasper's father was the King's right-hand man, they were best friends as well, as Lord and Master. The King bestowed land and gold on him and Lord Hart served him tirelessly, not as a member of the King's Guard but as his friend and ally. When Kasper's mother died Hart took it badly, and poured all his energy into his son, trying to make him into the best he could be, but Kasper rebelled against him, wanting to be wild and free. Wanting to do nothing but play in the castle grounds."

Emelda thought of the boy she had run through the fields with, gazing up at the clouds and laughing until her sides hurt. He had been so free. Life had been so simple.

"Their relationship suffered as Kasper grew. I remember the grey spreading through Hart's hair almost overnight, the lines appearing on his face. Then when the Rebel King started to menace us Hart refused to let Kasper fight, despite pushing him so hard to train. He didn't want to lose all he had left. So Kasper joined the King's Guard because he knew his father could do nothing to stop him. Lord Hart and Kasper were assigned to be your protectors, to watch over you and your hiding place until it was time for you to return Your Majesty, and that is how Lord Hart died, killed by the sword of Matthias Blake, the one man who got closer to you than any other assassin. Kasper became Lord of all his father had owned, but he's never had an interest in land or possessions."

As Lord Wolf finished his explanation there was a sadness in his eyes. The memory of his old friend still haunted him, but now Emelda knew where Kasper had come from and some of the things that had made him the man he was. Emelda didn't say anything, gazing ahead of her as the rows of men and women that waited for her grew steadily. She was thinking, remembering the boy she knew, the young man full of fire and passion; he had awoken things in her she knew she could never feel for anyone else, that she could never forget.

They reached the edge of the clearing where the encampment stopped and the trees began again. Here the trees had been thinned down so that the army would have a clear path through them to the open ground that surrounded the crumbling castle, yet could remain undercover as long as possible. There was a large, grassy mound that gave a good view of the army and at its base a boy waited with a horse clothed in green and gold. As Emelda approached he bowed low and came over to meet them. Emelda recognised the horse immediately, it was the same one she had ridden into the woods with

Kasper in her arms, although it had been brushed and groomed so that its coat shone majestically and its eyes gleamed, a horse fit for a Princess. She stroked the horse's nose and it pressed into her hand, recognising her. She swiftly mounted the horse, glad that she had not worn the dress, it was hard enough wearing a breastplate. The boy then handed Emelda her sword, it had survived the fire and had been sharpened and polished so that it shone in the early light. The weight of it in her hand gave her confidence. He also passed up a helmet but she didn't wear it, tying it to her saddle instead.

"Go, Your Majesty, they are waiting," said Wolf, ushering her horse forward.

Slowly and gracefully Emelda made her way up the mound until she could see the mass of people below her. There were more there than she had anticipated but not as many as there should have been. Her heart was filled with pride and she felt the hot tears at the back of her eyes; blinking them back she took her horse as close to the edge of the mound as she could so that everyone could see her. She felt their eyes on her as every head turned to listen. Silence fell over army as they gazed up at their Princess, the reason they had gathered here and the one they were fighting for. Emelda suddenly realised she had not prepared for this moment. All the talk of war and strategy and her worry for Kasper had consumed her thoughts so much that she had no idea of what to say now the moment was upon her. Taking a deep breath, she looked down at the faces that stared back up at her, then she caught a glimpse of Prince Eric, dressed in armour that shone silver in the sun, his blonde hair tied back and his helmet under his arm. He was sitting on a large, white war horse and next to him a soldier carried his banner portraying the white stag in all its pride and glory. Eric smiled at her and gave her a nod. Fixing her gaze on his blue-grey eyes she spoke as if it was only he that was listening, and she imagined Christian and Kasper standing beside him as they should have been.

"Men and women of St. Dores, your patience has been great and your suffering greater. Now is the time for change, now it is time for a new life and a new existence. I may be your Princess but I am just like you, I hate the darkness and I am fighting for the light, I am fighting for you. Let us bring about an end to our oppression, let's set ourselves free once more!" she cried, raising her sword above her head. There was a mighty cry as her people raised their voices in agreement, "For freedom!"

Prince Eric grinned at her, joining her in a war cry, confirming that she had done well. She watched as they hurried forward, disappearing into the cover of the trees, before replacing her sword in its sheath, turning and heading back down the mound to Lord Wolf. He waited for her with a proud look on his face.

"Well done, Your Majesty, come now let's get you to safety," he said, "some of the King's Guard are waiting for you back at the encampment."

"I have to see Kasper first," she told him, and not waiting for his answer she pushed her horse forward.

Finally she was able to go to the new infirmary, Lord Wolf trailing after her. He was keen to get back to his troops, to guide his men into battle but he could not leave her before he had delivered her into the hands of the King's Guard. She quickly dismounted outside the infirmary and handed the reins to Wolf.

"Your Majesty, I need to join my men."

"Then go," she said, "I will stay here; tell my protectors to come to me."

He sighed and tethered the horse to one of the tent posts. It began to casually nibble at the dried grass.

"Do not leave this tent, I will return momentarily." he said begrudgingly, bowing and leaving.

Emelda pushed open the tent door and entered, her eyes immediately searching for Kasper, desperate to see him sitting in a chair waiting for her, but he was still motionless, lying in a bed not far from the door. As she approached she could see that his chest still rose and fell with the same steady rhythm, that was surely a good sign? The physician bowed to her as she sat next to Kasper, but when their eyes met he gave Emelda a little shake of his head before disappearing off to continue preparing bandages and medicines to heal wounds and stop the inevitable flow of blood that was about to ensue in the battle. She was left alone with Kasper and for some time all she did was watch him, taking in every feature of his face. She memorized the scar across his left eye, the appearance of stubble on his pale skin, the fine lines that had started to collect around his eyes. Her hand brushed his black hair from his face, then she stroked his cheek before tracing the elegant swirls and shapes of his dark red tattoo. She touched the scars on his chest and felt his fingers between hers. She committed all of him to memory, wishing that she had immortalised him in this way when he had been animated, alive and vibrant. She stood up and glancing quickly around to make sure they were alone, took his face in her hands and kissed him tenderly on the mouth, lingering a moment before pulling away. She had almost believed that his eyes would open and he would kiss her back, but he didn't move, locked in a sleep so deep she was unsure he would ever wake up. Leaning close to his ear she whispered to him, in the hope that wherever he was he would hear her and come back to her.

"I remember you, I love you," her words were simple and heartfelt, there was no other way for her to put it. She could read a thousand sonnets and love songs to him but nothing could tell him how she felt more effectively than those three words.

Taking one last look at his face she turned and left, returning to her horse. Lord Wolf had not yet returned, but she could see a group of men on horseback in the distance heading her way. Pushing her helmet onto her head and swinging herself up onto her horse she turned towards the battlefield and headed for the trees, a look of grim determination on her face. She had meant every word of what she had said, she was going to fight for her people, she was one of them. As she rode her head suddenly began to spin and the world around her began to distort and blur. She held on tight to the reins, panic rising in her chest. There was a sharp jolt in her chest that shook her entire body. She could hear the cries of the men sent to guard her and she felt herself slip from the horse. Another jolt and her body convulsed against the hard ground, and then everything went black.

Inside the infirmary Kasper's eyelids flickered and his eyes flew open. He sat up and looked around, confused. He had heard Emelda's voice but she was nowhere to be seen. Then he heard the men outside calling after her, panic in their voices. He threw back the blankets and clambered out of bed. His legs felt weak and almost gave way beneath him. He steadied himself on the chair next to his bed for a moment, waiting for the weakness to pass and his head to stop swimming. After a moment, he ran as fast as his legs would carry him out of the tent and out into the sunlight. The bright light hurt his eyes and it took them a moment to adjust. As they did he saw her, surrounded by soldiers, lying on the ground, unmoving, just as he had been. He raced over to her, pushing the men out of the way, ignoring the amazement on their faces as he, Lord Kasper, knelt half-naked at the Princess's side and carefully pulled her into his arms. Deciding to trust no one, Kasper slipped the willow from around Emelda's neck and pushed it into his pocket.

"Emelda!" he cried, "Emelda!"

She languished in his arms, her heart silent, her breath still in her lungs. He cradled her head against himself and cried out in agony as if his own heart had been ripped from his chest.

Chapter 15

"What's her name?"

"Emma, Emma Dores."

Silence.

Then the slam of doors and the sound of an engine.

"Found in her flat...hypothermia...successful defib at the scene."

Silence.

Then lights and the beep ... beep of the life support machine.

Emelda struggled to make sense of where she was. She could hear voices, the sound of the world around her, but she couldn't work out where she was. Everything sounded alien to her. She couldn't see, she couldn't speak, nor could she move. As she waited in the darkness she listened.

"She's stable but we don't know what caused the coma, or whether she will come out of it," it was a woman, her voice detached but empathetic.

"There must be something you can do?" A man, his voice very familiar and reassuring.

"I'm sorry, Mr Penn, but we can do nothing but wait; she has made it through the first few hours and that's the worst part."

Penn, that name stirred something inside her. Emelda heard footsteps leaving and then more approached her and she felt someone's hand in hers, it was warm and safe. She tried to grip back and she felt her fingers twitch a little but nothing more. The sound of gentle tears filled her with sadness; someone was crying for her and she didn't know who it was. She tried desperately to move, to speak, but it was if the words were stuck in her throat, her body paralysed and she was left alone with only her thoughts, the world outside of the darkness passing by without her.

Emelda wasn't sure how much time had passed since she had heard someone crying at her side, she guessed she had slept. The face of Kasper still lingered in her mind, but she awoke to blackness again and the quiet hum of the world outside the darkness. She tried again to move her hands and for a moment she felt a tingling sensation and she managed to close her hand into a fist. She heard someone take a deep breath near her and her hand was clasped tightly in response to her movements.

"Emma! Emma!" A man was calling out, then there was a loud beeping followed quickly by the opening of doors and the drum of footsteps.

"She moved, nurse, she held my hand," he told them.

Emelda felt someone pulling her around, squeezing her hand, then it all stopped.

"These things do happen, Mr Penn, involuntary spasms are quite common in coma patients - don't pin too much hope on it," a woman told him.

"I understand, but she held on so tightly," he sounded dejected.

"Mr Penn, please go home and get some rest," replied the woman in a resigned manner, as if he were a little child and she had explained it to him a thousand times already. Emelda heard footsteps leaving.

'No' thought Emelda, 'I am still here.'

Determined to prove the irksome woman wrong Emelda focused hard on opening her eyes, willing them to open. She tried so hard it hurt, she felt like there was a fire burning behind her eyes but she didn't stop. How could it be so hard just to open your eyes? Eventually she began to see light from behind her eyelids and slowly they crept back, heavy and gritty. The world before her was bright and harsh. Everything was bleary and she almost immediately wanted to close her eyes again but she fought against the urge and continued to blink, slowly looking around.

"Wait! Nurse!" The man's voice hung above her and she slowly turned her head away from the transfixing lights.

A man's face slowly came into view, soft blonde hair framing his anxious face, his eyes fraught with worry. His mouth was moving but she couldn't focus on what he was saying.

"Christian?" she tried to say, but it came out as a dry croak.

Then suddenly it hit her like a slap in the face, a wave of noise and commotion. People flocked into view, pushing the man out of sight. She turned her head her eyes clumsily, trying to find him again. She was bombarded by lights in her eyes, people pulling at her hands and talking about her but not to her. She was scared and confused, where was the battlefield? Where was St. Dores? Where was Kasper?

Finally the people around her seemed to be satisfied with the tests there were doing and began to disappear out of view. A kindly looking woman stayed behind, along with the man. She wrote something on a clipboard at the end of the bed and offered to help Emelda sit up. Emelda nodded and the woman pressed something beside her and she was lifted up to the sound of whirring. She could see her surroundings a little better from an upright position, a bleak room painted pale green with grey lino flooring, bright unflattering lights and a large window with white plastic shutters. She was propped up on a single bed with bars that ran down both sides and tubes and wires protruded from her body as if she were a puppet. Her initial thought was to pull them out of her hands and arms but the man had sat down next to her and was holding her hand as if trying to make sure she wasn't going anywhere. He saw the terror in her eyes.

"It's ok, Emma, you're going to be fine," he said reassuringly, stroking the back of her hand.

Emelda looked at him confused, "Who are you? And who is Emma?"

She saw disappointment in his eyes and he didn't answer her. Instead he looked at the woman who was still lingering at Emelda's bedside. She nodded to him and made a few more notes on her clipboard.

"It's me, Nicholas, your brother," he said smiling at her.

She smiled back, still none the wiser, "I'm sorry but you are not my brother, my brother died a long time ago."

"Emma it's me, Nicholas, come on, don't play games," he said worry creeping into his voice,

"You seem kind, Nicholas," she said, "but I'm afraid I'm not this Emma you seem to think I am."

"Then who are you?" he asked.

"My name is Emelda, Princess Emelda of St. Dores. Where am I? This is not the infirmary at the

235

encampment." Emelda looked around again nervously, wishing Kasper was there.

"Encampment?" replied Nicholas, it was his turn to look confused.

"Mr Penn, I suggest you leave Emma to rest, she has had a very traumatic experience and from looking at her medical records it would appear she experienced similar mental difficulties following another trauma, the car accident that killed her parents," reported the woman.

Nicholas nodded sadly and looked back at Emelda with a forced smile, "Get some rest, Emma. I will be back tomorrow morning and we can catch up then."

Emelda watched him as he got up and gathered up his coat. He bent to kiss her on the forehead but she moved out of the way of his approaching lips and he looked hurt for a moment before taking her hand instead and kissing it. He waved as he left the room. The woman remained.

"Emma, my name is Doctor Phillips, you've been through a lot and its perfectly normally for your brain to block out those traumatic events, even fabricate things to make up for the damage done. It's my job to help you recover your memory and get you back on your feet. But for now, get some rest, I will send someone to take your food order soon," the woman explained.

"But I don't need to get my memory back," Emelda told her, "I know who I am. I just need to get back to St. Dores."

"Please get some rest - we can talk about St. Dores in the morning," with a clinical, fixed smile, put on for her difficult patients.

The doctor left the room, leaving Emelda alone and confused. She felt scared and anxious, she still had to get back to St. Dores. She shifted a little in the bed, her body felt weak and cold as if she had come back from the dead. She wondered where Kasper was and whether they had taken her far away. She wanted to get out of the bed, to pull the tubes from her arms and go to the window to get a better look at where she was. But she didn't have the strength - she felt exhausted so instead she reached down the side of the bed to where Doctor Phillips had pushed something and found a keypad. She studied it for a moment before working out how to lower the bed and lie back down, drifting off into a fitful sleep.

She dreamt of Kasper, his body motionless on a stone slab, his scars and wounds wide open, blood pooling on the floor around him. Demons with long fingers dipped in and out of his body, some licked the blood off the floor with relish, splattering it across their ghastly faces. She tried to get to him, to reach out and stop them but the more she ran towards him the further away he seemed to get.

She woke in a cold sweat to the sight of a nurse checking the bleeping machines and bags of fluids that hung on poles next to her bed. The nurse smiled at her and jotted something down on the clipboard before wheeling a portable table over to her. There was a blue tray with a plate covered with a metal lid on it.

"They brought you your dinner, Miss Dores, but we were told not to wake you. Want me to get it warmed for you?" she asked kindly.

"No, thank you," replied Emelda, pushing herself up. The nurse quickly reached for the buttons and adjusted the bed for her.

Emelda smiled at her and the nurse poured water into a plastic cup, placing it beside her plate before hurrying off. Emelda looked down at the plate, her hand hovering over the metal lid. Cautiously she lifted it, but the food beneath it was soggy and colourless and it smelt like cabbage although there was no cabbage on the plate. Two shrivelled sausages swam in a thin

237

gravy accompanied by a stodgy looking mashed potato and a scattering of watery carrots. Emelda put the lid back on and sipped at the water, it was at room temperature and tasted stale. Pushing the table away she proceeded to remove the grey peg from her finger. The machine next to her gave a long beep before falling silent and she watched the number on the monitor drop to zero. She then began carefully pulling a tube from her arm; the needle that followed surprised her a little, stinging as it left her flesh. There was a spurt of blood that sprayed over her bed sheets until she stemmed it with her fingers. With one tube out she reached for the one on her other arm and removed it in the same way, pushing hard on the skin to stop the blood. Once she was confident she wasn't going to bleed everywhere she pushed back the bedsheets and looked down at her legs. They were shorter than she remembered and plumper. Her gaze ran up her legs to her stomach - it was softer than she could recall - then to her bust which had significantly increased in size. She held a breast in each hand and wondered what on earth had happened to her.

Swinging her legs over the edge of the bed she placed them gingerly on the ground, slowly letting them take her weight. At first they felt as if they were going to buckle, but after a moment she felt some strength returning to them and she stood, holding onto the edge of the bed. Her room was small with a chair next to the bed, a door out to the corridor and another to where she did not know. With slow, concentrated steps she edged her way over to the window and peered between the slats of the blinds. Night had fallen since she had been asleep and she was faced with an endless flow of traffic that sped around below Emelda noisily and she watched it for a while, mesmerised. It was then she noticed her own reflection in the glass. She gazed at the face in the glass in amazement; it was not the face she knew, rounder and wider and crowned with an auburn fuzz.

Her hands went straight to her face as she felt her features one by one, who was she? Then it struck her, she was back. Back in the world she had left, the world that had become a distant whisper on the wind, growing quieter and quieter until she had almost forgotten it. Now she was back and it was blaring at her at full volume.

"No," she murmured, banging her fist on the glass and slumping down to the floor. She sat with her head in her hands, back against the wall for some time before a nurse came in and seeing her on the floor, rushed over to her and helped her back into bed. She attempted to put the cannula back in Emelda's hand but she refused and in the end the nurse gave up, making her promise to keep drinking to rehydrate. Then like a mother putting her child to bed she tucked her in and took the untouched food away, turning the lights down as she went. Emelda resigned herself to sleep. This time she dreamt of her brother, Luca, his wicked face as he defied her father, and then she saw the bloody scene of his murder. There was so much blood, too much blood in her opinion for one person. She had never shaken the horror of it, but even so she still wished she could be there, not in this cold, harsh world of bright lights and unfamiliarity. Lastly, she dreamt of Kasper and Christian; she reached out to them, her fingertips brushing theirs as she was dragged away from them by invisible hands that tugged at her clothes, her hair and her skin.

She woke with tears in her eyes to the sight of Nicholas at her bedside. He was reading a newspaper that he quickly folded and placed on the bedside table when he noticed that she was awake. He smiled at her and she returned it noncommittally. She wanted to roll over and go back to sleep, back to Kasper and Christian, who were separated from her by more than just death.

But she forced herself to sit up and look at the man who had been waiting for her to wake.

"How are you feeling today?" he asked her.

"Tired and confused," she replied. She had expected him to call her 'Your Majesty' and was a little taken aback when he didn't, until she remembered she was not a Princess in this world. She was no one and that was precisely why she had come here all those years ago.

"Do you remember me?" Nicholas ventured.

"No, I'm sorry, I don't, you seem familiar but that's all, like a smell you can't quite put your finger on," she explained.

He produced a large brown envelope.

"Here, I brought you something," he said, handing her the envelope, "as well as some of your own clothes, got to be better than hospital gowns."

Nicholas gestured at a large black holdall on the floor beside her bed. She looked down at it and nodded. Then she turned her attention to the envelope. Carefully she opened it and reached inside. She pulled out a thick wedge of photographs. The top one appeared to be of her and Nicholas outside a shop with 'Dores and Penn' written above their heads. The people in the picture looked happy.

"The Doctor said it might help for you to see some photographs, bring back some memories. Mum and Dad want to come see you too but I told them to give you a day or two first. Maybe tomorrow?"

He was babbling away at her but she wasn't really paying attention, instead she was passing the photographs through her hands, taking in each one, studying it. The faces seemed familiar but she couldn't have named any of them; sometimes she didn't even recognise herself. Nicholas dutifully went through each one of them and explained who everyone was but it was no use. It made no difference seeing them over and over again; she could not remember the places or the occasions and she didn't want to. She just wanted to go back.

"Nicholas," she said on the third round of the photos, "I need to rest, please can we stop."

"I'm sorry Em, I'm just so pleased you're ok, I just want you back, all of you. I know I need to give you time, but you really scared me back there. Got me thinking..." His voice trailed off.

She waited for him to finish but he didn't, he just looked down at his hands, his blonde hair flopping into his eyes.

"Do you want me to go?" he asked quietly.

"Yes," she said.

He looked a little surprised if not hurt before nodding and quietly getting up. He paused, hovering over her before deciding not to do whatever he was going to do or say, and giving her a little wave he left. Once she was sure he had gone she slid out of bed and gathered up the holdall. She rummaged through it until she found some clothes she was prepared to wear and got herself dressed. Then she opened the second door and found a little bathroom. She examined her reflection in the mirror somewhat disappointedly before washing her face and tying her hair back as tightly as she could. Going back into the bedroom she headed straight for the door to the corridor, and opening it, she peered out. The corridor was empty, filled with nothing but the hum and bleep of machines and the coughing and spluttering of other patients. Seizing the moment, she crept out of the room and down the corridor. She was gazing up at the signs wondering which way was the way out when Doctor Phillips appeared around the corner.

"Emma," she called out, but Emelda didn't take any notice, "Emma."
She placed a firm hand on her shoulder before Emelda looked at her.

241

"What are you doing out of bed and out of your room?" she asked, "you should be resting."

Emelda shrugged her hand off, and making a snap decision, she ran. She didn't know where she was going but she knew she had to try and get away. She had to get back to St. Dores. Who knew what was going on in her absence, or how much time was passing by while she was sitting in a bed looking at old photos of someone she didn't know? She glanced over her shoulder and saw Doctor Phillips staring after her, a look of amazement on her face. Emelda turned around and was met head on by two large men in uniform; they blocked her path and she had to stop. With careful yet firm hands, they escorted her back to her room, where she sat on her bed, her arms folded across her chest. Doctor Phillips sat in the chair next to her.

"I know you are confused, Emma, but you have to work with us, give it time and hopefully you will start to remember who you are," she said, "running away is dangerous, especially if you don't know where you are or who you are."

"I know who I am," she said, looking straight at Doctor Phillips.

"And who is that?"

"Princess Emelda of St. Dores."

"No, you are Emma Dores, you live in a flat ten minutes from here."

Emelda looked away, her gaze falling on the window. Her way out.

"Please stay in your room, Emma and try and rest, you've been through a lot. I have you booked in for a session with a psychiatrist tomorrow afternoon and then we can assess when you can go home."

Emelda didn't look at the doctor as she left the room, an idea was forming in her mind. When Nicholas had found her she had been near to death, her body cold and lifeless. She was almost gone from London, leaving behind the shell of Emma; she had almost returned to her home, to St.Dores, to her people, to her fight. She remembered something Kasper had said to her all those days ago when she had first awoken.

"For your transition back to our world you need to regain all of your memories and forget all of those you made in the other world. Otherwise you are no use to us, half in one world and half in another."

Half in one world and half in another. There must have been a tiny part of her left in London, just enough for the paramedics to reach out and bring her back. She knew what she had to do; to die in London, to let Emma go meant to return home, to Kasper, to the war that was raging in her name. She gazed around the room and her eyes fell on the window. She jumped off the bed and dashed over to it. She tried to open it but it had been painted shut. Cursing, she walked back over to the bed and lay down on it, staring blankly up at the ceiling. She wondered how else she could escape this life.

Her thoughts were interrupted by a knock on the door and a lady came in with steaming pots of tea and coffee as well as a menu for lunch and dinner. She quietly declined tea or coffee, accepting the menu and glancing at it briefly before lying back down on the bed. A short while later the lady returned to find Emelda exactly where she had left her except that now she was sleeping soundly. She collected the menu which hadn't been filled in, and rolling her eyes she left.

Emelda didn't wake until late afternoon to find a plate of dry sandwiches on the table next to her. She looked at them then rolled over and stared at the window, willing it open with her mind. She must have lain there until the sun started to disappear beneath the horizon and the cars switched on their headlamps, shining passing lights into her window. There was a knock at the door and her untouched sandwiches were replaced with another meal she had no desire to eat. She sat up on the bed and picked up the envelope again; she sifted through the pictures again. Glancing over at the door as someone walked past, the plate of food caught her eye, and the knife and fork alongside it. She reached over and picked up the knife. It was blunt and useless but she wondered whether it would be enough to chip the paint away from the sealed window. She tucked it under her pillow and continued looking through the pictures.

Her meal was once again removed and she pretended to be asleep until the lights went down to a dim glow and the corridors fell quiet. She crept out of bed and began chipping away at the thick white paint. It was a slow and laborious process that gave her uncomfortable blisters on her hands but she did not stop. The hours passed slowly and it wasn't until the first light of morning that she finally winkled the window free and pushed it hard so that it swung open. The morning breeze hit her like a bucket of cold water, refreshing and bracing. She leant out of the window and looked down. She was definitely high enough, she must have been four or five floors up from the ground. A drop from this height was certain to take her back to her world or kill her. There was only one way to find out.

There was noise outside of her room and she spun around, hastily pulling the blind down to hide the open window. It was only the cleaners with their squeaky-wheeled trolley, ambling past unobservantly. She looked up at the large white face clock on the wall. It wouldn't be long before the ward started to come alive and her opportunity would be lost.

She dashed across the room and pulled the heavy chair over to the door and wedged it under the handle to make sure no one could get in. She could hear voices coming down the corridor as she hurried back over to the window. Throwing up the blind she let the sunlight into her room. Feeling it on her face she remembered that moment in the monastery when she had regained her confidence, her determination, and she had felt the sun on her face for what seemed like the first time.

"I'm coming back," she said hoisting herself onto the window sill.

She gazed down and her stomach lurched, her legs dangled over nothing but air and for a moment she wondered if she could do it. There was a banging on her door and she looked back to see Nicholas standing there, looking through the glass panel in the door with a fearful expression on his face - there was an older greying man and woman with him who looked equally frantic. She could hear him calling out to her, hear his fists on the door, see the terror in his eyes.

She turned around and looked down again, her stomach lurched and she gazed back over her shoulder. The two large, uniformed men were there now trying to force the door open and she could see the chair starting to slip. She turned back again - she had to do it now before it was too late, before they could get to her, but something in Nicholas' voice made her pause.

"Emma, please don't!" he cried desperately, "Emma!"

She looked at him, meeting his eyes one last time, there were so dark, so sad. If it hadn't have been for his eyes he would have reminded her so much of Christian.

"Please Emma, don't."

"I'm sorry," she told him, shifting on the window sill.

Then she turned away, ignoring that little voice inside that screamed at her to stop, and closing her eyes she let herself fall.

"Emma, please," called Nicholas, his voice growing fainter.

The men broke in the moment she fell and Nicholas sprinted across to the room to the window she had just disappeared out of, calling desperately to her as she went. But there was nothing there, no sign of Emma or a body, she had simply vanished.

Chapter 16

Emelda's lifeless body was moved to a private tent, away from the chaos of the infirmary, while Kasper remained at her side in a tireless vigil. He barely spoke, barely ate, and barely moved. He listened to the sound of fighting and knew he should be there amongst his fellow men, fighting for freedom but he couldn't force himself to leave her, not even for a moment. Minutes became hours and hours became days and still she did not wake. Kasper watched for any sign of life, constantly checking for a pulse in her neck but with each passing day he felt nothing, her chest never rose with the rhythm of life and the colour seeped from her skin. He had toyed with the idea of using the willow, but how could it heal her when there was no life left to start with? What if she had gone back to that other world? It wasn't the same as in the Grey Man, they couldn't disconnect her from the willow and bring her back. She was gone, just an empty shell.

As the dawn broke on the fourth day of her deathly sleep, Kasper began to lose hope; he refused to let anyone see her or touch Emelda but him. He felt as if he, too, was fading; they had come so far and yet she was still so far away. Every time he got close it seemed that something pulled her further away from him, some invisible force determined to keep him away from her. Now they were at the encampment he knew she would have met Prince Eric. He knew how handsome and charming he was, how attractive he was to women and he knew he didn't stand a chance against someone like Eric but he had hoped with a tiniest part of his soul that she would see past all the charm and just see him, Kasper.

Kasper held Emelda's hand in his and, making sure no one was around, brushed his lips against hers. They were stone cold; he could almost taste the life slipping away from her, he felt tears forming at the corners of his eyes. He couldn't remember the last time he had cried, the last time he had felt so desperate and so helpless. He was a man of the sword, a soldier, a protector, not a man who bowed to his emotions. But he couldn't hold it back, someone else long-buried was resurfacing, the man he once was, the lover of her sweet soul. A young man who picked hundreds of flowers to fill her bedroom on her birthday just so he could see her smile, who would sit for hours listening to her dreams and worries because he liked to hear the passion in her voice and see the joy in her emerald eyes. So that he just might have a chance to comfort her, to hold her to him and feel the warmth of her gentle form.

A thin stream of light poured in through the door of the tent, bathing Emelda in a pale glow. As Kasper pulled away from her he felt any hope of her waking up die inside him.

"You can't die, not now, there is still so much I have to say to you, so much I want to do with you," his voice shook, a tear escaping the corner of his eye, "Emelda, I love you."

He felt her hands start to move, then her whole body began to shake and convulse as if she was having a fit.

He stepped back for a moment in shock, then coming to his senses he cried out for help, fear gripping his chest as he dashed forward to try and stop her banging her head. There was a flurry of people in the room in an instant, they surrounded her bed and tried to hold her down, pinning her to the bed and her body writhed on the bed, contorting in all sorts of unnatural shapes. Kasper's helplessness grew so much so that it turned to anger. He shouted and raged at the physicians and nurses in his desperation, a wild look in his eyes, until suddenly she fell still.

Emelda had kept her eyes closed as she fell, feeling the air rushing past her, waiting for the ground to rise up to her. But it never came. When the wind suddenly ceased and the sound of the traffic below disappeared, she forced herself to open her eyes and she was back. Hovering above St. Dores she could see the battlefield - it was a hideous mess, gruesome and stifling. Men and women fought at close quarters, swords slicing through flesh and shattering bone, cleaving limbs and drenching the ground in blood and sweat. The smell of death hung in the air, thick and choking. Emelda could almost taste it and it made her gag as she fought back the urge to vomit. Everything was dark and bleak as if the colour had been sapped out of it. Her heart sank at the brutal, bloody chaos that stretched out beneath her.

Her people were fighting hard but they were greatly outnumbered. So many bodies littered the ground that men stumbled over their comrades as they fought and the ground was stained red. Great swathes of soldiers dressed in black, gleaming metal continued to pour out of the crumbling castle that was once her home. Where they came from Emelda did not know, but they seemed relentless, an inexhaustible cache of swords and bows that advanced, wave upon wave. She saw Prince Eric, his silver armour gleaming, his banner still flying and his men fighting valiantly. She saw Lord Aryan with his men with skin like silken ebony and eyes like coal fighting under the proud eagle of their land, and Lord Chen with his samurai, slicing down men in every direction. Her soldiers filled in the gaps and manned the long bows, sending showers of arrows toward the enemy that took out row upon row of them, but still they came. It was as if they were being formed in the fires of hell and spewed up onto the battlefield in a constant stream - they could not be mere men but something unnatural.

The Rebel King must have had a piece of the willow, bark or ash with only a fraction of the living willow's power, and mixed it with all his hate and greed to bring forth this tireless army. Then Emelda saw him, swathed in darkness, standing on the buttress of the castle watching the scene of destruction, a grin on his face. He held a small bag in his hand and he scattered a pinch of its ashy contents over the earth before him, followed by a few drops of red liquid that looked suspiciously like blood. To Emelda's horror creatures that walked like men, swathed in black armour with hooded faces erupted from where the ash and blood fell. It brought forth life but mixed with so much darkness it was twisted and corrupted. Emelda was filled with disgust as she looked down on the man who had savaged her land and imprisoned her people.

Moving away from the castle, she hunted the battlefield looking for Kasper, for his gleaming katana flashing in the morning sun but as she looked she felt herself being dragged away towards a small solitary tent and it was as if she was falling again, plummeting towards the earth in a rush of wind and noise. The sound of fighting and of urgent voices grew louder and louder as she drew nearer to the tent and then she heard Kasper's voice, desperate and strained. A shudder ran through her body as she passed through the roof of the tent and towards her convulsing body. She caught a glimpse of herself surrounded by men and women holding her down with Kasper at her head, and then it was as if her soul was being pulled toward her body by magnetic forces. She moved faster and faster until she collided with herself and there was a moment of silence before she sat up, her eyes wrenched open and she took a deep breath. She breathed in and out again and again making her empty lungs fill with life-giving oxygen. She had made it back.

"Princess," whispered Kasper, "Emelda."

She looked around to see Kasper pushing the doctors out of his way, forcing his way to her side. Her eyes widened in amazement as they met his, his dark eyes were full of relief and anguish. She wanted to reach out and draw him to her, to feel the safety of his arms around her. She had never thought she would see him again, let alone be able to touch him again or to tell him how she felt. The last time she had seen him she had said goodbye to him. He had been alive but unmoving, unreachable, and now he was standing next to her, his large hands warm in hers. Not caring what the people around her thought she pulled his hand to her face and closed her eyes, rubbing her cheek against his rough palm. It felt so warm, so alive! He clasped her face with both of his hands and pressed his forehead against hers. She opened her eyes and smiled at him.

"You came back," he said, so that only she could hear.

"I never meant to leave," she replied, they were so close she could feel his breath on her lips, and her skin tingled.

There was a gentle cough and Emelda broke away from Kasper. She looked up at all the faces that were staring at her in amazement. Coming to their senses they all bowed their heads in respect, but no one said anything for a long time; no one had expected her to come back to life. She had been dead, lost to this world, but now she sat before them breathing the same air that they did, her eyes alight with a new fire.

"The willow?" she said to Kasper.

He reached into his pocket, "I took it from your cloak before they brought you here. I trusted no one."

Nodding, she reached out her hand and he handed her the willow. Carefully she fastened around her neck once more, back where it belonged, before turning her attention on the men around her.

"Bring me my horse and my armour, my people need me," she said with authority.

"Your Majesty, I don't think that's a wise idea..." began one of the physicians.

"Do as I have asked," she said abruptly, and the people around her quickly dispersed, leaving only her and Kasper.

"What are you doing?" he said. She could hear the anger mixed with concern in his voice.

"I am doing what needs to be done, what has to be done," she replied with determination.

"You were dead, Princess," he replied.

"And yet I sit before you now, telling you what must be done. You are either coming with me as my protector or you need to let me go."

"If you will not stay here where is it safe then I will go with you to keep you safe."

"I do not fear death anymore. My people are dying out there for me, they are fighting a losing battle while I sit here. I am the only one who can save them now."

"I will be your sword and your shield, Princess, no one will lay a finger on you while I am at your side," Kasper placed his hand on her cheek.

She smiled, "Very well, I would have it no other way."

There was noise outside the tent and Kasper turned to see Maximus standing with one hand on the tent flap.

He stood up straight when he saw Emelda, and bowed low.

"Your Majesty, I have your horse and your armour, would you like me to bring it in or take it to your tent?" he asked.

"Tether the horse and bring me my gear, there is no time to waste, Bigge," she told him.

Maximus ducked his head and entered the tent - he seemed to fill the space with his giant form. He quickly placed her armour in front of her and her sword before bowing and asking if she required anything else.

"I need Jena to help me dress," she told him, "please find her quickly."

"Yes, Your Majesty," replied Bigge, attempting to leave, but Kasper called out to him.

"Wait!" Then he turned to Emelda, "I will help you, Princess."

Emelda looked shocked for a moment, but then she nodded. Who knew armour better than a soldier? His skill would be far greater than Jena's, but the thought of him touching her made her heart pound and she felt her face grow warm.

"Very well," she said quietly, "Bigge, leave Jena, gather all the King's Guard and bring them to the tent immediately."

"Yes, Your Majesty," he said, before bowing and ducking out of the tent.

Emelda looked at Kasper, her eyes flitting from his mouth to his eyes. There was warmth in his eyes, something she hadn't seen before and it sent her heart into overdrive. He reached out a hand to her and gently helped her down from the bed. She expected to feel weak, but it was as if she had been renewed by her brush with death. Her body felt strong, her reflexes sharp and her mind quick. She was still wearing the trousers she had fashioned, and a shirt, but her bodice was gone.

She watched as Kasper reached into the pile of armour and clothing and found her bodice. He held it out for her to slip her arms into, then he brushed her hair from underneath the collar and began to button the bodice. The touch of his fingers on her neck made her skin tingle and the hairs on her body stand on end. He did not look at her face once as he lifted the breastplate over her head and fastened it at the waist, although he could feel her eyes boring into him. He dared not look at her, otherwise he wouldn't be able to dress her, to send her out into harm's way. He couldn't bear to lose her again.

As he adjusted her sword he forced himself to look at her. There was such determination in her eyes that for a moment he was at a loss for words.

"Are you sure you want to do this?" he asked her one last time.

She looked at him. Kasper knew she was becoming the Queen she was destined to be, and soon she would be lost to him in an arranged marriage . . . she was beautiful.

"I have to do this, Kasper," said Emelda.

He nodded and led the way out of the tent. Outside Emelda shielded her eyes from the harsh brightness of the sun; it took her a moment before she could take in the scene before her. A small group of men including Maximus Bigge waited with their horses for her to give out orders; their chatter stopped as she approached and untethered her horse. They bowed deeply to her before Maximus stepped forward boldly.

"My Princess, tell us what you need us to do and we shall do it," he said, bowing.

"I need to get to the castle, Bigge, I need to speak with the man who oppresses my people," she told him.

Bigge looked as if he was about to argue with her but there was something in Emelda's eyes that made him nod resignedly. He turned to the men behind him and called out orders to them. They shouted out a battle cry in response and quickly mounted their horses, armour clinking. There was a horse waiting for Kasper too and a serving boy standing at its head, laden down with his armour. With quick practised movements, the boy dressed Kasper and it was a matter of moments before he, too was seated upon his horse, battle-ready.

"Your Majesty, please follow us," said one of the men from beneath his helmet, his dark eyes shining in anticipation of the fighting ahead.

The sounds of the fighting grew louder as they made their way through the encampment, it was mixed with the agonised cries of those left wounded and dying around the camp. Some had managed to drag themselves to the infirmary or been carried by friends who left them and returned to carry on the fight. Emelda looked around wide-eyed, she had never seen so much pain and suffering and they hadn't even reached the fighting yet. She swallowed hard and pushed on; had she stopped her heart would have broken and she wouldn't have been able to carry on. She wanted to bring water to every parched mouth and wash every bloody wound, to hold the hands of the men who had given their everything for her. But she had to carry on, they needed her to be strong now that they had been made weak in her name by the enemy's blade.

Kasper turned to look at Emelda - he saw the sadness in her eyes and the hesitation.

"Princess, there is no time for weakness, your men have given their lives for you. If you don't have the stomach for it go back now," he told her bluntly.

She looked at him and he could see the anger and the passion returning to her face. He smiled to himself as she berated him.

"I am your Princess, do not speak to me like that," she scolded him, but inwardly she smiled, she had needed the familiarity of his harsh tongue to bring the fire back again.

They passed the grassy mound that she had given her speech from. Many men and women milled around, sharpening weapons and hammering out armour. There were great burning fires with large cauldrons of stew that bubbled over them; boys dashed around with buckets of water and others helped the injured and dying get away from the fighting. There was so much happening that Emelda struggled to take it all in and no one noticed her in the middle of her guards heading out to fight. She was just another face in the crowd, another sword for the fight. As they forced their way out onto the battlefield the reality of war hit Emelda hard. The acrid smell of blood that soured the air was so pungent and overwhelming that Emelda had to steady herself in the saddle, mouth closed tight. Blood ran like rivers as far as the eye could see and the ground shook with the pounding of hundreds of feet battling upon it. The body count was higher out here and as they pushed on Emelda could see more and more bodies, organs spewed across the ground, hacked off limbs and eyes, so many eyes dead and staring. She cursed herself for not coming sooner and focused her sights on the castle, tearing her gaze away from the death that surrounded her.

Her guard formed a tight circle around her, cutting down any enemies that came close. But to her amazement none approached her. Instead they seemed to cower away from her, dropping their weapons and covering their shadowy faces with their hands. They were quickly vanquished by the men they were fighting, looks of amazement coming over the weary faces of Emelda's people as they gazed up at their saviour.

"Stop!" called out Emelda over the clash of metal on metal and the agonizing cries of the injured and dying. Her guard came to an abrupt halt.

"Your Majesty?" replied Kasper.

"I need to dismount," she told him, "I need to walk among them."

He looked at her, confused, "But why?"

"Look how the devils flee from me, they cannot look at me, they cannot touch me."

"Then we will stay in a circle around you."

"No, I must walk alone."

"Don't be so naïve, Princess, you are not indestructible and I will not lose you again, not to your own foolishness," Kasper said.

"Then walk with me, you must follow behind me and I will make a path through the darkness," she told him before dismounting gracefully.

The other men looked confused but Kasper gestured for them to remain on their horses and form a row behind the Princess. They watched as Emelda sheathed her weapon, and spreading her arms wide headed boldly into the fray. The enemy's soldiers cried out in unearthly shrieks as she touched them, the merest brush of her fingertips like an agonising fire that scorched their skin and devoured their flesh. Her men began to cheer as the enemy began to flee, howling like wild creatures. They were not men, they were things of the darkness and she was a blinding light that cast away the shadows. Her influence seemed to grow and spread, and soldiers further and further away began to cry out in pain as her power reached them. She sensed a great wave of relief run through the battlefield as the tide began to turn; her men began pushing forward, gaining the ground that they had lost. Yet still the black clad soldiers came, like ants scurrying up from the beneath the ground, escaping from within the castle walls. She fixed her eyes on the castle, on the man who stood cloaked in shadows watching over the pandemonium.

Emelda's heart was pounding by the time she reached the castle entrance, not with fear but with confidence, with a boldness that couldn't be stopped.

Her presence at the gate stemmed the flow of soldiers from within, yet she could still hear them jabbering and clicking like insects hiding in the shadows. The King's Guard stopped behind her and dismounted, drawing their weapons and surrounding her as much as she would let them. Kasper stood at her side, so close she could feel his breath on her neck.

"Here I am!" she cried out.

A strange silence fell over the battlefield behind her and the fighting came to a stop, the last few enemy soldiers slaughtered by her army. The air was filled with tension so thick that Emelda thought she might choke on it but still she held her ground.

"I heard you wanted me, so here I am," she shouted louder this time, her voice bouncing off the stone walls.

There was movement in the shadows and the chattering from inside grew louder until a figure cloaked in black emerged. He stepped out into the pale light of the sun and beckoned her forward. She took a step towards him and Kasper grabbed her arm, almost hauling her back. She shrugged him off angrily and glared daggers at him.

"You have to let me go," she hissed at him.

"I can't, he will kill you," he replied, his tone equally cross.

"Trust me, please," she said softening her voice, she didn't want the last thing she said to him to be in anger, "I will return, I promise."

Kasper let go of her reluctantly, "Princess, if you don't come back as quickly as I think you should we are coming in."

Emelda nodded, "And once I have returned you must start calling me by my name, Kasper."

She smiled at him and he forced himself to smile back, despite the dread welling in his heart and turning his stomach. Every ounce of his being wanted to run after her, to hold her in his arms and run away with her but he remained dutifully where he was, watching her small figure disappear into the shadows. As she entered the gateway of the castle the portcullis dropped down behind her with a heavy clang. Kasper sprinted towards it, reaching it as it reverberated around the stone walls. He pounded on the metal bars and cried out but it was no use - she was gone.

Chapter 17

Emelda heard Kasper's cries follow her into the
darkness as she approached the figure that stood before
her. As she reached him he turned and walked away and
she followed him deeper into the castle, crossing the
large courtyard. He turned and waited for her in the
middle, his face hidden by his hood. Emelda looked
around at her once beautiful home; every corner was
shrouded in shadows in which creatures of nightmares
lurked. As she stood before him in the centre of the
courtyard she saw more figures dressed in black appear
from the surrounding corridors, edging closer.

"Show me your face," she demanded, her voice
echoing gloriously around the courtyard.

She felt his smile before she saw it, cold and
calculated yet deeply familiar. He pulled back his hood
to reveal a shock of auburn hair that shone like fire and
eyes like emeralds that mirrored hers, except that there
was a lifelessness about them. His eyes were filled with a
hate that she had never seen or experienced before, so
deep and ingrained that it was blinding.

"Luca?" she uttered, in amazement.

Cautiously she reached up to touch his face but he grabbed her by the wrist, holding her hand inches from his face. He turned and looked at it and then looked at her. There was a cruel smile on his face as he pulled her closer to him and with his free hand he took hold of her chin and forced her to look into his eyes.

"Sister, I had hoped I would never see you alive," he spat at her, releasing her and pushing her away just as he had done as a bitter and spiteful child.

Rubbing her wrist, Emelda stepped forward.

"But you died...I found you..." she murmured.

"You found nothing, your stupid little brain filled in the gaps," he growled at her.

"Luca, what happened to you?" she asked him gently.

He laughed coldly, "What happened to me, dear sister? I got away, I became a man greater than our pathetic father, I took all that I knew he would never give to me. It was all you, always was."

"What?"

"Stupid girl, you never even knew. This is all your fault, he loved you more, he couldn't see you for the airheaded idiot you are,"

"Luca, I don't understand what you are blaming me for."

"The kingdom, the power, everything! He was naming you heir to the throne, our own father had nothing but contempt for me. I was never good enough for him, but you on the other hand could do no wrong - but I saw you for the manipulative little bitch you are!"

Emelda flinched at his words, so twisted with years of hatred and bitterness. She knew it was all lies but it still cut deep. She had never realised her own brother had felt so strongly about her.

"But look at me now, I hold the power, I hold the respect. Hundreds at my beck and call and all I need to do to secure it is to kill you. I will finally be rid of the perpetual thorn in my side! The willow will be mine and so will St. Dores and all the kingdoms as far as the eye can see!" His voice had become a shout that even the shadows seemed to hide from.

There was shuffling from the edges of the courtyard and several figures came forward, swords raised, eyes burning from beneath their hoods. But Luca lifted his hand and they all stopped immediately.

"No," he said softly, "I want to kill her myself."

He pulled his sword from his belt and brandished it with glee. He let out a loud, unnerving laugh that sent shivers down Emelda's spine. Lifting the sword above his head Luca was about to strike her when she spoke.

"Luca, I am so sorry, I didn't know," she said quietly, her eyes fixed on his.

The malice in Luca's eyes seemed to lessen a little as he stood poised to end her life; he hesitated, his blade hovering above her. Something inside of him wavered for a moment and she saw the sad little boy he was, alone and angry, desperate for an end to his pain. But in the next moment it was gone and his blade was moving swiftly towards her face. Moving quickly, she dodged his blow and unsheathed her sword, ready for his next attack.

"This makes it more interesting," he laughed, lunging at her again and again.

She parried his thrusts, imagining herself moving in the same way she had seen Kasper and Christian move, as if she were dancing, so that her blade became an extension of her body. Luca's men watched with blood lust in their eyes, they whooped and cheered for their king, keen to see her blood spilt across the stone floor.

The deadly dance carried on as Kasper watched Edwards and several other members of the King's Guard climbing nimbly up the castle walls. They disappeared over the top and he listened for the thud of their feet on the ground. He was soon rewarded with the sound of clashing weapons and then the youthful face of Edwards peered through the bars of the portcullis.

"They have cut the ropes, Lord Kasper," he told him.

Kasper cursed and turned to the men behind him who were waiting expectantly.

"Any man with the strength to, get over here and help move this gate, now!" he cried.

There was a cry in response and the ground shook as the men descended on the castle entrance. Slowly the portcullis began to scrape its way up out of its grooves, and Kasper, throwing his armour off, managed to slide himself underneath.

"Get it secured," he said to Edwards, who nodded and called out orders to the men as Kasper disappeared into the castle.

Emelda pushed hard against Luca, her own blade cutting into her hand. With all her strength, she managed to throw him off balance, and knocking the blade from his hand she thrust her sword towards his own throat. He reached for her sword and pulled it closer to his throat.

"Go on, you little whore, do it," he hissed at her.

As she hesitated for a moment he grabbed the sword and wrenched it from her hand. He clasped her round the waist and pulled her close. Emelda felt the cold blade of the sword against her skin, then a searing pain as Luca buried it deep into her stomach. She cried out with the pain as he embraced her tightly. Over his shoulder she saw Kasper running towards them across the vast courtyard that had been their arena, a wild look in his eyes. She mouthed his name as Luca relinquished her from his grasp, laughing as he watched her fall to the floor clutching at her stomach.

Luca did not see Kasper, nor did he feel his blade on his throat until it was too late. His blood spurted in a glorious crimson fountain, covering Emelda in the thick, warm liquid as he fell to his knees next to her. Their eyes met for a moment in the bleakness of death, before he slumped forward face down on the ground. Emelda felt herself growing faint as her body could no longer keep her upright, she collapsed onto the ground next to her brother, their faces almost touching. She looked into his dead eyes as their blood mingled together in the very place they had grown up side by side.

"Luca," she murmured, reaching out a bloody hand to brush the hair from his face, "brother."

She felt her body grow cold as she turned her gaze away from Luca's face. Staring up at the sky she smiled to herself. It was over now, he could finally be at peace, away from the hatred and the lies that he tormented himself with. Shaking, she reached into her breastplate and pulled out the little willow bud that was fastened around her neck. She tugged the cord until it gave way and opened the little vial before letting her hand drop to her side, willow bud clasped tightly; she was exhausted at such a small effort.

'This is it,' she thought, 'the end is finally here and I've only just begun.'

She could hear fighting going on around her and she tried desperately to see Kasper for one last time but she was too weak to move. Instead she gazed up at the clouds passing across the pale sky and imagined she was a girl again, lying with Kasper in the wheat fields, the golden corn bowing around them and the afternoon sun warming their skin. She smiled and closed her eyes, she could see it better that way, she could reach out and touch him. His skin felt soft and warm, untouched by the ravages of time and anger. Kasper's smile was carefree and innocent. Oh, how she had loved him even then, before she became a woman and her flesh was awakened, before his touch made her tremble and her heart beat fast in her chest. His fingers stroked her cheek and she placed her hand over his, relishing the warmth of his touch. She wondered if it would be alright to lie here forever with nothing but Kasper and the golden sheaves of wheat. She turned to speak to him but he was gone, her cheek felt cold as if he had never been there, and the sky turned black.

She scrambled to her feet, calling his name, searching for him but before her eyes the wheat withered and died, turning to ash around her feet. She could see her home in the distance and she ran towards it but as she did the walls began to crumble and the gleaming stones turned black. She felt the cold sting of rain on her skin and she looked up to the heavens. She found herself under the boughs of a great willow tree, its bark scorched and charred, its leaves turned to dust around its roots. Emelda reached out and touched it, and as she did she felt something coursing through her body like a wave of energy and a bright light radiated from her fingertips. The tree seemed to cry out, to surge with the light; buds sprouted from its barren branches and lush green leaves began to erupt from the new buds.

The ground began to tremble and she held onto the tree to keep her balance. Gazing up into the branches she saw eagles soaring down from the sky to perch on the tree, mighty lions appeared, bounding across the ruined landscape and noble stags prised the new leaves from the branches with their rough tongues. She watched in awe as the animals surrounded her, bowing down to her as if they were men, their horned heads and flowing manes touching the floor. The eagles cried out in unison as if they were calling to her. The sound got louder and louder and the eagles began to circle her, getting closer and closer until their voices began to sound like words, like someone calling her name, desperate and pained.

The eagles got so close that she closed her eyes and ducked down for fear of being struck in the face. She could hear the flap of wings so close that she could feel the air swooshing against her cheek. When she opened her eyes, the eagles were gone and she was lying in the courtyard next to Luca. She turned her head with what little strength she had, cold blood congealing on her face and in her hair, sticking her to the ground. She could see the cloaked men circling a lone figure who fought hard to hold them back whilst in the distance a swarm of men came pouring into the courtyard, swords raised, a battle cry on their lips.

"Emelda, Emelda!" came a voice over the roar of the men and the sound of fighting.

She tried to fix her eyes on the direction the voice came from, attempting to lift her head off the ground, but she was so weak she could barely move. As she watched she could see Kasper's black boots come pounding towards her, her name on his lips. He fell at her side and without a moment's hesitation he gathered her into his arms and rose to his feet, pulling her in close to his chest. She could hear his heart racing, feel the sweat seeping through his clothes. She breathed in his sweet scent of lavender. He had come for her. With all her strength, she clasped onto his clothes, desperate to stay close to him, to never let him go again. He felt her fear and held her even tighter still.

"I've got you Princess, I will never let you go," he whispered softly in her ear, "everything is going to be alright."

Emelda nodded, fighting the urge to close her eyes and to drift into unconsciousness. She fixed her eyes on Kasper's face while everything else drifted by around her. If she could see him then she could hold on, she could make it through the pain. With each step she took the wound in her side sent pain coursing through her body and she gritted her teeth against it, trying not to black out. She could feel the warmth of fresh blood blossoming beneath her breastplate and she knew she had lost too much blood. Determined and as stubborn as ever Kasper ploughed on out of the castle and under the portcullis to where Emelda's army milled around an empty battlefield, confused and lost. The battle that had seemed doomed to end in a sea of bodies and the blood of St. Dores had come to an abrupt end. Four days of relentless fighting was over yet they were unsure whether to celebrate or to mourn. They had watched their Princess enter the castle, seen the shadowy figure of the Rebel King and now they waited anxiously, wondering who would emerge from the castle entrance.

Prince Eric wiped the blood from his face, his gleaming armour stained and spattered, and gazed towards the castle. He had seen Emelda from a distance, her auburn hair flowing like fire in the sunlight, she had stood out amongst the killing and maiming like a beacon of hope. He sheathed his sword and headed towards the castle, gathering men as he went until every man and woman out there was following him in a great surge towards the castle. Either Emelda would come out alive or they would go to their deaths avenging hers. As he stood at the entrance, sword drawn, he could hear a fight going on inside and he wondered if he should take his men in. Lord Aryan and Lord Chen quickly appeared at his side ready to fight on; the men nodded at each other knowingly and raised their weapons, ready to let out a deafening war cry. But their cry fell silent on their lips, unheard; from within the castle entrance came the figure of a man walking slowly, a precious treasure in his arms. Prince Eric held up his hand for the men to wait, he could hear the creak of the bowmen's bows as they took aim, ready for his command.

"Hold your fire, stand down! Stand down!" he called as loudly as he could. The other Lords joined in the chorus, spreading it across the expectant battlefield.

Emelda heard Prince Eric's voice and smiled to herself, at least one of them would survive to get the chance to be happy now. Kasper came to a halt as he emerged from under the old portcullis taking in the scene that lay before him. Barely able to keep her eyes open Emelda tore her gaze away from Kasper's face and looked out at her men. A sea of faces turned towards them in amazement. Prince Eric dropped to his knees, head bowed almost to the ground. Lord Aryan and Lord Chen followed suit as it spread like a tidal wave across the silent battle field until every head was bowed in reverence.

Kasper stood unsure what to do. He knew Emelda was dying, there was no way she would make it back to the infirmary and even if she did her chance of recovery was slim. Suddenly feeling the weight of his burden Kasper dropped to his knees, exhausted. He cradled her in his lap, looking into her eyes and telling her it would be ok as Prince Eric approached. He placed a hand on Kasper's shoulder and he looked up at him, shaking his head. Emelda's body felt heavy, every breath was laboured and painful, but she tried to smile at Kasper anyway, trying to ease his sorrow. Prince Eric knelt at Kasper's side and placed his hand on his shoulder, Lord Aryan joined him on the other side and Lord Chen in front until the great Lords and Prince of the Kingdoms surrounded their Princess, their Queen. She was the bringer of light, she had seen out the darkness and they were eternally in her debt, yet despite being the most powerful men in the land there was nothing they could do to save their saviour from the clutches of death.

"Kasper," she murmured, her voice little more than a breath.

She reached up and touched his face. He was crying soft, sweet tears and she tried to brush them away but he shook his head.

"Let them fall," he told her, "I am not ashamed."

She smiled at him before wincing in pain.

"The willow? I can use it, where is it?"

"Gone...back where it belongs," breathed Emelda.

There was a loud cry from behind them followed by the drum of feet. Kasper glanced around, tearing his eyes from Emelda's face. Edwards was running towards him, his face smeared with blood and a deep gash across his chest but still he ran as if his life depended on it, cradling something precious in his hands.

"Lord Kasper, wait!" he cried, dropping to his knees beside him in a shower of mud and blood.

He opened his hands for Kasper to see and he peered into Edwards hands, eyes wide in amazement. Before him was a small seedling that seemed to be growing before his very eyes, small bright green leaves unfurled and twisted themselves towards the sun, taking in its life-giving rays.

"And there are more, so many more!" he told Kasper excitedly, "I saw the Princess give you some of the bark from the willow bud, I thought this might help her."

Kasper carefully took the small plant from Edwards and handed it to Prince Eric, then he laid Emelda gently on the ground and began undoing her breastplate as fast as his trembling hands would let him.

"Just hold on," he told her, "hold on."

With the breastplate removed he could see her chest was barely moving, so he placed the tiny seedling into the wound and waited.

Emelda felt her eyes close, there was nothing she could do to stop them. The pain was finally easing off and she could feel herself slipping away. It was a blissful relief as a cold numbness overcame her body. She could hear Kasper telling her to 'hold on' but he was so far away and so quiet she could barely hear him. She wanted to tell him that it was ok, that the pain was gone and that they could lie together in the wheat fields once more under the warm summer sun.

A tearing pain tore her out of her numbness and she opened her eyes wide in horror. The fuzzy image of Kasper leaning over her came into view. He was mouthing something but she couldn't hear it, but she could feel the heat of her own tears running down her face. Another excruciating pulling at her side made her cry out in pain and grab at her stomach, then her vision was filled with a blinding light. She shut her eyes tight against it. When it had finally passed she could hear crying and someone breathing hard and fast. It took a moment before she realised it was herself. She could see Kasper and Prince Eric's faces, filthy and creased with concern, peering down at her. The pain in her side had eased but it still stung with each shallow breath. She tried to sit up but she felt too weak; strong arms reached underneath her and propped her up a little.

"Princess," said Kasper, her hair was plastered to her head with blood and sweat and he brushed it out of her eyes, "how are you feeling?"

"Am I dead?" she asked.

"I hope not," he replied gently.

"I thought I had died," Emelda took as deep a breath as she could, wincing at the pain.

"Go easy, Princess," Kasper told her.

"What happened?"

"The willow healed your wounds, it saved you in the same way you saved it," Prince Eric told her with a smile.

Gingerly Emelda reached down to her stomach. She could feel the rough edges of a recently stitched wound - it was tender and sore to the touch but she was beginning to feel stronger and stronger as the moments passed. She closed her eyes and relaxed into Kasper's arms. The others nodded to him and he gathered her to him and she nestled into his chest, home at last. He climbed to his feet, a new lease of life flowing through him and stepped boldly towards Emelda's army. He was greeted with an almighty cheer that rose from the hordes of men and women the pressed forward to see her, bowing as Kasper passed by. They parted like a

269

great sea, then swarmed back around them as they passed through, eager to follow in an immense procession. Some of the King's Guard remained at the castle flushing out anyone or anything evil that remained; others stood mesmerised by the wonders going on inside, the new life that was exploding out of every nock and cranny.

As he walked Kasper heard murmurs of amazement and glanced back over his shoulder. He stopped in his tracks, addressing Emelda hastily.

"Princess, look!"

She slowly opened her eyes, unwilling to move away from Kasper's warmth. He turned so that she had a good view of the castle over the crowds. The men and women parted so that her view was unobstructed and she could see the full glory of her journey. The castle was slowly being engulfed in a swathe of pale green and silver; every stone, every turret was awash with bright green leaves and stems. They twisted in and out of the windows and exploded out of every crack in the masonry like a great green blanket, covering everything dark and sinister that had ever been there with life. The sky was beginning to fill with birds of all kinds, that were landing within the castle, claiming it as their own. Life was returning to St. Dores.

Emelda's lips parted in awe at the sight, before her thoughts turned to her brother, his body lost forever in a tomb of foliage. He had wanted the willow bud and the power it held so badly that it had devoured him and now he himself had been consumed by it. Emelda let a single tear fall for Luca, the boy she had called brother, but that was all; she felt nothing for the man that had stood before her just moments ago. Any trace of humanity had gone from him, hate and jealously had stolen that from him, the boy that he was had been lost. She decided to believe he had died that night when she found his room covered in blood. He was the body that had been found

270

out in the woods wearing his clothes and his rings. That was him, robbed of his youth at the hands of cruel men. She could still cry for that version of him, she could still love him.

She closed her eyes again and Kasper headed for the encampment. He walked the distance slowly and steadily, fixing his eyes on the row of trees that signalled the end of the battlefield. As he walked he whispered to her that he had her, that it would be ok, and she trusted him. She drifted into a sweet sleep in the warmth of his arms and the sway of his step lulling her deeper and deeper. She barely noticed when he placed her in her bed back at the encampment and carefully removed her blood- stained clothes. He washed her wound and her face before pulling the blankets over her and sitting down at her side.

Kasper leant his head on the edge of the bed and closed his eyes. He must have drifted off as he was woken by the concerned face of Lord Wolf, who looked a little battle-worn. Wolf glanced down at Kasper and placed a hand on his shoulder. Kasper was still wearing his sword and his clothes and hair were matted with blood and dirt.

"Come, let her rest, she is safe now," he said gently, "you need to rest as well and wash."

Kasper slowly turned around and stood up. He nodded at Wolf, rubbing the sleep from his eyes and glanced back at Emelda.

"I will stay with her and find you when she wakes, fear not, Lord Kasper," Wolf said, giving him a little nudge, "now off with you."

Reluctantly Kasper left Emelda's bedside, unable to stop himself glancing back at her until he was out of the tent. As he stepped out he took a deep breath - there was something different about the
air he was breathing. It was as if it was cleaner, richer, sweeter. It was as if there was something that had

been contaminating it and now it had been purified. He gazed around. The trees, the people, even the earth seemed to be more alive. People rushed around tending to the wounded and the hungry, celebrating and drinking. There was a hum of excited chatter; it brought a smile to Kasper's once cold face, and with it a part of him returned, a part of him he thought he had lost long ago.

He walked slowly over to one of tents that had been erected for the King's Guard and entered. It was quiet inside, most of the men were still out on the battlefield gathering in the wounded and moving the dead. They had no family, no one to come back and celebrate with so they carried on tirelessly and obediently with their duty to the Princess and to St. Dores. Kasper thought about how he would have to go back to that life now that the Princess was safe. He began to undress slowly, his body tired and sore from fighting. He tended to the new wounds he had sustained and then went to get soap and water to wash in. Upon his return, he took his knife and went out to the back of the tent where it was quiet and sheltered and he knew he was unlikely to be disturbed. He knelt down and washed his face in the bucket, scrubbing it with the lavender smelling soap, not caring about the sting of it in his eyes, before carefully shaving by feel until his skin felt soft once more. Then he stripped off completely and splashed the water over himself before scrubbing his entire body. He picked up the bucket and poured it over himself, shivering as the cool liquid ran over his skin. It felt good and refreshing, it was cleansing his soul. He then turned to his hair, washing that too in the same manner until he felt entirely clean and new.

Still dripping he headed back inside and to his surprise he found Prince Eric waiting for him. The prince looked surprised for a moment as Kasper stood before him, totally naked and unashamed. His eyes ran over his war-torn body, lean and strong, before he looked him in the eye.

"Tell me about my brother!" Eric asked, his eyes full of grief, "what happened to Christian?"

"Let me dress and I will explain everything to you," said Kasper. Eric nodded and watched Kasper disappear into the dressing room, then sat down at a small wooden table.

Kasper was only gone a few moments before he returned, dressed in the usual dark green uniform of the King's Guard, the emblem of the lion and the sun stitched into a badge on the chest of his jacket. He went to a wooden chest and pulled out a bottle of amber liquid, then he retrieved glasses from a cabinet filling each with a generous measure of the liquor.

"The finest whiskey, a perk of the King's Guard. Good grief, there has to be some," he said, handing a glass to Eric and sitting down at the table opposite him.

"I know that Christian was killed on your journey here, but this is the first chance I have had to speak with you. Tell me, hold nothing back," Eric said, taking the glass and gazing into it as if he would find his brother's face there.

Kasper then began to explain what had happened with Indira down that dark alley all those nights ago; the way Christian had carried on fighting despite his injury, strong until the end, and loyal. He told him of the place that they had buried him, that was not fit for even the worms let alone someone as valiant as Christian. He told of how Christian had smiled at the end – although he knew his death was coming he was still thinking of the Princess and his duty. Kasper watched as the tears gathered in the Prince's eyes as he told him how it was his fault that he had let Indira run loose as long as she had, that he should have killed her the moment he had laid eyes on her, the moment he suspected she was making designs on Emelda's life, the moment Christian had warned him.

Kasper finished his tale and reached for the bottle again - Eric held out his glass expectantly. The amber liquid tumbled into the glass, the sweet aroma of raisins rising out of it. Prince Eric lifted his glass high and gestured for Kasper to do the same.

"I'm sorry…" he began, but Eric silenced him.

"There is enough sorrow here, do not add any more. He lived a life worth celebrating," his voice was soft and understanding, "to Christian, beloved brother and friend."

"To Christian!" shouted Kasper, getting to his feet.

"To Christian!" Prince Eric joined in his cry.

The two men threw their heads back and swallowed the fiery whiskey in one gulp. It burnt all the way down to their stomachs, making them suck their breath in through their clenched teeth, but it felt good and purifying. Kasper lifted the bottle again but Prince Eric waved his hand.

"I have someone I need to see," he said, shaking his head, "but thank you."

Kasper nodded, he was sure that Eric was going to see Emelda and he had every right to. She was his fiancée now; she would be his wife and his Queen, the mother of his children and heirs to the Kingdom. The whiskey suddenly left a bitter taste in his mouth and his chest felt as if it was being crushed. Breathing deeply, he bowed to Prince Eric who was making to leave.

"Thank you for bringing the Princess back safely, she has set me free from all this formality. We are so lucky you and I, to know a heart like hers," and smiling at Kasper, Prince Eric turned and left.

Kasper's heart sank as he poured himself another drink; he finished it and lifted the bottle again. He decided against it, standing up and throwing the bottle in rage. It smashed on the floor as he let out a heart-wrenching roar. It was time for him to leave, he would make sure Emelda was recovered and then he would go as far away as he could go, to a place where she could only haunt his dreams and he could be alone with his grief. He stormed out of the tent, the last drops of the King's Guard's whiskey seeping into the dry ground.

Chapter 18

Emelda spent two days drifting in and out of consciousness, the pain in her side becoming less every time she opened her bleary eyes to glimpse the world around her. The faces of Kasper, Prince Eric, Jena and even Lord Wolf drifted across her line of vision, each one looking as concerned as the last. Around her the men and women of St. Dores slowly packed up the encampment and returned to their homes, desperate to get back to their families, to start their lives again. Many were only farmers or labourers who had turned their hand to the sword in an attempt to finally break free from the oppression of the Rebel King. They left the battlefield and the encampment as free men and women, taking victory home to their loved ones as well as the swords of those who had been lost in the fight for freedom. The sacrifice had been great, but not in vain - they counted that as some small consolation. There had never been such sadness mixed with such joy.

Kasper saw it on the faces of the men and women as they gathered their belongings. Some looked lost, other wept as they went, but most were quiet, lost in their thoughts. The Princess's tent came into view around the corner and he approached nervously, hardening himself to what he was about to do. He had practised what he would say over and over in his tent but every time it came out wrong. In the end he had decided to be clear and straight to the point. No emotion, just the bare minimum and then leave. He had watched Prince Eric come and go from the tent; he had heard him speaking gently to Emelda, whispering sweet nothings into her ears as she slept and he knew he had no place here now. He had done his duty and now he had to move on, to leave the King's Guard.

He stood outside her tent in the deepest part of the night and wondered if he should just leave without seeing her. It would be easier, but cowardly. He took a deep breath and fixed his face into its usual cold look before ducking under the door. Emelda was asleep, but she roused as he entered, a smile appearing on her sleepy face. She brushed her hair over her shoulder and sat herself up in the bed with relative ease. Kasper was pleased to see her moving so freely again.

"What brings you here at this hour, Kasper?" she asked.

He approached her bedside and bowed before sitting down. She immediately noticed his swords strapped to his back and her eyes widened.

"Kasper?"

"Princess, I must leave. You are to be married soon - you will be Queen, there is no place for me here, there never was," he told her bluntly.

"No, no, I…"

"I hope you will waive the promise I made to the King's Guard."

"I will not," her voice wavered.

"Then you will have to hunt me down and execute me."

"Kasper, wait, you don't understand…"

He cut her off again, "I understand all too well. I have no place here so I am leaving."

He got up to leave and she reached out to him, despair and desperation in her eyes.

"But I love you."

He hesitated for a moment, just long enough for Emelda to get hold of his hand. She clung to him with all the strength she could muster but he tugged his arm away and turned his face away. He headed for the door, determined not to look back so that she couldn't see his heart breaking or he hers.

"Kasper! Kasper!" Her voice followed him out of the tent, thick with tears but he didn't stop. He gathered his horse and the few belongings he had and disappeared out into the depths of the night.

Jena found Emelda asleep at her dresser, her arms folded under her head, her precious hairpin clutched in her hand. She didn't stir when Jena entered, and when Jena touched her skin it felt cold, as if she had been there all night.

"Your Majesty," Jena said softly.

Emelda stirred a little and slowly sat up, she looked at Jena with bloodshot eyes, her skin pale and puffy. With no regard for her status Jena swept Emelda into her arms and held her tight like a child, as her body shook with uncontrollable sobs.

"He's gone, he's gone," she whispered, her words choked with tears.

Jena said nothing, letting the silence fall around them. She stroked Emelda's back and wished there was something she could do. They remained in this unlikely embrace until Jena felt a calm come over her Princess. She gently pulled away from her and wiped the tears from her face.

"It wasn't supposed to end like this," murmured Emelda, getting up and walking over to the wash basin, her steps slow and a little unsteady.

Jena went to help her but Emelda ushered her away, filling the basin herself from the pitcher of water next to it.

"Can I get you some hot water, Your Majesty?" Jena asked.

"No, no this is fine," Emelda replied, her eyes fixed on the whirling basin of water.

Emelda didn't speak for a while, her heart so heavy she could barely form the words she wanted to say. If she said them, if she told Jena what had happened then it would all suddenly become reality. Kasper would really be gone, he wouldn't appear through the tent door, his expression full of concern and kindness. She washed her face in the cold water, rubbing away the tears until her skin was red, then she turned to Jena.

"I need to get dressed and see my people," she instructed.

Immediately Jena got to her feet and began rooting through the clothes that had not been destroyed by the fire. She thought about how Emelda would need more clothes and she pictured herself wandering through the castle market, touching the fine cloth and reams of intricate lace. How beautiful she would make her Princess, she could never leave her. Then her thoughts turned to Prince Eric - he would want to return to the Greylands and he was already talking of taking Jena with him but there was no way she could leave Emelda now. Her heart throbbed as she reached for the dress made of rich purple velvet.

Emelda stood like a doll, letting Jena dress her and prepare her for the world beyond the tent, a world without Kasper. She watched herself being readied in the mirror and it was like looking at a stranger. Her face was so blank, so empty that should almost couldn't look at herself. This was her face now - she knew sadness would fade, that time would heal the hurt but she knew she could never love anyone like she loved him, and she didn't want to. A future of loneliness lay ahead of her.

"You are ready, Your Majesty," said Jena, interrupting Emelda's thoughts.

Emelda took one last look in the mirror and reached for the hairpin Kasper had given her. She held it out to Jena who took it and arranged it in Emelda's hair that fell loose down her back. She couldn't bear the tightness of it pulling at her scalp, it seemed to be so much more painful now and she had always preferred her hair long and flowing. Whether it was appropriate or not, she didn't care.

"You are beautiful, Your Majesty," Jena told her with genuine feeling.

"Maybe once, now all I see is sadness," Emelda replied, her voice distant and detached.

"I still think you are," Jena ventured.

Emelda looked at herself in the mirror before turning it in its stand so that all she could see was its wooden back.

"That's better," she remarked, "go fetch Lord Wolf, please."

Jena curtsied and disappeared out of the tent. She returned a few moments later by herself and informed Emelda that Lord Wolf was waiting for her outside. Emelda nodded and took a deep breath; she tried to put Kasper's face from her mind, focusing on the task at hand. She would be relieved to leave the stuffy tent she had spent the last few days recovering in, to feel the sun on her face and the breeze in her hair. As she stepped out of the tent she saw Lord Wolf standing at the door of the main tent. He was alone; he looked greyer than she remembered, but very much alive. He bowed low to her then came over and took her hand in his.

"It warms my heart to see you up and about," he smiled at her, but she could still see worry in his eyes.

"Thank you, Lord Wolf, but you needn't concern yourself over me anymore, I feel well," she lied to him. Her body may have been healing but inside she was broken.

"Then your people await you, Your Majesty," he said, gently leading her out of the tent.

The wind whipped her hair around her face and the sun beat down on her from a clear blue sky but she felt nothing. No warmth from the sun or coolness of the wind. The world around her seemed to be filled with colour again, but to her it was still black and white.

'So this is how it will be,' she thought, as she approached the crowd of people that had gathered outside the main tents to see her.

Forcing a smiling onto her face she gazed over the crowd. So many expectant faces looked back at her, waiting for a revelation about what was going to happen next. A young man appeared at her side with a horse for her to sit upon so that she could be seen by all, and with his help she mounted it before addressing her people.

"Finally we are free!" she called out, "together we have defeated the enemy and we can return home to our loved ones, knowing that our lives are our own. I will begin to rebuild St. Dores and the surrounding city, but the old castle will be left as it is. I want to build a new St. Dores, one that is greater and more wonderful than the last."

There was a cheer from the crowd, which sounded hollow to her ears.

"Those who have no one to return to or wish to start a new life here will be employed in the building of the city and castle. For now there is little to pay you with except the promise of land and a home to call your own. It will take time for life to return to normal but we must

281

be steadfast in our labours; the easy part is over and the hardest part now begins.

For all of you who wish to remain I will set up a tent for you to register. Lord Wolf and the King's Guard will oversee the distribution of work and land. They are my eyes and ears amongst you, they are my representatives and they will be treated with the same respect that you would give me if I were to walk amongst you. The same respect I will give to each and every one of you. I do not wish to be a ruler detached from her people. I want to celebrate in your joys, to weep with you in your times of sorrow. It is time for change in so many ways. Now the time for fighting is over, we must celebrate this turning point in our lives."

There was a loud roar from the crowd, drowning her out. Emma waved at them and there was another cheer.

"Now go make merry!" she shouted over them.

She turned to Lord Wolf who stood at her side, "I must go see the castle."

"Yes, Your Majesty."

Emelda and Wolf were brought horses and began to push their way through the crowded encampment, hands reaching up towards Emelda, trying to touch the hem of her dress or the heel of her shoe, any part of the woman that had saved them. They called out their thanks to her as she passed by and she reached down to the outstretched hands, her fingertips brushing against the hands of those who had sacrificed so much for her. She thought of those who were not there and said a silent prayer for them.

Eventually the crowds dispersed and they left a hubbub of activity behind them. They headed for the row of trees that edged the battlefield. Emelda could feel her pulse quicken as they made their way through the trees; she thought to herself that the trees ought to be cut down. The emerged out onto the still battlefield. It was eerily quiet - nothing moved, not even the trees in the wind. The King's Guard had been busy burying the dead; freshly dug mass graves covered the ground in neat rows covered with hundreds of wooden grave markers. There were no names - there were too many for the King's Guard to know who every man or woman was, but everybody was accounted for and there would come a time when the families and friends of those who had died would come from across the lands to write the names of those who had been lost to them on the grave markers so they would never be forgotten. Emelda had already decided to leave the land as sacred. Nothing would be built here and little did she know that nothing would grow here either. There was too much blood, too much death for life to thrive here again.

She bowed her head in respect to the dead as they made their way through the graves. She attempted to count the grave markers but she soon lost count, there were too many. Fixing her eyes on the castle she cursed herself for not getting there sooner, for not escaping back to this world more quickly, for not coming fully across in the first place. If only she had been stronger, if only she had remembered who she was sooner.

The crumbling castle stood like a beacon of life amongst the killing fields, covered with a blanket of green that moved with the wind and twitched with an abundance of animal life. Emelda stopped at the entrance; the portcullis was now being held up with twisted green branches that covered everything. Feeling anxious she urged her horse on and it reluctantly entered the green cave, whinnying a little as they went. They headed towards the courtyard, the sound of the horses' hooves deadened by a thick carpet of moss. They emerged from the corridor out into the boughs of a great willow tree. Its uppermost branches stretched up into the sky and beyond, the dappled golden light of the sun filtering down through them like golden rain. It was breath-taking and Emelda had to dismount to enter its boughs further in her hunt for the heart of the tree. She tethered the horse and disappeared deeper into the foliage until she came to a thick trunk at the heart of the courtyard.

Gazing up at the wondrous green canopy her foot caught on something on the ground and she almost fell. Lord Wolf, who was close behind, caught her before she could hit the ground. As she prised herself away from his arms she looked down at what she had stumbled on; the ground was littered with the bodies of the Rebel King's followers, each wrapped in their own shroud of green. She bent down and tried to pull back the plants from their faces but the tree was not prepared to give them up.

"Your knife, Lord Wolf," she ordered.

"Your Majesty," he said, offering her his knife.

She cut the greenery from the closest body to reveal the face of a young woman not much older than herself who looked as if she were sleeping peacefully. Emelda got up and made her way over to the next body until she had cut open every cocoon and only one remained. The last body lay under the very roots of the tree as if it had claimed this one for its own. Looking around Emelda guessed they must be in the centre of the courtyard, in the very spot where she and Luca had lain face to face in a pool of their own blood. Carefully she cut back the roots to reveal the face of her brother. The blood was gone from his face and his eyes were closed as if he were asleep, just like the others. He looked peaceful at last. The pain and hatred was gone from his face and Emelda stood up, her hand to her mouth. Though she had known that this one would be her brother it was still a shock to see him. She stood staring at him, the knife dangling by her side. As she watched the roots slowly engulfed him again, pulling him further under the tree.

"Goodbye, Luca," she whispered.

"Let us go, Your Majesty, we have seen all we need to see," breathed Wolf, not wanting to break the peaceful atmosphere of the courtyard.

"I took the willow bud from my neck just before I lost consciousness. It must have landed in our blood and taken root," said Emelda quietly, "I want cuttings taken from the willow and distributed across the land. Send it to the Greylands, to Lord Aryan and Lord Chen. It is too much power for one person."

With one last look at her brother's final resting place she turned and walked back to her horse. She finally felt that it was over, she could breathe again.

Chapter 19

That evening a great feast was held in Emelda's honour. People came from the towns and villages to celebrate her victory, her recovery and their new-found freedom. As she sat at the head of a long table with Prince Eric on her right and Lord Aryan and Lord Chen on her left, she heard stories of the land springing forth wheat and oats, of the animals rising up from their ashen remains. The trees had begun bearing fruit and the hedgerows and skies were alive with the sounds of life again. Emelda smiled at every story, desperate to share her people's joy, but she found herself feeling empty and alone amongst the crowds of people. She sipped at her wine disinterestedly, her eyes wandering up and down the table. She found herself looking for the familiar faces of Christian and Kasper, the ones she longed to see, but no matter how hard she looked she knew she would never see them again.

Once the sweet course had been served Emelda excused herself and returned to her tent with Jena. They sat and talked in the flickering lamplight until they could no longer keep their eyes open and they both curled up in Emelda's bed.

Time passed by and days turned to weeks and weeks to months. Lord Aryan and Lord Chen returned to their lands, although Prince Eric remained on the basis that he was the Princess's fiancé. Building work was started on a temporary building that Emelda could call home, a place where she could receive guests and administer orders. She had it built in the heart of what would be her new city so that she would see the buildings rising from her window. It filled her with anticipation to see the city growing up from the ground before her very eyes. She spent many hours every day going over the building plans and walking the rough streets, making sure things were going to plan. She reviewed the taxes and the legislation her father had put in place, dismissing some and improving others. Under her fair rule the Kingdom gradually grew strong and the peoples' love of her grew exponentially.

The day of her coronation loomed. The finally preparations were being made to a grand hall in which it would take place. She had visited it once or twice - it had tall windows and a beautiful tiled floor that made her footsteps echo as if she were a giantess. At one end was a large throne that had been her father's. It had been rescued from the old castle and restored to its former glory. Early one morning as the sunrise was staining the sky pink she crept from her rooms and out to the grand hall. She took her shoes off and walked barefoot to the throne so as not to make her presence known, and placed herself gingerly upon it.

This was the first time she had let herself sit on the large wooden throne adorned with the lion and sun of St. Dores. The sight of it made her feel nervous, it was so big and lonely up on its platform and she was so small, she was only Emelda. She sat in the throne, her feet barely touching the floor, gazing up at the high ceiling, wondering where Kasper was now and what he was doing. So many times she had thought about ordering

Lord Wolf and the King's Guard to go and find him, but they were so busy building the city, collecting taxes and overseeing her orders that she didn't feel she could put her foolish heart before her people's future. Feeling all alone she sighed to herself.

The door at the entrance to the hall creaked open and she jumped off the throne in surprise. Prince Eric stood in the doorway, his tall figure handsome in the morning sunlight. He didn't say anything, striding across the hall until he was standing at the bottom of the platform and then knelt down, head bowed.

"Eric?" she said to him, stepping down towards him so that they were on level ground; he was her equal.

"Emelda, I have come to ask for your blessing. I wish to marry Jena, but she refuses to leave you," he told her, looking up at her.

"Get up," she said with a smile, offering him her hand, "I am fond of Jena and I will be sad to see her go, but I will speak to her. My sadness should not stand in the way of her happiness."

Prince Eric looked at her fondly and took her hand in his, pressing his lips to it tenderly.

"Thank you, Emelda, but there is more, she may already be with child," he said a little blush forming on his cheeks.

"Then you must marry her immediately," she grinned, "I would be honoured to organise it. Please do not deny me this happiness."

Eric looked at her; despite her broken heart Emelda still had space to share his joy and he admired her for that. She would have made a good wife, he could have been very happy with her. But she was not Jena.

"I would never deny you anything that made you happy," he said with a laugh and there was a moment between them when they both wondered what would have been if neither Kasper nor Jena had stolen their hearts. Life would have been easier, simpler, they would have been happy, but there would have been that moment when they wondered who else was out there.

Prince Eric kissed her hand again and again before bowing low, then disappeared out of the hall. Emelda followed soon after, not bothering to put her shoes on. She snuck back into her rooms and slid into bed smiling to herself, knowing that somewhere nearby Prince Eric was proclaiming his love and his intentions of marriage to Jena.

Emelda drifted off to sleep, the warm rays of the morning sun filling her large room. She was dreaming about Kasper again, the feel of his skin beneath her fingertips and the taste of his lips on hers. A loud banging on her door woke her with a jolt and she lay motionless in her bed trying to hold on to the last fading moments of the dream. The banging came again, faster and more urgent.

"Your Majesty," came a small voice from outside.

Emelda sat herself up in bed and pulled her hair over her shoulder, "Enter, Jena."

The door swung open and Jena hurried in, her dress dishevelled and her hair in her eyes. Her breath came in short, sharp gulps and her skin was flushed. She closed the door quickly behind herself and scuttled over to Emelda's side. She dropped to her knees and grabbed Emelda's hand, placing her forehead upon it.

"Jena, what is going on?" Emelda asked, lifting Jena's chin with one hand so that she could see her face.

"Your Majesty..." murmured Jena looking at the ground.

"Please call me Emelda when we are alone," she smiled, "we are friends now."

"Emelda, Prince Eric has asked me to marry him..." she began.

"That is wonderful news," grinned Emelda, but Jena did not smile.

"He is your fiancé and I fear I am already with his child."

There was worry in her eyes and Emelda could see the tears starting to gather in the corners. She pulled Jena up onto the bed and wrapped her arms around her like a mother comforting a child.

"You are not the first and you will not be the last, Jena," hushed Emelda, "that is why you must marry him. You love him, do you not?"

"With every fibre of my being," she said pulling away from Emelda's embrace and wiping her face, "But I cannot leave you, not now and not ever. I told him so."

"Then you are a fool."

Jena looked taken back, "A fool?"

"You would give up all your heart desires, a chance at happiness and fulfilment to stay with me? Now that would be foolish. I order you to marry him - the day after my coronation shall be your wedding day. It will be perfect."

Emelda left no room for argument, but Jena still looked worried, until an idea crossed her face. She clasped Emelda's hands in her own, her eyes alight with excitement.

"I will do as you ask, but on one condition. I will marry Prince Eric if, after the wedding, he finds Kasper and brings him back to you," Jena exclaimed.

Emelda smiled at Jena, "If only it were that easy. I have no idea where he would have gone or what he is doing with his life, I wouldn't know where to start."

"You don't have to, Eric will find him, I know he can."

The morning of the coronation dawned bright and clear. Emelda rose early and called for Jena who appeared wide-eyed and expectant at her door. She let Jena dress her in the way she always had in a gown of silver and green, a matching cloak adorned with the lion and the sun of St. Dores heavy upon her shoulders. She sat as Jena brushed her hair until it gleamed like gold, the little hairpin fixed neatly into it. Emelda reached up and touched it gently; her heart leapt a little at the thought that soon she would see Kasper again, and she couldn't stop a grin spreading across her face.

As Jena finished she turned to her and clasped her hands in her own.

"Tomorrow I will be doing this for you, you will be radiant!" she laughed.

"But today it is your turn to be radiant, Emelda, today you are to be Queen," replied Jena caught up in Emelda's infectious laughter, it had been so long since she had heard her laugh.

There was a knock at the door.

"Come," called Emelda.

Lord Wolf stood in the doorway, dressed in his finest clothes.

"My, don't you look dashing," teased Emelda.

Wolf cleared his throat, "Are you ready, Your Majesty?"

Emelda nodded and she and Jena followed Lord Wolf out of the house to a carriage that awaited her. The three of them began their journey through the newly-laid streets of St. Dores. As the carriage bumped along the paved roads Emelda peered out of the window at the masses of faces that lined the roads. She could see nothing but smiles and hands waving to her. They held banners high and waved flags with the lion and sun on them. Emelda waved back, her heart cheering at the sight of so many adoring faces.

The trip to the Grand Hall was over almost as soon as it started and as they arrived Emelda found herself lingering in the carriage, gazing up at the mighty building that stood before her. Despite all she had been through to get here she still felt apprehensive, it was as if she had been playing Queen before and now it was no longer a game. She prayed that her crown would not be too heavy.

Emelda took a deep breath, pushed a smile on to her nervous face and emerged from the carriage out onto the steps of the hall entrance. There was a mighty applause from the crowds and she turned and waved before entering the hall with Lord Wolf at her side and Jena behind her. Once she was inside and the doors closed behind her the noise of the crowds was deadened and an air of solemnity fell upon them.

Emelda felt her heart drumming in her chest and she put on her most regal face and fixed her eyes on the throne at the end of the hall. Her eyes lit up when she saw a familiar face waiting for her at the other end.

"Brother Icka," she whispered excitedly.

Remembering the sobriety of the situation she stopped herself from skipping down the aisle and continued in the slow, regal pace she had practised in her room. There was delicate music coming from some unknown corner of the hall and flowers lined the walls and arches as well as her throne. Brother Icka waited for her, a gentle smile on his face, like that of a father awaiting his daughter on her wedding day. He held a small green velvet pillow in his hands upon which sat her crown, the one her father had commissioned for her. Emelda felt a little lump in her throat as she approached him and he bowed to her. Sweeping her cloak out from under her she sat upon the throne, her hands neatly folded in her lap. The music faded out as Brother Icka cleared his throat and began to speak in a loud, booming voice that echoed around the room.

"Princess Emelda, do you come before your people as the rightful heir to the throne of St. Dores?" he asked her.

"I do," she replied, her eyes drifting around the room. She saw Prince Eric sitting next to an empty seat and she imagined Christian there beaming up at her.

"Do you promise to rule this land fairly, upholding all the laws of the land and protecting its people?"

"I do," she declared, letting her eyes drift around the room once more, but the face she hunted for was not there. She had let herself hope, just a little, that Kasper might have come, that he might have shown his face one last time.

"Then it gives me the greatest honour to crown you Queen of St. Dores, all hail Queen Emelda!" He cried, placing the crown upon her head and falling to his knees.

There was a cry of 'All hail, Queen Emelda' and she rose from her throne and descended from the platform. She wanted to run but she made herself walk until she reached the doors and escaped the suffocating sedate hall to greet the jubilant crowds. They called and cheered as she emerged feeling a little breathless. Straight away she headed for her carriage and it wasn't long before she was joined by Brother Icka and Jena. She watched out of the window as Lord Wolf and Prince Eric climbed into a second carriage, then Brother Icka called out to the driver who drove the horses slowly forward. Now that the coronation was over Emelda wanted to get out of the new town and back to Brushmire, back to the spot where she and Kasper had buried Christian so that she could uphold her promise to him. She couldn't leave him buried in a nameless grave like a forgotten soul any longer; the very idea of it tore her up inside and she twisted her hands together nervously as they rode through the town. She knew she ought to be waving and smiling at her people, but instead she sat back and stared out of the window as if there was no one there. In her head she urged the horses on, but she knew she had to parade herself through the emerging town as was expected.

Brother Icka reached over and touched her hand kindly. He didn't say anything but he squeezed her hand tightly and her eyes filled with tears. Trying to choke them back she felt Jena shifting next to her as if she wanted to comfort her but couldn't in the presence of Brother Icka.

"Your Majesty, you don't have to be strong in front of me," said Icka softly, he nodded at Jena who pulled Emelda in close and held her as the tears came.

She cried until she felt dry, until there was nothing left in her anymore. She cried for Christian, for the space he had left behind in her heart; she cried over the empty seats at her coronation that should have been filled by her mother and father, by her brother and by her lover. She cried for her people, for all the death that tainted the celebrations and she cried with relief that it was all over and she could move on. She held on to the thought that she would see Kasper again soon, that she would tell him that she loved him and he would hold her in his arms once more. She longed to be near him, just to see his face and hear his voice, she wanted to be his lover, his wife and bear his children.

As the left the city borders they quickened the pace, quickly making up time. It took the rest of the day to reach Brushmire, where the town's people threw flowers over her carriage and called out to her in elation. Emelda called the carriages to a halt just outside the town and let Brother Icka climb out ahead of her; he turned and reached out his aged hand to help her down the steps. Outside a large group of men had gathered. They all carried spades and others carried a stretcher and blankets. A lump came to her throat at the sight of all the people that had come to help her. They bowed to her and she nodded her head at them, before leading the way on foot across the countryside. She barely recognised the land and she struggled to remember where Christian was buried, until she saw a mound of earth littered with tiny white flowers appearing on the horizon.

"There," she called out, quickening her pace.

The men hurried past her and carefully began to toil in the loose earth. The grave was shallow and it wasn't long before there was a cry and the work came to a halt. Emelda crept a little closer so that she could see the folds of Kasper's cloak, full of dirt, laid over the shape of a body just visible underneath. Her breath caught in her chest and she swallowed back tears, but she did not cry. She held her composure as she nodded to the men and they knelt down at the grave and began brushing back the earth with their hands. She felt a large, warm hand on her shoulder and she looked up to see Prince Eric standing next to her. She had been so focused on the men at work she had not noticed him approach her, nor had she thought about how he was feeling, this was his brother. She cursed herself for her selfishness and placed her hand on his. His eyes were full of sadness.

"I'm so sorry," she murmured, but he shook his head.

"He died in the most honourable way, protecting you. By doing his duty he helped save us all, he is a hero, Your Majesty," replied Prince Eric, his voice calm and steady.

Emelda nodded and looked back at the body that was almost free of its unworthy grave. Eric let go of her shoulder and stepped forward. He knelt and helped remove the last handfuls of earth, not caring for the mud on his clothes and with total disregard of his status. He finally reached in and pulled back the cloak. Emelda turned away, catching only a glimpse of Christian's still golden hair. She could not bear to see what death and decay had done to him. Eric replaced the cloak and stood up. He gestured for the men to bring the stretcher and blankets and they hurried over. Carefully lifting him out of his grave they placed him on the stretcher and covered him with a white sheet. Emelda watched as the body went past her and she said a quick prayer. Prince

Eric followed, brushing his hands off on a handkerchief. He stopped in front of her but did not take his eyes off Christian's body.

"I want to take him back to the Greylands and bury him there. After the wedding I shall depart, I will leave Jena with you and then I shall go find Kasper as I promised her," he told her.

"Then I will come with you for the funeral," Emelda said.

"No." Prince Eric was a little abrupt and Emelda was taken back for a moment.

"No?" she questioned.

"Forgive me, Your Majesty, but Greyland funerals are quiet affairs, it will only be my father, mother and I. Please say your goodbyes here," he explained, his curtness hiding the sorrow he felt.

Emelda bowed her head, "Very well, Prince Eric, I will see to it that his body is stored appropriately and ready for your departure the day after tomorrow."

"Thank you," replied Eric, taking her hand and kissing it before following the body back down towards the carriages.

The journey back to St. Dores was quiet but Emelda felt at peace. She had fulfilled her promise to Christian and now she could move on without thinking about him lying in a pitiful grave with no acknowledgement of the sacrifice he had made for her and for her people.

There was a feast and a celebration for Emelda's coronation that evening and Emelda found herself sitting between Lord Wolf and Prince Eric, but she struggled to keep the sadness from her face and when she turned to speak to Eric he was staring into nothingness, a distant look in his eyes. She looked up at him, she could see Christian in him, they were alike but very different. Prince Eric was elegant and charming, every movement was made with finesse whereas

Christian had been brash and bold, his face sweet and endearing - but she knew both were loyal.

Emelda made her excuses, complaining of a headache and left before the celebrations ended with Jena following her up to her rooms. She undressed with Jena's help and climbed between the sheets as Jena sat on the end of her bed. Her very soul felt weary and she was desperate to sleep, for this day to end, but there was something about the look on Jena's face that told her she wouldn't be sleeping just yet.

"I had them bring you a bed," she said, gesturing to the small wooden bed in the corner.

"Yes, Your Majesty," Jena nodded but did not move; she swallowed as their eyes met and Emelda could tell something was bothering her.

"What is it Jena?"

"You will think I am foolish."

"Never."

"I am scared to go to the Greylands. What if his mother and father don't approve of me? He was supposed to marry a Queen and he is returning with a serving girl. I won't know anyone but him, I will be alone there and you here," she blurted, "I'm not you."

Emelda smiled, "When they see how much he loves you, they will love you too in the same way I love you. That is why I want you to go and be happy. I am never far away. And I won't be alone for much longer, I pray."

"But what if..."

"No what if's. Tomorrow you also become a Queen. Once you are married in the eyes of God, that is something no mortal man can undo. You carry his child, there is no way a grandparent can say no to a grandchild!" laughed Emelda.

Jena smiled a little and pointed to the bed, "May I sleep here?"

"Of course, now get undressed, you need your sleep, it's a big day tomorrow."

Jena quickly stripped down to her undergarments and climbed under Emelda's sheets with her. Together they drifted off into a sleep full of dreams of lovers and sweet kisses.

Chapter 20

Emelda enjoyed the wedding day. There were surprised looks on her courtiers' faces when Jena instead of Emelda emerged carrying a magnificent bouquet of flowers and dressed in a flowing lace wedding dress of icy white, with Emelda herself following behind, dressed modestly in a gown of pale green. It amused her when Brother Icka raised his voice over the objections, quashing them without hesitation, a mischievous grin on his old face even though he was not privy to the secret. The day carried on as if it were Emelda herself that had gotten married - no expense was spared and no glass ever ran dry.

Ignoring the rumours and whispers that spread amongst the people, Emelda danced and laughed, full of the joy of love. She danced with Prince Eric and Lord Wolf, even Jena herself, encouraging others to follow her informality. She was a Queen but she wanted her people to know that she was human too, just like them. She let her hair flow loose down her back as she was spun by Prince Eric, a heart-warming smile on his face, before Maximus Bigge cut in and stole her away. He bounded around with her until she was almost dizzy with dancing but she didn't care. Eventually she found herself a seat back at the head table and watched Jena and Prince Eric dance. They had eyes for no one else, it was as if they were the only couple in the room. Emelda's heart sank for a moment as Kasper's face crossed her mind and she lost herself in thoughts of him.

There was a gentle cough nearby and she awoke from her daydream. She looked up to see Lord Wolf watching the lovers dance too.

"Let me go with Prince Eric, Your Majesty," he said to her.

"Sorry, what do you mean, Lord Wolf?"

"I know where to find him but I may need to use a little more than persuasion."

Emelda's heart leapt as she looked up at Lord Wolf and she nodded at him.

Kasper sat watching the waves break on the shore, his bare feet pushed into the cool damp sand. He took a long drink from the bottle in his hand and pushed it into the sand. The woman next to him blabbered away, her fingers attempting to trace the scars on his hand, then up to the tattoo on his bare arm. He could hear noise but he couldn't hear what she was saying, nor did he care. As her fingers reached his bare chest he grabbed her wrist and turned to face her, his eyes burning. He had thought she resembled Emelda and across the smoky bar he had thought for the briefest of moments that it was her, but she was ugly in comparison now that he saw her in the light, and full of empty words, a shallow copy of the woman he loved.

"What did you say?" he asked her, seeing the fear in her eyes.

"There was a royal wedding, after the coronation a few months ago. Now the Queen is with child," she replied timidly, "please let go, you are hurting me."

He threw her wrist back at her and she scampered away like a frightened animal. He didn't even watch her go, turning back to the lapping sea. He looked down at the bottle and then back at the sea. If he drank enough and went out into the water he knew he would drown. No one would find him until he was bloated and stinking, if the fish didn't eat him first. He got up and went back to the small fishing hut he lived in and gathered up as many bottles of whiskey he could find and returned to his spot on the beach as the sun was sinking below the horizon. He had thought he would have been able to let her go, to move on - even if he never loved another again he was at least alive. But he had discovered that a life without Emelda was no life at all. He was tired of living with ghosts.

The whiskey burnt on its way down and he thought of Christian, hastily buried in a grave so unfit for him. He raised the bottle towards the setting sun, the light illuminating the amber liquid.

"Here's to you, my friend," he murmured, taking another long drink from the bottle.

He drank as much as he could without vomiting, his sight blurred and his head spinning. Dragging himself on his hands and knees he inched himself towards the water until he could feel its coolness pulling him in. He turned onto his back and let the waves pick his limp body up and then drop it again on the rough sand. He felt himself drifting deeper and deeper out into the sea, the salty water washing over his face and into his mouth. It stung his eyes but he didn't care, he just wanted to hurry up and be consumed by the dark coldness.

In his delirium, he thought he heard voices over the lap of the waves in his ears. Then he felt hands on his body and he closed his eyes waiting for them to pull him down into the water. He felt sweet oblivion close in around him as the water filled his nose and mouth; he took his last breath and blacked out.

Kasper woke to a violent shaking; he rolled over onto his back and opened his eyes. Everything was blurry and he was immediately sick, he choked for a moment before turning his head to the side. He coughed and spluttered, struggling for a moment before he realised his hands were bound behind him. He screwed his eyes shut and then opened them again, hoping for clarity. This was definitely not heaven, it was dark and uncomfortable and he was pretty sure no one tied you up in heaven. His head pounded and he felt horribly sick, feeling the vomit rising in his throat, he rolled onto his side and heaved. The smell of stomach acid mixed with sea water and alcohol filled the air as Kasper rolled onto his back and breathed heavily, waiting for the cold sweat that consumed him to subside. As his eyes adjusted to the dim light he could make out the four walls of what seemed to be a wooden crate. Light seeped in through the hastily constructed walls leaving lines of light over his body. He shuffled himself painfully up into a seated position, the rough wood tearing at his bare torso, and took a better look around. It only then occurred to him that they were not stationary but moving; the crate swayed with the movement of a cart and bumped along the ground. Now that he concentrated Kasper could hear the crunch of stones under wheels and the clatter of hooves. There were also voices that he recognised.

"Wolf!" he shouted angrily.

The voices outside fell to a quiet whisper so that he couldn't hear what was being said.

"Wolf! Why couldn't you just let me die in peace?" He swallowed the urge to be sick again as the cart lurched over a hole in the road.

"You know the punishment for desertion is death, even for you, Lord Kasper," Lord Wolf's voice came close to the side of the cart.

Kasper slumped against the side of the cart heavily, "I was living in hell, death will be a sweet release."

There was silence from outside, just the steady sound of the horses' hooves. He leant his head against the wall and closed his eyes. He tried to ignore the pounding in his head and pictured Emelda's face as he left and the way he had told her that she would have to hunt him down and execute him. He had never thought she would. For a time he had hoped she would come after him, declaring her love for him. He would take her into his arms and they would be united again. But as the months had passed he had let his hope die; he had stopped gazing out of the window at the road that led to the sea and turned his attention to drinking and sleeping, until that night when even that had gotten too much for him to bear, that coupled with the news of her marriage to Prince Eric and their child. He pictured them together and wanted to leave it all behind. He hadn't realised how hard it would be to leave her behind, to forget. He had shut himself off to it all once, but now that floodgate had been reopened there was no stemming the flow, not again. It was unbearable. At least this way he would get to see her face one last time.

Kasper drifted in and out of consciousness as he was ferried back to St. Dores in the uncomfortable cart. He knew the journey was at least a week long. He had ridden as far as he could until he met the sea and could go no further. He had gone to his father's old fishing hut without even thinking about it. It was the place where his father had met his mother, where they had fallen in love after he rescued her from the drowning currents of the sea. She had been coming across on a merchant ship that had gone down in the storm, she was the only survivor. She had captured his father's heart the

303

moment he had laid eyes on her, cold and bedraggled. She had passed on her black hair and dark eyes to their son before she had died.

The journey was long and arduous, the constant shaking of the cart rattled Kasper until he thought he could take it no longer. His wrist hurt from the constraints and his body was battered and bruised from the rough roads. They stopped periodically for food and water. Once they even poured a bucket of cold water over him and sluiced out the cart, but he was fed very little. But he didn't care, he had given up, he longed only to see her face once more before he died. This physical pain was nothing compared to the emotional agony he felt. He only ever saw Lord Wolf when he emerged from the cart; he spoke to Kasper very little but looked on him with pity.

He woke on the eighth day of their journey to the sound of hooves on cobbles and he knew they were back in St. Dores. He wriggled himself upright and waited for the cart to stop. When eventually it did the door was flung open, letting in the dewy morning light. His heart in his mouth, Kasper peered out from the darkness of his confines to see the sun beginning to rise over a large empty courtyard. Kasper was hauled out roughly, almost losing his footing, but before he could get a good look around he was dragged off to a dark back entrance out of the way of prying eyes. In the fleeting glimpse he got of his surroundings he assumed he was in the Queen's newly built castle, or at least part of it - he had seen evidence of building work still taking place. He was impressed at what had been accomplished in the months he had been away. He didn't have long to think as he was pushed up a narrow servants' stairway and along a corridor. They reached a small door at the end and Lord Wolf turned to him before knocking.

"I'm sorry it had to be this way. I knew you wouldn't come even if I told you the truth. You are too stubborn," he told him, then he knocked, not giving him a chance to respond.

"Come," came a woman's voice.

Kasper felt his whole body tremble at Emelda's voice. He longed to see her but at the same time he wasn't sure how he would be able to look at her after their parting. He wasn't sure he could bear to see her full of another man's child.

Lord Wolf pushed open the door and entered the candlelit chamber. Emelda was sitting at a desk next to a large four poster bed with her back to the door, writing busily. She looked up as the men entered and put her pen down. Kasper's heart leapt at the sight of her and he was barely able to remain standing. Emelda pushed the chair back and stood up; she was fully dressed despite the early hour, as if she had been waiting for them. He dropped to his knees and bowed his head low, staying that way as she straightened herself out, not daring to look at her.

"Cut his ropes and you may go, Lord Wolf," she ordered.

"But, Your Majesty..." he protested.

"I told you to go," she told him with authority, and Wolf took out his knife, freeing Kasper's hands before bowing low and leaving them.

Kasper let his hands drop to his sides, still not daring to look up at Emelda as he listened to the sweep of her gown on the floor as she crossed the room to him.

"Why won't you look at me?" she asked him, but he remained silent, "Kasper?"

She reached down and lifted his chin gently, looking down into his dark eyes with more love than he had ever seen. His eyes travelled from her face down her body to her flat, taut stomach and back to her eyes. Her authority had grown so much since he had left her on the cusp of her sovereignty, she had become the Queen he knew she would be.

305

"After everything you still doubt me?" she said, with such sincerity that any resolve he had left melted away.

"But..." he murmured confused, "Where is Prince Eric?"

"Probably with his wife feeling their child kick within her belly," she said, with a smile.

Emelda knelt on the floor in front of him, tears in her eyes, and reached out to touch his face. He took a moment to register what she was saying to him before the realisation struck and he gathered her into his arms and kissed her forcefully, his tears mixing with hers.

"Why did you leave me?" she asked him, pulling away.

"I thought...Prince Eric..." he started, but he found his voice fading.

"You thought wrong," she told him, pressing her forehead against his, not caring about the dirt or the sweat, "I love you, it was only ever you."

He held her face in his hands and kissed away the tears as they fell from her eyes, again and again, murmuring his love for her in between each one. She pulled away, getting to her feet and taking him by the hand. He stood before her dirty and battered and she wept even more. Leading him over to the bed and sitting him down upon it she gathered a bowl from her washstand and filled it with water from the jug. She flung the cloth over her arm and carried it to him. He sat watching her, his heart in his mouth, as she carefully dipped the cloth into the water and tenderly washed the dirt from his chest, kissing each and every bruise or cut as she went. She knelt on the floor in front of him and proceeded to wash his face, her fingers tracing the scar across his eye so gently he could barely feel her touch.

Nervously she reached for his trousers undoing the button at the top with tentative fingers. She felt his hands over hers and looked up at him as he pulled her on top of him, laying them both down on the bed and with a gentle hand on her chin he brought her face close to his. He kissed her with little lingering kisses as he reached round and unbuttoned her dress. She sat up, letting it fall away from her body and slide to the floor before he pulled her into his body again, kissing her over and over, his lips travelling down her neck and along her collar bones. The rest of her clothes fell away along with his until they were both naked, their flesh pressed against each other, warm and trembling. His hands traced the shape of her breasts, her stomach and her thighs until he could take it no longer and he made love to her. He was gentle at first but as his passion grew he couldn't hold himself back, he rolled her over onto her back and pinned her to the bed, kissing every inch of her skin until they both cried out with pleasure.

He gazed down at her lying beneath him as she breathed hard, a beautiful smile on her face.

"I love you, Emelda, I will never leave you again if you will have me," he told her.

"Nothing would make me happier," she grinned, pulling his lips towards hers. Just before she kissed him she whispered, "I love you, Kasper."

His dark eyes came alive with passion as he kissed her with all the love and longing of a decade. It poured into her and shook her very soul and she let it happen, his love washing over her again and again in blissful abandonment. At last she was his and he was hers.

The End

About the Author

Lydia Baker was born in October 1988 and grew up in Horsham. Now, aged 28, she lives in Crawley with her husband and four children. Writing has been a passion of hers since childhood and now she has published her first novel 'The Return of the Queen', it's time to start work on the next one!

22942471R00182

Printed in Great Britain
by Amazon